About the Author

Linda Fawke has always loved writing but only seriously indulged her passion on retirement. She writes fiction and non-fiction, preferably late at night. She has a degree in Pharmacy and a PhD in Pharmacology and her pharmaceutical background is evident in both of her novels. A Prescription For Madness is the sequel to A Taste of His Own Medicine

Linda Fawke is married and lives in Berkshire. She has three children and six grandchildren.

Also by Linda Fawke

A Taste of His Own Medicine

A Prescription For

Madness

Linda Fawke

Acknowledgements

Many thanks, yet again, to Jonathan Veale, my editor and fellow Kindle novelist, for his help, advice and encouragement. I know I can always rely on him.

My son, Joe Fawke, a consultant neonatologist, provided valuable information about potential genetic problems in the newborn and checked the medical content of the book. Any errors in this area are mine, not his.

I'm also grateful to Caroline White, whom I met at the Henley Literary Festival, and her book, 'The Label' for insight into coping with Down's Syndrome.

My patient husband, Tony, is my constant support, whether it is putting up with me writing late into the night or proof-reading (and re-reading… and re-reading) the book. I could not manage without him.

Belonging to the Wokingham Writers' Group has been invaluable and I thank the members for their critiques and support.

Finally, I would like to thank Fiona Routledge for creating the excellent book cover for me.

For Joe, Anna and Tim

Chapter 1

'Stop phoning me!'

Kate slammed the study door. She did not want her words echoing around the house for Neil to pick up. She hated outbursts; never slammed doors.

'Leave me alone!' She cut off the call, grabbed her coat and car keys and left the house.

Her sports car made her smile: a Mazda MX5, a treat to herself, her "baby". Anger ebbed away as she opened the door and climbed in. She leant back into the comfort of the leather seat and stroked the smoothness of the gearstick. It was January; the glitter of frost still adorned the bare branches of the trees. Not the weather for having the hood down but what the hell! She wanted to feel the wind in her hair. She pulled her scarf tighter round her neck and turned up her collar. As she accelerated, the engine roared. How she enjoyed that noise! She changed gear as late as possible, soaking up the power, feeling it in her bones. She headed away from town, away from traffic. These roads were familiar; she ignored the speed limits and put her foot down. The police were never around and she knew the sites of the speed cameras. It was risky but that was part of the fun.

The wind would blow thoughts of Jonathan and his phone calls away. Her mind emptied, her thoughts soothed by the rays of an ineffective sun. The tyres squealed as she took a sharp bend but she kept control. An approaching car flashed its lights and she saw a fist in the air. She thought the driver mouthed something rude. She didn't care. Quite the opposite. Making her presence felt was one of her pleasures.

A rabbit ran across in front of her and she swerved on the slippery road. There was a bump, more felt than heard, and she saw the body in the rear-view mirror. She sighed and screwed up her face. A man appeared in front of her, emerging from a farm gate. She got too close, her eyes still on the inert mound of fur. 'Shit,' she cried, veering across the road. I could have killed him. The farm-hand jumped sideways and she earned herself another fist in the air. He looked like Jonathan: same hair, same height, same build. For a moment she thought it *was* him. I could have killed Jonathan. But she hadn't and it wasn't. No, she thought, I don't want Jonathan dead. Do I?

She fought memories of their past, the pregnancy, her hopes and her hatred.

An icy puddle cracked as she drove through it, muddy water splashing upwards. Bugger, the car will need washing. Dirt did not feature in Kate's life. She skidded at another bend and was glad to be the only car on the road. Pushing my luck, she thought, laughing out loud. Her cheeks were tingling and the cold air was making her eyes run. But it was like a roll in the snow after a sauna. Totally worth it.

She could cope with him now. The drive had worked. As she headed home, her mobile rang. She knew she shouldn't answer it. No desire for a fine. Rashness, curiosity and the empty road won.

'I'll stop calling when we come to an agreement. You said you'd meet me.'

'I thought you would come to your senses, Jonathan, and leave me alone.'

'That's the point. I *have* come to my senses.'

'I don't know why you keep chasing me.'

'Meet me and we can discuss it.'

She changed down a gear so that the engine roared and she had to shout. 'What is it you want? A quick fuck?'

'Well, that's an option, I suppose. Or even a slow one. A delicious sharing of pleasure, entwining our bodies together, the stroking of velvet, the steaminess of passion.' Jonathan laughed at his deliberately extravagant words. 'I think you know, much as I'd enjoy it, that's not what I'm talking about.'

Kate did not reply.

'You said you'd meet me.'

'I did.' She was a woman who kept her word. 'I'm driving. I'll call you back.'

She'd lost count of how many times Jonathan had phoned over the last few weeks. He was tenacious. Kate thought he'd forget about the events of the reunion, would ignore the emails they'd exchanged afterwards and return to the real world. Kate wanted nothing to do with him. They had little in common any more; just distant student memories, the vestiges of physical attraction and the impact of her revenge.

She'd left her mark on him as he had on her. That was it. Finished. Move on. But the dislike, repugnance even, she hoped to inspire was missing. Jonathan, recently remarried Jonathan, pursued her with his eyes at the reunion. And, afterwards, continued to contact her. Well, she would keep her part of the bargain.

She called him from the study, her body still tingling from the drive.

'Where?' Jonathan asked.

'Not near here. I don't want to be seen with you.'

'OK. I've got to go to North Wales next weekend for a travel magazine. I need to spend the day on photos but then I'm free. Why don't you join me for dinner? We can both stay at the hotel and return on Sunday. I'm sure you can think of a reason to be away that will satisfy your undemanding husband.'

Kate ignored his remark about Neil.

'I'll book separate rooms.'

'Alright. Send me the address. I'll arrive Saturday afternoon. But remember, Jonathan, this is a one-off. Not the start of a relationship.'

Kate could hear the smile in his voice as he said, 'Fine.

One step at a time.'

An excuse. She needed a cover. There was the possibility Neil would also be away – he was rarely home – but Kate needed to be prepared. She thought for some moments and picked up her phone. It was worth a try.

'Hi, Becky. How are you?'

'Kate – nice to hear from you. I'm fine. It's been a while. Is it a social or a professional call?'

'It's social. Need a bit of help.'

'How is it you only contact me when you need help?'

'Because I'm a demanding, selfish friend who takes advantage of you. I'd refuse to listen if I were you!'

'But you know I won't. What is it now?'

'Next weekend. Should anyone ask, could I be going somewhere, say the theatre, with you and staying Saturday night away from here?'

'It's possible. Would that "anyone" be Neil?'

'You know what I always say – info on a "need to know basis". I don't want you to have to lie more than necessary. "Anyone" means just that. It includes him.'

'I suppose it's alright. But I'll be here and don't intend to lock myself away from anyone's sight.'

'That's fine. Thanks, Becky, you're great.'

During dinner, Kate told Neil she'd bumped into Becky who'd asked if she'd like to see a play in London with her on Saturday; that the friend she was intending to go with was ill. What was it? Shakespeare. Have forgotten which one.

'If you don't even know what the play is, why do you want to go?'

'Just being friendly. Haven't seen Becky for a while – she's always fun. And I like Shakespeare.'

'It's all the same to me. I have a meeting on Saturday. I won't be here anyway.'

***

4

Kate spotted Jonathan sitting on a stool at the bar. He had left a message for her. "Dinner at eight o'clock. Meet in the lounge beforehand." Trust Jonathan to set it all up, to choose a good but not extravagant hotel, to give her nothing to complain about. She surveyed him. He looked relaxed, chatting to the barman, a glass in his hand. He wore a fresh blue-striped shirt and chinos. They looked good on him – all clothes did, a throw-back to his days of modelling. His hair was neat, well cut. He was clean-shaven; he would smell of an expensive after-shave. And she felt the unwanted adrenaline rush his appearance always stimulated.

Perhaps he sensed her presence. He turned.

'Join me in a gin and tonic?'

'A small one, please.'

He guided her with the lightest touch of his hand on her elbow to a table in the corner, then sat and looked at her. Kate knew one of them would have to break the silence. If she did, it would be his triumph, so she said nothing.

'Why have you come?'

'Because I agreed I would meet you once more and I don't go back on my word.'

'So exact. Do you hate me, Kate?'

'I did. Long ago. You're not part of my life now. I feel nothing.'

Could he tell she was lying? Did he detect her raised heart rate? She didn't want to be affected by him; she did not. He could have stayed with her, could have married her. Who knows whether she would have lost their baby if he had cared? It was a question she debated until she could debate no more.

'I thought you weren't part of *my* life until the reunion. Then I realised how much you still mean to me. You may think this is stupidity but I do believe we can pick up old threads. Can't you feel the electricity, the tension between us now?'

Kate cut him off before he could say more. 'Jonathan, for God's sake, we're both married. What did you tell me? You married last year? Your third marriage. It hardly inspires trust.

5

Why would I leave a good husband for you? Why would you leave your new wife? This is ridiculous.'

'I have a confession, Kate. I told you I decided I would never marry again after I split from my second wife, after that disastrous marriage. I expected you to ask me why I married a third time but fortunately you didn't. The truth is, Kate...'

He stopped and moved closer to her, leaning towards her, gathering in her gaze.

'The truth is, I didn't remarry. I have a partner but I'm single. I told the lie so you wouldn't think I was a predator. I thought you would find me "safer" if I was married. It was a spur of the moment choice. Possibly wrong. But now I'm being honest.'

'Why should I believe this story rather than the previous one?'

'I don't know. Maybe because this one's true.'

'It doesn't matter either way to me. The presence or absence of a third wife is not an issue. And if you've got a "partner", as you say, it comes to the same thing.'

'So you're still totally in love with your pleasant, staid husband, who likes "the good life", a night in with a take-away and a film. A guy who gives you no excitement. You told me all this at the reunion, Kate, you told me! I haven't invented it. Come on, Kate. Don't become middle-aged.'

Did he guess how much she hated being in her fifties?

'Don't turn down what life can offer.'

A waiter arrived to show them to a table, giving Kate a moment to think.

'My life is no concern of yours.'

'You implied you had the odd affair so I don't believe faithfulness – or lack of it – bothers you. Anyway, I'm not suggesting we have an affair. I'm asking you to consider a proper relationship with me.'

'I'm not having a relationship of any sort with you, Jonathan. I will admit to physical attraction which is outside my control. If you've detected that...' Her voice trailed away and she shook her head. 'Don't misinterpret it. We'll eat together tonight. We'll sleep apart. I may even have breakfast with you tomorrow. But that's the limit of our involvement.' Kate wished she had dressed less well, had not used perfume, had not tried to impress. But she needed the props. That was her way.

Jonathan smiled. It seemed her words passed him by like a brief breeze on a still day. He did not ignore them; he simply focussed on Kate and heard something else.

They ate a delicious meal, which Kate did not enjoy. Jonathan ordered Sancerre, remembering how much she liked it. Curse him! Why did he have to be considerate? The longer she spent in his company, the less control she had over her emotions.

'I have a suggestion, Kate. We need to go away together.'

Kate started to speak and he put his hand up to stop her.

'Wait.'

'Jonathan, I'm going to bed now. I don't want to hear any more.'

As she stood up, he put his hand over hers, gently, without force. But it could have been a shackle; she could not move.

'Just listen, don't be so impulsive. We had something special between us. I know it's long ago and we're not the same people now. And I acknowledge the break-up was my fault. I was immature, confused and naïve. I don't need to tell you that. But it's not something either of us can forget. You needed to get your revenge. I accept that. If our relationship had been insignificant, you wouldn't have bothered, wouldn't have devised such a plan.' He rubbed his ear.

Kate tried to move but his hand still held her. She had to listen.

'I've given this considerable thought. I've been too impulsive, expecting you to react to our "reunion" in the same way I have. I need to give you more time. And I will. I'll stop phoning you. I won't contact you for a week. Perhaps two. But I'm not letting go. I want you to think what sort of future we could have together. Examine your relationship with Neil. Has it run its course? I'm not asking you to hate him, just to decide if you want to spend the rest of your life with him.'

His speech finished, Jonathan sat back in his chair and watched Kate. Their silence cut them off from the hum of conversation in the bar and the faint sounds of background music. Lives went on around them, a play performed on a distant stage. Kate knew she had to say something. Could she trust Jonathan? Should she share some of her worries about her marriage with him? He said he lied about his present wife, partner, whatever she was. He wasn't trustworthy. She would become vulnerable if she confided in him.

'Tell me about your partner. You want me to leave Neil. Are you prepared to leave her or do you fancy the idea of having two women on the go?' Kate's voice was edgy with sarcasm.

'I expected that question. Okay, you deserve some information. At the reunion I told you my first, much loved, wife died. Later, I made a disastrous marriage out of loneliness. It failed quickly. And I said I would never remarry. I haven't. But that didn't mean I intended to live the life of a monk. I've had relationships. My present one works after a fashion. We live together. She gets on well with my daughters and they like her. That's really why it's lasted.'

'But you said you'd been married a year.'

'We've been together a year. Just rearranged the terminology.'

'So you'll "rearrange the terminology" again to bring me into your life?'

'I don't think those are the right words. You'll be more than just another relationship. That's why I think we need to go away together for a few days. Somewhere new without the trappings of everyday life, the responsibilities and ties that limit our thinking.'

'I can't just disappear from Neil's life.'

'You can, for a few days. You've come here this weekend.

It seems you managed it without too many problems. You can do it again. You must have friends who can help out. Someone who can provide an alibi.' He gave Kate a questioning look. 'I'm often away with my work – it isn't a problem for me.'

'Not a problem for you. How convenient! Everything nicely organised to fit in with you. I'm not at your beck and call, Jonathan. I was once, I know. I'd have done anything for you. But you're asking too much. I came here saying it was a one-off, a single meeting because I'd promised it. I haven't changed my mind.'

'Like I said, I won't pester you. But I know you well enough, Kate, to know you'll have to think about my proposal.'

The meal was over. Jonathan kissed Kate chastely on her cheek and wished her goodnight. She left the restaurant ahead of him and did not look back. But she put her hand up to touch the spot where his lips had been and imagined she could still feel the slight roughness of his face.

She left the following morning before breakfast and drove home. Jonathan ate alone, optimism his only company.

Chapter 2

She leapt out of bed and ran to the bathroom. The previous night's dinner decided it wished to leave.

'You alright?'

'Does it sound like I'm alright?'

'Anything I can do?'

'Keep out of my way.'

'Fine. Just asking.'

Kate washed her face, took a few sips of water and made her way back to bed, collapsing in a heap on the duvet.

'Get into bed properly.'

'No. I'm too hot. Think I must have picked up the twenty-four-hour sickness bug that's doing the rounds. Hope I don't get the runs as well. Had loads of people coming into my pharmacies asking what they should take for it.'

'Well, then, you know what to do.'

'Neil, stop being a pain in the arse. Keep rehydrated is the answer and it will pass. Don't eat. Even a non-scientist like you should know the basics.'

'Kate, you're the worst person in the world when you're ill. You don't have to bite my head off with every sentence.'

'Shut up. I don't do "ill". Who else do you know who hasn't had a "sickie" in the last fifteen years? I don't intend to start now.'

'So you'll go into work, spread your bugs about, and end up with all of your staff off sick. Sensible, that.'

'I'll work from home. I don't have any particular

commitments today.'

'I should know better than argue with you. Do as you please. I need to get up, anyway. Off to Manchester for a meeting. Hope I don't take your bug with me. All about the next exhibition. Got to start planning early.'

'Exhibitions, exhibitions. You think of nothing else. Back tonight?'

'No. Away one or two days. I'll let you know.'

Kate turned over, dragging the duvet with her and drifted off to sleep. Neil went to the bathroom and she half-heard the rush of the shower. He bustled around the bedroom, rubbing his hair on a towel as he put assorted items into a holdall and found the day's clothes. In her comatose state Kate registered his movements. She knew exactly how he stretched before pulling his shirt over his head, lazily not undoing all the buttons, how he tucked it into his trousers. The wiggle of his hips as he adjusted the zip. The practised one-leg stance as he put on his socks; a skier's balance. Then the careful opening and closing of the bedroom door. She noted the sound of coffee being made downstairs, snippets of conversation that moved around the kitchen as he spoke to someone on his mobile phone, the popping of the toaster and the smell of burnt bread. Finally, the click of the front door. Neil was gone.

Half an hour later she was drinking a cup of tea and feeling slightly better. Unhealthy places, pharmacies, she thought. Little better than hospitals. First place the suddenly sick call in, the nearest and quickest way to get a remedy and feel better. Victims of our own success, she mused. But Kate was rarely caught out. She was the one who stood in for her own staff when they were ill. With six pharmacies to her name, it was a significant call on her time. Well, there was a mass of paperwork to do; that would be today's job. Neil was, unfortunately, right. She should keep her infection to herself.

By mid-afternoon, she was feeling more human and even a little hungry. She ate a dry cracker and it stayed down. Maybe it's just a mild attack and won't last the day, she thought. Let's be positive, it won't hurt me to lose a pound or two of weight. Perhaps unwisely, she had a cheese sandwich later on but there were no ill-effects. She was even pleasant to her husband when he called to say he wouldn't be home that evening.

'Sorry I was a bit short with you this morning.'

'I know what you're like. You have little sympathy for yourself when you're ill. So I just ignore you when you are abominably rude to me if I try to help.'

'Well, you'll be glad to know I'm feeling better. How did your meeting go?'

'Really well. They raved about my ideas for the next exhibition. It's going to be called 'Ups and Downs'.

'You've chosen more original titles.'

'Ah, but you don't know what it's about. Tell you when I get back. Won't be for a few days, I'm afraid. These things always take longer than expected.'

He was bursting with enthusiasm. She knew he was already somewhere else in his head. Photography was not only his career, it was his obsession. Once it had been her.

'Okay. We do seem to lead separate lives these days. Give me a call tomorrow.'

It was true. They shared a bed, ate together a few times a week and chatted inconsequentially. But the jigsaw of their lives interlocked less well now than it once did. There were pieces missing. Since the success of his "Love Hurts" exhibition a couple of months before, he was in demand. From being a talented but little-known photographer, his name was appearing in journals and magazines, he was interviewed and praised and collaborative offers were appearing. I should be delighted for him, Kate thought. I am delighted; he deserves all the accolades he's getting. So why do I feel uncomfortable? Why do I snap at him whenever I can? Jealousy? No. I'm successful, too. I've been successful for several years. My pharmacies are thriving, I have independence. I look and feel good. I can spend what I want on myself. She looked down at her clothes. Even today, a not-going-anywhere day, she was wearing designer jeans and an expensive sweater. But there was a niggle. Kate knew what the problem was. How to solve it was the issue.

***

It was a shock when she threw up the following morning. Her stomach hurt as there was little in it. Must be more virulent than it seemed, she thought. She stayed in bed for an extra hour but the day followed a similar pattern. She drank plenty, was not sick again but did not feel like eating. Nothing appealed to her even though she felt hungry. She picked at a bread roll. Tomorrow, I'll go along to the North Street pharmacy, she decided. I'm bound to feel fine by then.

But the same thing happened. The day started with vomiting. Everyone she knew who had suffered recovered within a day, two days maximum. If it's not the usual tummy bug, what is it? No diarrhoea; sickness mainly in the morning. My God!

Kate sat down with a thump on the sofa. Her mind flew back to the university reunion. How long ago was it? Over three months. She had sex with Jonathan. It was necessary, part of her scheme to get revenge on him, to help her cope with what he had done to her. And all went to plan, she made him suffer. That she might become pregnant as a result had not crossed her mind. She was over fifty, for shit's sake!

Let's be logical. Kate solved problems by attacking them in a precise and analytical way. Pregnancy at her age was possible. Her periods were erratic now; they had always been irregular. Had she missed one? Or two? Maybe she had. Shit. Here am I, a pharmacist. Someone who advises on birth control on a regular basis, who knows which methods are recommended and which are unreliable, a source of comfort and advice to fifteen-year-olds and women near the end of childbearing. And I can't look after myself. I shall be the laughing stock of the town! Kate shivered as these

13

thoughts rushed through her head. Her standing in the community would be diminished. But what else could it be?

She thought about Neil. They had regular sex. His recent success had restored passion to their love-making; success was sexy. But no! It can't be him. She thought back to the early days of their marriage, to the shock of discovering he had a low sperm count; a bad time. Then they accepted a family was something neither of them needed. And still didn't need.

Men with low sperm counts do have babies; it can happen. But it was more likely to be Jonathan's.

On the other hand, it could be a nasty bug. Morning sickness normally starts earlier in pregnancy. A frisson of relief ran through her but she knew well enough all pregnancies were different. How often had she said that?

There was a simple way to find out.

Kate realised she was still sitting on the bed, dishevelled and disorganised. This would not do. She shook her head to get her mind in order and prepared to go out. I shall simply ignore any feelings of nausea and they will go away, she told herself. She dressed with particular care, made sure she spent longer than usual on her make-up, and headed for the North Street pharmacy.

'Haven't seen much of you lately as I caught that awful tummy bug. Think I must've had a double dose as I've felt really nauseous and threw up a lot.'

'Gosh – glad you didn't come in! We've all escaped and don't want any gifts from you.'

There was no problem in discreetly acquiring a pregnancy test. Patience was not one of Kate's strengths but she forced herself to remain all morning in the pharmacy, giving time to each member of staff, and doing the paperwork she would normally do. She went home after lunch as usual.

Her hands shook as she went through the simple procedure of the test. As she held her breath, the blue line appeared. She had confirmed her pregnancy.

She could not tell anyone. She could definitely not tell

Neil. She could not go to the doctor's surgery or the Medical Centre where everyone knew her professionally. Her staff must not know. Once, when she lost her first baby, part of her longed for another. She should not have been so rash. This was no longer her wish. Absolutely not.

Kate was not a problem sharer. She preferred to make her own mind up. But now she longed to confide in someone. She had decisions to make and talking would help her. But who?

The phone rang.

'Good news, Kate. I'm coming home this evening. Shall we go out for a meal?'

It was the last thought in Kate's head.

'That bug has been really persistent and I'm barely over it. I don't think I'm up to eating much. It'd be a waste of money. Why don't we get a take-away? You can eat most of it and I'll just have a little.'

'Okay. Whatever suits. I've got loads to tell you. Hope you're up to having a drink! See you later.'

Neil was so much in his own world Kate doubted he would notice hers had been turned upside down.

Chapter 3

'Mum, I thought I'd come and see you at the weekend. Just me. Neil's busy. Arrive Saturday, leave Sunday. Is that okay?'

The pause was so long, Kate wondered if her mother had heard her.

'This coming weekend? Oh, I don't know. Yes, I suppose so. I mean, it'd be lovely. You usually give me more than two days' notice. But I can go shopping tomorrow. Don't keep much in the fridge these days. And I'll find time to clean up the house a bit. Yes, of course you can come.'

'Stop flapping. I'll take you out for a meal and your house is always immaculate. I'm your daughter. I'm coming to see you, not inspect the property.'

'You know what I'm like. A place for everything and everything in its place.'

Clichés embellished her conversations in the way originality never could.

'I'd better phone the hairdresser's if we're eating out. Hope I can get an appointment at short notice. I'm sure they'll fit me in. I'm a good customer. Would you like scrambled eggs for breakfast?'

Kate had no desire for eggs in any form.

'Toast suits me better.'

'Jam or marmalade?'

'For God's sake, Mum, it doesn't matter!'

'Alright. Don't snap. Just want to make you welcome. Have some little treats for you. I thought you really liked scrambled eggs. You always used to. It's not that you come very often.'

Kate felt the guilt of a daughter who neglected her mother. It was always there, usually hidden under a blanket of mundane tasks, coming to light unexpectedly when she was feeling reflective. They had never been close, did not have the instinctive bonds she saw among other mothers and daughters. But it suited Kate. A mother was a mother. Not a best friend, not a sister: a mother. She was the person who delivered you to the world, brought you up and cared for you, but also the person who set you free. And that was the problem. Her mother never wanted to let her go. The constraints of her childhood still chafed like physical bonds when she allowed them. But in spite of the past, it was a comfortable enough relationship and infrequent visits were sufficient to keep it that way.

'I know I should come more often. I do try but you know how busy I am.'

What a dreadful excuse! Kate regretted her words.

'See you on Saturday for lunch. A small sandwich will do. Don't go to any trouble. You choose where to eat in the evening.'

Kate knew her mother would be pursuing the vacuum cleaner round barely used rooms and stocking the fridge with enough food for several weeks. It was her way and she was unlikely to change. Working out what she was going to say was a more pressing issue. They did not discuss intimate matters, never spoke about sex and even the delicate matter of puberty was handled via a book. She spent her childhood believing her parents selected her from a showcase, her tiny self wrapped up in silver paper on the top shelf. The most prized package. Learning about birth was a shock.

This was new territory. But at least she knew whatever she said would go no further. Her mother was discreet. And did not live locally. It would be good for them both to talk, to talk seriously. For the first time in their lives. At least, she hoped it would be good.

17

The small sandwich turned out to be an assortment of cheese and pickle, ham with mustard or egg mayonnaise. Her mother beamed with delight as she laid the table with an embroidered cloth, put a small vase of flowers on it and arranged the best plates. She told Kate to tuck in, doing the same herself. She was making up for the recent absence of much in the fridge. As she bobbed up and down, getting drinks, finding serviettes and loving being busy, she did not spot Kate hiding sandwiches in her handbag rather than eating them.

The house smelt of fresh laundry and lavender furniture polish with a slight undertone of bleach.

They talked about the new neighbours (pleasant enough although the young boy kept kicking his football over the fence), the problems with Auntie Valerie's errant son (sacked from his latest job for poor time-keeping and swearing at the manager), the faulty double-glazing (fortunately still under warranty) and what Kate would like for her next birthday (she had no idea). The afternoon disappeared. Her mother had an inexhaustible supply of topics she produced at random, jumping like a flea from one to another.

'It's good to have a chat. I miss conversation now your Dad's gone. Not that he ever had much to say. You're amusing and such a good listener.'

Kate smiled and nodded. She had not contributed much where amusement was concerned.

'You're a bit quiet today, Kate. Are you feeling alright?'

'I'm not totally myself. In fact, there was something I wanted to talk to you about.'

Her mother sat upright as if someone had a gun to her back. She opened her eyes wide and put her hands to her cheeks.

'You haven't got some dreadful disease, have you? It's not…you know…is it? Is it treatable? If it's a matter of money, I'll try to help. Don't have much but you can have what there is. Private treatment is quicker. You shouldn't wait around for some appointment months away. But you know all about these things.

Why didn't you tell me sooner? Or have you only just found out? Oh, my poor darling!'

The questions came ever faster and she stopped when she ran out of breath. She looked at Kate in horror. A piece of pickle dropped out of the sandwich she was holding and landed on her lap.

'Calm down, Mum. I'm not ill. It isn't cancer. Stop panicking. Just listen for a moment or two and I'll tell you.'

'Well, what a relief that is! But you've come specially to tell me something so it's got to be important. Is there a problem with your businesses? Are you in debt? You're not in trouble because of a wrongly dispensed prescription, are you? There was something on the radio recently about a case like that. Is there a lawsuit? My God, what will the neighbours say?'

Kate's silence eventually got through to her mother.

'Sorry, Kate. You asked me to listen. And all I've done is talk. I *will* listen now.'

Kate waited. She needed the silence; she needed her mother to feel the silence, too.

'I'm pregnant.'

There was a long pause. Kate could see her mother struggling to take in the information, to find the right words.

'I've come to talk to you about it and try to get my head straight concerning what I'm going to do. It's called seeking parental advice.'

'I didn't think you and Neil wanted children. Isn't it a bit late now?'

'Mum, I think you've missed the point. I didn't intend to become pregnant.'

'You, Kate? You're always so organised, you don't have accidents. I bet you were on the pill and it failed. Always thought it was risky. A bad idea.'

Kate recalled a conversation they had years ago, prompted by a television programme about the pill. Her mother didn't believe it worked and was uncomfortable discussing it. Kate tried to explain its mode of action but her mother would not listen and was adamant in her views. Instead she turned to finding negative, unscientific comments in newspapers or magazines, cutting them out and posting them to Kate. It was the closest she got to advice on contraception.

'No, Mum, I wasn't on the pill. I stopped it a while ago. And it does work. If I'd been on it, I wouldn't now have this problem.'

This was proving harder than she expected. Her mother was either naïve or being deliberately difficult. Surely it could not still be embarrassment?

'So what does Neil think?'

'He doesn't know.'

'Shouldn't you tell him?'

'Okay, Mum. Let me give you the whole story. It'll surprise you, probably shock you, but hear me out.'

A stunned face looked back. 'I need a cup of tea. Just let me put the kettle on and make a pot.'

Tea was the answer. Her mother would make it whatever she said. Kate was standing looking out at the garden, manicured and neat, all character having been removed with the weeds, when her mother returned. With a shaking hand, she poured out two cups, trying not to look her daughter in the eye. Twice she started to say something and stopped herself. Kate broke the silence.

'Do you remember a boyfriend I had in the last year at university? A guy called Jonathan.'

Her mother's face brightened. 'Lovely lad. I do remember him. He had lunch with us on one of our visits and was a delight. Chatted away to your dad and me as if he'd known us for years. And he brought you here when I had to go into hospital to have that gallstone operation. Me and your dad, we hoped it would last. Fancied having him as a son-in-law. Would have been an asset to the family. Not that I have a problem with Neil, of course. But suddenly he wasn't around anymore. You never did tell us why and I didn't like to ask.'

'Well, I met him again at the reunion a few months ago.'

Her mother looked blank.

'You remember – I told you about it. We went back to the pharmacy department to celebrate thirty years since we all graduated. Without giving you unnecessary details, Jonathan and I ended up in bed and I think the baby is his.'

Her mother let out a cry worthy of a third-rate, sensational film.

'Oh, Kate, how could you? What a sluttish thing to do! And with your upbringing! I can't believe a daughter of mine would behave like that!'

'Which century are you living in, Mum? It's 2006, people hop in and out of bed with each other all the time. Anyway, there was a reason for it, a serious reason which I don't intend to go into. It wasn't just lust or trying to turn the clock back. And I don't sleep around; I object to being called a slut.'

Her mother gave her an unbelieving stare and made a guttural grunt.

'I was stupid, I admit, and didn't consider I might get pregnant at my age. Now I don't know what to do. I cannot contemplate parenthood but I'm against abortion.'

'But it could be Neil's! It's got to be Neil's!'

Her mother announced this as a revelation, her face lighting up with relief. A solution to the problem Kate had missed!

'You're right. There is a possibility it could be his but I've not got pregnant before and we have an active sex life. Neil has a low sperm count.'

Her mother blushed, unable to cope with such information. Sex lives and sperm counts were not in her repertoire. 'You never mentioned Neil's…condition before.'

'I know. He preferred not to make it public knowledge although it didn't bother him. Just something he lived with.' Not a choice but a fact of life, like an ugly mole, she thought.

'Folk believed we'd decided to concentrate on our careers and not have a family. As, no doubt, you did. And it was, in fact, true.'

'Yes.' She sighed. 'Always hoped to be a grandmother, though. Like most of my friends.'

'I went through a bad period when we got Neil's news. A time when I wanted what I couldn't have. Always perverse, that's the way I am.' She sighed. 'Suddenly I needed a child. Everyone I came across seemed to be pregnant or a mother. The pharmacy was flooded with babies. It was difficult. I couldn't talk to Neil about it as it sounded like an accusation. I suffered on my own.'

The impact of the memory was more forceful than she expected. Losing Jonathan's baby, then not being able to have Neil's. She had felt like a victim, felt fate was against her. She had to push these memories away. Weakness was intolerable. She overcame it then and would not succumb now.

'But logic won and I realised I didn't need or even want a baby. And I've managed well without one.'

'I'd have been "Grannie Annie". That sounded just right to me. I wouldn't have minded a girl or a boy. One of my friends has twin grandsons. I'd have been delighted whatever.'

'I became more than ever motivated to make my businesses successful.'

'They come to stay with her regularly. Lovely, mischievous, little lads.'

'And it worked. I've had a brilliant career.'

'I met them in the park once and we went to the café together. I bought them ice-creams.'

They were in separate worlds, talking to each other but not communicating. Kate broke the strange atmosphere that surrounded them with a new tone of voice.

'So what do you think I should do?'

'What? Why are you asking me? I've no idea. I can't think…don't know what to…can't get my head around your actions or your attitude.' She was struggling, tripping over words and stammering. The hand she put up to her face was shaking. 'And as for Jonathan, he's gone right down in my estimation.

Your dad would be shocked! I'm glad he's not around to hear all this.' Then she muttered, 'Never thought I'd say such a thing,' and tutted to herself. She was a practised tutter.

'I need to make a decision soon. If I decide to get rid of the baby...' Her mother winced. '... nobody other than you and I need know about the pregnancy. I've told no-one else. My life would carry on. Not as normal, but it would seem that way from outside.'

Kate took a deep breath. 'If I have the baby, do I keep it, do I pretend it's Neil's? Do I tell him how lucky he is finally to have fathered a baby? Would he believe me? He might not want it.' Kate was trying to sort out the options that were going round her head like a tangled ball of string. She was talking as much to herself as to her mother. 'Or do I tell Jonathan the truth? What would he say?' She decided not to mention Jonathan's keenness to re-start their relationship. 'Maybe I should put the baby up for adoption? I don't know if I could cope with that. What should I do?'

'Oh, Kate! How on earth do you think I can solve your problems? I never could. You always went your own way, did your own thing. You rarely asked for advice about anything.' She gave an enormous sigh. 'If we tried to offer it, like when we suggested you went to a university closer to home, you ignored us. "Miss Independent" we used to call you. We accepted that was how you were. You stood on your own two feet and we were proud of you. I don't think I can start advising you now. It's too late.'

Yes, thought Kate. Once I was old enough, I was determined to do my own thing. I was over-protected, cosseted, kept in a safe cocoon of possessive love for my entire childhood; the polite little girl on display, the one who always did as she was told, the goody-goody who passed her exams with ease. But the break-away was difficult. It took time and nerve to make the escape.

She remembered her parents' rules. Bedtime at seven

o'clock. No exceptions. Allowed to read for twenty minutes. They would come upstairs at half-past to check the light was off. All her friends went to bed at eight. One evening, she went downstairs to ask if she could read for a little longer and received a slap on the leg for cheekiness. She didn't do it again. The following day she heard her mother telling a neighbour she needed her wings clipping now and then. Wings clipping! She was not a bird although sometimes she felt like one, a creature whose ability to fly was hampered. She tried hard to be good but only the transgressions were noticed.

Transgressions, however, were rare. She could recall one incident. Her mother said she could play in the front garden but not open the gate. Her friend, Gillian, was playing in the street. She didn't want to disobey but the temptation to go outside for just a few minutes was great. And it would stop the taunting, the "Mummy's little pet" and "Baby, baby!" jibes. So she escaped. She was caught, of course. Her mother had eyes everywhere. She was sent to her room with a sore bottom, her mother's words, "I'll break your spirit, I will!" pursuing her. Yes, the break-away was difficult.

Kate was about to comment on the thoughts rushing through her head, to say something hurtful as a form of defence, when her mother's demeanour changed. She seemed suddenly smaller, the bustle and bounce disappeared from her body and she wiped the back of her hand across her eyes.

'I've struggled with problems of my own. Problems I couldn't bear to talk about. But I'll tell you now. There never seemed the right moment to say this before. But as we are being honest with each other…' Her voice faded and she inhaled deeply, looking around the room as if the roses on the wallpaper or her aunt's antique mantelpiece clock could help her.

'I lost three babies before I had you. Two at four months and the third at six. It was heart-breaking, especially the last time. The doctor said I probably wouldn't be able to carry a baby to term.'

Kate tried to say something but the revelation robbed her of words. She managed, 'How sad!' and muttered a few more broken sentences. Annie carried on without listening.

'And to make matters worse, your dad's sister, your Auntie Jane, had an abortion just as I was losing the third baby. I don't remember exactly why but she didn't want another child – she had four already – and was worried about the baby having something wrong with it. She was a lot older than me.

'She was probably worried about Down's Syndrome. It's more likely in an older mother.'

'What's that? I think she said the child might be a mongol. Is it the same?'

'Oh, Mum! Don't use that term. It's rude and unkind, not politically correct these days. The disorder is called Down's Syndrome.'

'I'm just telling you what happened, what she said. Don't get on your high horse with me! I didn't have your advantages or your education. I can only say what I know.'

'These days it's like calling someone from the West Indies a "Blackie". It's just wrong, unacceptable.'

'Your Uncle Bob still calls black people "Blackies". Doesn't seem to worry him. But then he lives in Birmingham so it might be alright there.'

'It's not alright anywhere and Uncle Bob is a racist. I've told you that before.'

'You've told me lots of things before. How am I supposed to remember them all? Uncle Bob's always been kind to you. Why are you hard on him? And why are you shouting at me?'

Kate said nothing. This was not a conversation she wanted to continue. It should never have started. The atmosphere in the room was tense; a dull silence descended on them. Kate wondered how they had ended up arguing about political correctness when the purpose of her visit was to get some advice from her mother.

'I didn't come here to argue, Mum. Sorry I sound as if I'm lecturing you. It isn't my intention. But I'm a pharmacist and have to be aware of what is and isn't acceptable to say to people. I can't go upsetting my customers. And I don't like to think you might inadvertently use an expression that could upset someone.'

Her mother frowned, her bushy eyebrows almost covering her eyes. She got up and walked around the room, plumped a cushion on the small armchair in the corner and adjusted one of the curtains. She gazed out at her garden for some time then suddenly turned and walked back to the table. She nodded and patted Kate's hand. The uncomfortable episode was over.

Kate smiled. 'Let's go back to what you were saying about Auntie Jane's abortion.' She spoke softly, hoping she sounded more kindly than before.

'Alright.' Her mother took a deep breath and carried on. 'Jane said the pregnancy was an accident and she couldn't cope with a baby with something wrong with it. Any sort of wrong, whatever it's called.' She spoke the words deliberately, looking at Kate with a hint of fierceness in her eyes. 'I'd have given the world to have that baby. I didn't speak to Jane again. I couldn't. Fortunately, they lived miles away.'

'We almost gave up. But then you came along. A small miracle. I think I told you once I spent a lot of time in bed when I was carrying you. I couldn't bear to tell you why. It disturbed me. One day, I thought, when you were expecting, perhaps the right moment would arise and it would be natural to tell you my story.' She stopped and thought, leaning her head to one side. 'I suppose that's just happened.'

Kate put her arms around her mother who was now weeping, tears dripping on to her daughter's sweater, her chest heaving as she tried to control her feelings. They remained together for some moments, an unaccustomed sharing of emotion.

'It's alright. I don't think about those times now. Not like me to get so distressed. It's just that when you talked about what you might do…' She moved away from Kate, wiped her eyes on a tissue, blew her nose and shook her shoulders to dispose of her cloak of grief. She stood still for some seconds, her eyes closed.

Then she sighed heavily. 'I'll just pop upstairs to sort myself out. Have another cup of tea.'

Kate took a deep breath and breathed out slowly. Her mother's scent lingered on her, a mix of Nivea face cream and Pears soap. I wish I were not here, she thought. She looked around the familiar room. The carpet had changed and the curtains were new but the ornaments were those she was forbidden to touch as a child. She picked up a Wedgwood bowl, Jasperware, blue and white, and felt the same uneasy thrill she had at the age of eight. Her fingers tingled and she replaced it quickly. She touched the brown tiled fireplace with its unrepaired chip in one corner and remembered cutting her hand on it. And the tiny crystal vase still sparkled in the corner cabinet, as tempting as ever. She lived here until she was eighteen and had visited many times since. Why did the house still trouble her? There were mixed memories.

Her reverie was broken by footsteps on the stairs. The woman who emerged through the door was the mother Kate knew. Gone were the tears, there was a fresh splash of lipstick on her lips and a breath of perfume. Her shampooed and set hair was lacquered firmly into place. She grinned broadly, said the matter was over and was not to be mentioned any more. Kate started to talk but Annie put up her hand to stop her, insisting she was fine; they would have her home-made cakes, butterfly cakes with butter icing, Kate's favourite when she was little.

Something else for the handbag.

'Just one more thing I need to say, Kate. I suppose I should be glad you wanted to discuss your problems with me but really I'd have been happier if you hadn't.'

'Okay. Point taken. I won't do it again.' Heaviness dragged at her spirits. 'I just thought…' Kate decided it was better not to explain further. 'I know you'll not mention this to anyone. We'll leave it there. Forget all about it. Both of us. This conversation has never happened.'

'Too right, I won't mention it!' The moral righteousness returned. 'Let's change the subject. I think we'll both be happier on less emotional ground. Come and see the new wallpaper I've chosen for the bedroom.'

I should have known better, Kate thought. It was a mistake confiding in her.

'Look at the time! We'd better get ready to go out soon. I've booked a table at the Royal Oak. It's a gastro pub now and the food's excellent. You'll like it. And didn't you mention a few weeks ago you were thinking about buying yet another pharmacy? You must tell me all about it over dinner.'

Annie had not only planned the meal, she'd lined up a comfortable topic of conversation.

Kate sighed. Why did I think it was a good idea to ask for help from my mother? I'll have to look elsewhere. I have an idea.

Chapter 4

On the way home, Kate thought about her options. Pauline was the person whose name had jumped into her head. She's the kindest, most caring person I know. Well, knew, she thought. They were friends as students, had shared a flat. They were both delighted to see each other at the reunion and their friendship, much neglected, regenerated. They promised to keep in touch. Not to wait another thirty years! Or, more practically, not to wait until the next reunion in five years' time. Pauline will listen without being shocked. Talking to someone who will understand and have sympathy with me has got to help.

Several emails later, Kate was invited to visit and stay the night. Pauline was pleased and surprised that Kate contacted her so soon. Being Pauline, she accepted everything as it happened and didn't ask if there was a reason. Neil, unknowing Neil, was away again. Kate packed an overnight bag and headed the forty miles or so to Pauline's.

There was a large people-carrier on the drive and as she rang the doorbell she could hear the noise of running children and of someone shouting at them. It was a Saturday; were there other visitors? She expected Pauline's husband to be around but as they had never met, also expected he would leave them together to chat.

Pauline was welcoming as only Pauline could be. She threw her arms around Kate and talked non-stop.

'I knew you wouldn't mind. Ginny's here. She's my eldest daughter. I've told her all about our time at university and she's dying to meet you.'

Two small children ran up to Pauline and grabbed her legs. Their chatter stopped when they saw Kate and they wide-eyed her nervously.

'These are her twins. Girls, say "Hello" to Kate who's a friend of Granny's, and tell her what your names are.' Kate was clearly too scary to speak to. 'Well, this one's Emily and the other's Martha. They won't be shy for long. Usually, you can't shut them up.'

Ginny arrived, unwound the girls from their grandmother's legs, and told them to go and play somewhere else.

'Lovely to meet you, Kate. Mum hadn't told me much about her time at university until the reunion. Now I've heard all sorts of stories!'

Kate couldn't imagine what would have been so interesting. Before she had time to make a suitable comment, there were screams from around the corner.

'Mummy, Martha's pulling my hair!'

'She did it first!'

'I didn't.'

'Yes, you did! Ow, stop it!'

One of them burst into tears and both ran to their mother, talking at the same time, getting progressively louder.

'Oh, the joys of motherhood!' Ginny rolled her eyes at Kate. 'Come on girls, be quiet and let's find out what the problem is.'

Kate and Pauline were left on their own.

'They're just showing off because there's someone different here. Normally, they play well together. Once they've got used to you, they'll stop this nonsense. And Sarah will be arriving soon with her three so they'll have company. Sarah's my daughter-in-law, married to my son, Ben. Lovely girl. They've got two boys and a girl. One of the boys, Joshua, is older than the twins, the other, Thomas, is around the same age. Their girl, Clara, is the youngest at nearly two. It'll be a bit chaotic but I didn't think you'd mind. And I wanted you to meet my family. Don't know if Alice – she's my youngest daughter – will be able to make it. She said she'd try. Depends on how she's feeling as she's expecting her first. She's having a difficult pregnancy. A lot of nausea though it's getting better.'

Kate lost count of the names. Her memory was good, always had been, but the sea of unnecessary information flooded her. Ginny was the only name she remembered.

'Does Ginny live close?'

'Yes, they all do. Well, within an easy drive. Means we all see a lot of each other. Lovely for the kids to be able to play with their cousins, especially as they're close in age. And I can babysit. They do make good use of Eric and me!'

'Eric?'

'My husband. Of course, you don't know him. He's at a football match. You'll meet him later.'

An explosion of noise pulled everyone into the sitting room at speed. Kate followed slowly, unable to take in the blur of colour and movement flashing before her. After half an hour, she realised she had barely spoken.

'Alright, Martha, you can bring the pram in but be careful. Don't bash the furniture. Emily, you have the buggy. Go and show your dolls to Kate – or should they call you Auntie Kate? She'd love to see them.'

Kate shook her head. She had no wish to be their aunt.

She was surrounded by toys and given precious objects to hold. She'd not been near a doll for decades and although she made soothing noises to poorly infants as part of her job, it was just that. She had few social skills where kids are concerned, she realised. She tried. She asked what the dolls' names were, a few more labels to forget, and which ones were the best. She admired the pram but said the buggy was just as pretty. The girls stopped shouting and vied for her attention, bringing more and more offerings – a bottle for feeding, a dummy, some blankets, a pillow. Kate sank under the weight of the childish desire to please.

'Kate, you're incredibly good with them!' Ginny enthused. 'You must have grandchildren of your own.'

The pause was slightly longer than Kate intended.

'No, I don't have children. So, obviously, no grandchildren.'

'Sorry. I didn't mean to say the wrong thing. Martha, be quiet for a moment. Mummy's talking. But you must have lots of contact with little ones. I can see that. Did you hear what I said, Martha? Well, do as you're told, then.'

'Of course, parents bring their children into all of the pharmacies but I'm more familiar with children's illnesses than their toys.'

'Mummy, somebody's ringing the bell!'

Ginny laughed and covered her unease by answering the front door. A blast of noise and a stampede of feet rushed through the hall.

'Hello, Granny. Look what I've got! It's a new fire-engine and the ladder goes up and down. Me and Thomas got presents.'

'Wow! That's super, Josh. Have you got one, too, Thomas?'

'No, he's got an aeroplane.'

'Let Thomas answer for himself, Josh. We all know you're the chatterbox.'

Not another one, thought Kate. Temporarily, the new invasion went quiet when they saw the stranger on the sofa. Pauline did the necessary introductions and took her flock of followers into the kitchen for drinks and biscuits.

'Pauline, just plain biscuits,' Sarah called.

'Sorry. Too late.'

Five small children emerged, each with a chocolate finger biscuit. Emily was carrying two. She went up to Kate and gave her one.

'I gived one to the lady, Mummy.'

'Good girl.'

'I don't usually eat biscuits.'

Pauline, Ginny and Sarah all looked at her. To be given a chocolate biscuit by one of the twins was an honour not to be rejected.

'But as you've brought it especially for me, I'll have it. Thank you...Martha.'

'I's Emily.'

She handed it over and clambered on to Kate's lap. Both her hands, podgy and warm, were smeared with chocolate and there was a brown dribble from her lips.

'Be careful, Emily. Don't get chocolate on Kate. I always wear clothes that don't matter and can go in the washing machine. Yours look far too smart! Here, have the wipes. You might need them.'

Something else that was too late. She saw a brown smudge on her new, cream trousers.

'Don't worry. I'm having these dry-cleaned next week,' she lied as she took a small bite of biscuit and put it down on the table. Someone would eat it.

'Run off and play hide and seek,' Ginny said, giving her girls a push towards the door. 'Josh, you be seeker and the rest of you find good hiding places.'

There was the clatter of toys being dropped as they all rushed out. Doors slammed and there were screams of delight. Thomas came back complaining he didn't know where to hide. Pauline pulled him behind one of the sitting room curtains which he grabbed with delight. But the hiding place was too good so he left it after a few minutes as nobody came near. Gradually they all returned and conversation became impossible again.

'Who's going to help me sort out your tea in the kitchen?' Pauline asked the little ones.

'Me,' came a chorus and the flock gathered.

'What shall we have? How about worms?'

'Yeah, yeah, lovely worms. I wanna get them out of the packet.'

'And me!'

'I said first!'

'Spag Bol, Kate. Worms are spaghetti. I can see it's a foreign language to you.'

Pauline, the ever-capable grandmother, took the five children into the kitchen where she fed them their tea, gave them yoghurt for pudding, cleaned up the mess and returned them, wiped and satisfied, to their mothers in the sitting room. The wine bottle was on the table and the women were drinking.

'Watch out now the hooligans are back!'

Sarah grabbed the bottle and as one, they clung on to their glasses. Kate clutched hers to her chest like a favourite teddy bear rather than holding it delicately by its stem as she usually did. She'd appreciated the civilised break; it wasn't long enough. She got up and asked where the toilet was. Apart from needing to go, it was a few precious minutes away from the chaos.

'I need a poo!'

'And I do! Lemme go first!'

'No. I can't wait. You can't go on your own, anyway. Go and get Mummy.'

Joshua and Thomas lunged at the toilet door and almost landed on Kate's lap. The lack of a lock, a minor inconvenience, had now become embarrassing. The boys stopped dead and looked at Kate.

'Boys, go away and find your Mummy. I won't be long.'

Kate hastily sorted herself out, as both boys shouted at the same time about their need for the toilet that was occupied by "the lady".

'Sorry, Kate. Should have warned you and suggested you went upstairs. We don't have bolts on the loos or bathrooms anymore.' Pauline clearly thought the incident amusing. 'Josh locked himself in last year and we had to remove a window to get him out. Kids!'

'Finished! Mummy, finished!'

Sarah went off to wipe the appropriate bottom or two.

Toilet visits completed – the twins also need to go – the

two families began to gather their belongings and prepare to leave. Kate marvelled at how long it took. Finding the toys, putting on the coats, losing the gloves, getting shoes on the wrong feet, giving everyone a hug and a kiss.

'So pleased to meet you all. An unexpected bonus.' The words climbed unwilling out of Kate's mouth.

As the cars pulled away, two others arrived.

'Eric's back from the match and Alice is here, too. What a shame they didn't arrive a bit sooner!'

Kate felt a wave of nausea as she contemplated more socialising with people she did not want to know.

'Kate, I've heard all about you from Pauline and I'm delighted to meet you.'

Kate put out her hand but Eric ignored it and hugged her. His round, shiny face was creased with much smiling. He was plump where Pauline was slim but they were different versions of the same person.

Alice was more reserved. She stroked her small bump as if it needed comforting and either future motherhood or her natural disposition made her the quietest of the group.

'I hear you're not having the easiest pregnancy.' Kate felt obliged to make conversation.

'It's been bloody awful. I was in two minds whether I wanted a baby, anyway. I think this may be the first and the last.'

'Lots of women say that,' Pauline said. 'Kate, I'm sure you've heard it in all your pharmacies!'

'I have. But every pregnancy is unique and some women have a far harder time than others.' Kate, needing help herself, was dispensing advice. How did this happen?

'How were your pregnancies, Kate?'

Pauline jumped in and explained the situation, to Kate's relief. "Pregnancies". Yes, she was now on the second one.

'We're having the same tea as the children. Spaghetti Bolognese. Are you staying, Alice? Not much seasoning in it to suit the kids so it may suit you as well.'

'Okay. Thanks. As I've arrived late, I might as well eat here and go home afterwards.'

They all sat down to an unappetising tea – something Kate would call dinner, but Pauline was a northerner – which needed much salt and pepper. Kate was not hungry, anyway. At no point in the evening did Kate have a chance to talk properly to Pauline.

The following day, Eric decided the three of them should go for a walk as it was crisp and sunny, a beautiful winter's day demanding the company of warmly wrapped up folk with a determined step. They would have a pub lunch. Kate could set off home afterwards, he suggested.

A breeze disturbed their hair and cooled their faces. Kate felt composed and ready for a serious talk. They chatted comfortably about Kate's pharmacies and Pauline's hospital responsibilities, about the pros and cons of their different jobs. Kate mentioned Neil's recent photographic success and Eric talked about his physiotherapy practice. They moved on to how worried they were about Alice and her dislike of being pregnant.

'I do hope she comes to terms with it. It's still early days,' Pauline said.

'You don't think she might decide it was a wrong choice and have a termination?' Kate asked.

Two horrified stares answered her. Wrong comment.

'Just wondered. I've known it happen.'

All these were interludes, however, spacers between the anecdotes about their grandchildren. Pauline would never boast about her own children's achievements but grandchildren were a different matter. All the world loves a grandchild, it seems. Kate laughed at the story of how Joshua fell out of bed, rolled under it and had no idea where he was when he woke up; then she heard about the time Thomas ate an entire box of chocolates without being sick. Best of all were the "twins" stories. How they giggled at the various times they got mixed up, how folk could not tell one from another and the amusement it provided. The stories were so familiar, Pauline would start the tale and Eric finish it, a dual comedy act, polished to perfection through much practice.

Kate smiled. She did much smiling. She did much nodding and saying, 'How lovely.' The opportunity for the serious talk never arrived. As she got into her car and offered her thanks, her hosts were effusive about her visit. She must come again and bring Neil next time. It would be great for him to meet the family, too.

As she drove off, Kate breathed in the air of freedom.

It was a failure. No time to talk to Pauline on her own. No advice. No discussion. But an insight into the world of children. She hated the mess. Could not tolerate the noise. Did not relish getting her expensive furniture bashed by a toy pram. Disliked sticky fingers and the need to wear clothes that "don't matter". Did not want her silk curtains used as a hiding place. And she needed, absolutely needed, to have a lock on her toilet door. Perhaps it was a worthwhile trip after all.

Chapter 5

Neil arrived with an Indian take-away. 'Thought I'd pick one up on the way home. Didn't think you'd mind if I chose. How are you?'

He pecked Kate on the cheek and looked at her. 'Look a bit peaky. Will you eat?'

'A little.'

He bustled about in the kitchen, laying the table, finding the hot pickle, making a cucumber raita and chatting non-stop. Kate let him get on with it.

'Well, that was a successful trip. Have started to get plans in place. Must tell you about my ideas. It all started when I was in Becky's pharmacy a few weeks ago. A woman came in with a child with Down's Syndrome. It was clear from her appearance. I had my camera and various other bits of kit with me and this little girl – I suppose she was around seven – came up and started asking me what everything was. We started chatting. She was so sweet and so curious. Her mother apologised to me and said she hoped her daughter'd not been a nuisance. Said she was just being sociable and loved talking to people, to anyone. I said she was a delight and her mother beamed. "Not everyone reacts like that. Thank you." Those were her words. It got me thinking.'

Neil stopped for breath and to serve out the food. Kate stared at him. What was he doing in Becky's pharmacy?

'I know there's still a stigma about Down's Syndrome. Not as bad as it was, but it's there. I suppose unconsciously I contributed to it by being surprised how bright and sociable this kid was. And I wondered if I could help. Photography is powerful. It can influence and change opinions.'

'I know, Neil. You can skip that bit.'

Neil appeared not to have heard Kate's comment. 'I'd been searching for ideas for the next exhibition and this was my "Eureka" moment. The title came to me: "Ups and Downs". How Down's Syndrome kids integrate with the rest of the world. Showing them in their true light. But maybe also showing some who're having a bad time. Needs a lot of work, it's a sensitive subject. But I believe I can do it. What do you think?'

'What were you doing in Becky's pharmacy?'

'Sorry?'

'I asked why you were in Becky's pharmacy. Surely I have enough pharmacies to equip you with whatever you need.'

'I was asking what you thought of my ideas for the next exhibition. Something I've been working on in my head constantly for the last few days, something I consider a brilliant idea, an opinion-changing endeavour. Important for kids with Down's Syndrome, important to me, my career, my future. And you want to know why I was in a pharmacy? God knows. I can't remember. Perhaps my throat was sore. Maybe I'd got a headache from too much thinking. My nerves were probably frayed from your dreadful behaviour towards me. What does it matter?'

Neil, laid-back, easy-going Neil, was now shouting.

'I didn't ask why you were in any pharmacy. I asked why you were in Becky's. That's what interests me.'

'I know her, she's a friend, my friend as well as yours. Why shouldn't I call in if I want to?'

'You seem to be seeing a lot of her. I spotted you'd written a phone number on an envelope addressed to her. Your flyers for the last exhibition were in a wrapper with Becky's name on it. I noticed. Too many coincidences.'

As she said it, Kate realised these were the words of a petty-minded, jealous harridan. This isn't me. What am I doing?

'Kate, I've no idea what you're talking about. What are

these envelopes? When did this happen? What exactly are you accusing me of? Stationery theft?'

In spite of her acrimony, Kate smiled. Neil's words amused her. His usual tactic: break a bad mood with humour.

'This conversation isn't going well. I need a breath of air. You finish the food, open a bottle of wine and we'll celebrate your new ideas when I come back.' Kate pushed her dinner away and left the room.

Neil leaned back in his chair and examined the ceiling. He closed his eyes and saw the envelopes in question. Recycled scraps of paper of Becky's he'd used without thinking. Little errors of judgement, little moments of carelessness. He got away with it, produced plausible explanations at the time. Or so he thought. But Kate had noted it all and was challenging him. Why now? What did she suspect? Did she want to be reassured it was simply her wild imagination?

What would he say about Becky?

He was still debating with himself when he heard Kate's key in the door. Rapidly he cleared up the remaining food, most of which went in the bin. He found a bottle of Côtes du Rhône on the wine rack and went to join Kate in the sitting room.

'Sorry, Neil. Not sure what got into me. This bug seems to have affected my head as well as my stomach. Tell me more about your "Ups and Downs" ideas. I think it will work. And maybe I can help as I know something about the condition.'

Neil felt like a condemned man whose head had just been removed from the noose. Perhaps it was a temporary reprieve while further evidence was gathered. He chose to ignore that complication and launched into more details about the exhibition.

'So far, I've mostly been at the concept stage, plus arranging dates and venues. I've been asked to take the work to different places. Think of that! First time it's happened for me. But I need to work on where I'll get the right photos. I need to talk to some medics about the condition, some families with Down's Syndrome children. And I wondered if I'd be able to photo some of the more severely disabled kids, maybe those in "special needs" homes. Not sure about that. I have to think about how to present my case. Don't want to be seen as a "voyeur". I've never handled anything as sensitive before.'

Kate realised he was in his own world again. She listened and nodded, half-concentrating. They finished the wine and the ambiance was genial, the sort of atmosphere where delicate subjects could be broached. In a pause while Neil was scribbling in a notebook, Kate jumped in.

'I'm not a jealous wife, Neil. But I would like to know if I should be concerned. We've been married over twenty years. What happens then? Do folks drift apart? Do they accept complacency? Do they need the occasional affair to keep sex vibrant, to keep the relationship fresh? I don't know. I really don't know. Do you?'

'Wow! I wasn't expecting this. Suddenly so deep! I thought our sex life was pretty lively, anyway. You always seem satisfied. We have a good life together. I don't know what's got into you, Kate. I suggest you think about something else.'

Neil stood up. 'Another bottle?'

Clever Neil, Kate thought when she lay sleepless in bed. Avoided the issue – if there is one. But he's partly right. I do need to think about something else – as well as our relationship. Why should I expect him to be faithful if I'm not? I suppose I'm not worried about a casual encounter; I've had a few and Neil never suspected. As far as I know. Maybe he's done the same. But something more permanent? A total change in our lives? Neil leaving me? For Becky? I can't believe it.

Becky – amusing, great company, an asset to any party. And an efficient, caring pharmacist. But a partner for Neil? No, she is too lightweight. Something tells me he would not have a casual affair with her. Such things don't last and what an uncomfortable situation that would create. Kate felt the gnawing, insidious pain that told her she was being unfair, a poor friend.

But if he did leave me, would I turn to Jonathan? What a

gamble! How can we return to our student selves? We can't. We don't know each other now. She looked across at the sleeping Neil. I know exactly the position he likes to lie in, one hand tucked in by his face. I know he likes a down pillow, the window always open; I know the make of boxer shorts he wears in bed. He always starts the day with an over-hot shower which he stays in for three minutes. I timed him; he didn't know. Must be something in-built, automatic, out of his control. He shaves every day, always the left side of his face first. I bet he doesn't realise it himself. Dresses in his own style. Good quality, casual clothes which he hates until they've been washed or "worn in". Then they last until they are designer-scruffy. Gets irritable if he doesn't exercise but would say he's never anything but good humoured. Looks better than most men of his age. Most men. Better than Jonathan? There was an inevitable comparison which she did not want to make.

I don't know anything about Jonathan. Not the important facts nor the silly, insignificant ones. And those are the ones that make up a relationship. Maybe the test of a good, loving relationship, the degree of intimacy you enjoy, is whether or not you know your partner's bowel habits. Her own humour amused her.

I'm stuck in a rut. A comfortable, familiar rut. Do I want to stay here? What has happened to the adventurous Kate, the one who's always up for a challenge? The try-anything Kate? Maybe she is now a try-a-few-things-only Kate. Or a try-nothing-at-all Kate. Then the problem of the pregnancy crept up on her like a malignant disease. She was getting adept at pushing it to the back of her mind now the sickness was less severe. Pretending it was not there. Perhaps I should have drunk less tonight? No. The evidence that wine is harmful when pregnant is not conclusive. I'll lead a normal, independent life. It will not be run by an unborn child. I'll know what to do. I should not make a hasty decision. I am in control.

As she drifted off to sleep, she wondered where the nagging desire to discuss her future with someone fitted in.

Chapter 6

'We saw "The Tempest" in London.'

'Did we? When?'

Becky wrinkled her nose at Kate's comment, a question mark hanging between them.

'The weekend when I asked you to cover for me. Not significant now but I thought you'd like to know. It's on in London and that's where we went. The friend you were going with was ill and I took the spare ticket.'

'Well no-one asked me so it's irrelevant. But thanks for the flowers – not necessary, though.'

'Just so you know I don't take your friendship for granted.'

'Why do you always lead such a complicated life, Kate?' Becky sighed. She was without energy today.

'I suspect it's no more complicated than yours.' Although debatable at the moment.

She had not considered Becky as a suitable confidante, someone to help her get her head straight. But they'd bumped into each other; sometimes fortune throws unexpected opportunities around.

'Fancy a coffee?'

Kate led her towards the nearest coffee shop.

'Not keen on this one. Has some significant memories for me. There's a new one round the corner, 'Bean Bag'. Let's go there.'

'Makes no difference to me.'

'I nearly called you. I was considering it. Thought you

might return one of the many favours I've done for you. And now fate has taken a hand and given me the chance.'

And I thought fate was working for me, Kate thought. 'What mischief are you getting into?'

'None. It's more my past catching up with me. I need some advice.'

Becky chose a table in the far corner and sat with her back to the room.

'This is unlike you, secretive, hiding away. You normally shout your activities from the rooftops. What evil have you been up to? Robbed a bank or had sex with your sister's husband?'

Kate's amusement was cut short by Becky's expression.

'This isn't a laughing matter. I'm pregnant.'

Kate could feel her heart beating faster. Two of them, both in their fifties, both pregnant? Not the commonest age for such events, rare even.

'Are you sure?'

'Well, the test was positive. I know they can give false results but they're pretty good these days.'

'Do you feel pregnant?'

'Not really. Not had much in the way of morning sickness. Felt queasy for a few days but put it down to the horrible bug that's been doing the rounds.'

Kate nodded. 'So why did you do the test?'

'I'm still asking myself. I'd missed a period. I'm usually super regular and it could just have been the menopause knocking on the door. Something told me a test wouldn't hurt. Never done one before on myself. Folk ask about the tests all the time and I advise, of course. I really didn't expect to see that blue line.'

There was an inevitable next question.

'You know what I'm going to ask. But you don't have to tell me.'

'I think it must be Colin's.'

'At the reunion?'

'Yes. If you recall, we had a fling on the Friday evening,

44

fired by wild, student memories and too much red wine. Then he got unpleasantly drunk and I abandoned him. But we did have sex, full penetrative sex, and I've calculated back – it was around the right time of the month for conception.'

'You weren't on the pill, I assume?'

'No. It didn't suit me and I honestly didn't think there was a need.'

Kate mentally raised an eyebrow. Lively, attractive Becky. She didn't imagine sexual encounters were alien to her. But that was not today's issue.

'Oh, God, Becky! What are you going to do?'

The two women looked at each other. Kate saw hope spread across Becky's face while she felt the weight of a double burden pressing down on her.

'I don't know. That's the advice I thought you might give me.'

'Let's look objectively at the situation.'

Becky's shrug showed her attitude to being objective.

'We can consider the options.' Kate knew what they were; she'd spent many nights going through them.

'The first question is – do you want to have the baby?'

'I don't know.'

'Are you going to tell Colin? Does he mean more than a one-night stand to you?'

'I don't think there's much mileage in telling him. We have no relationship, we're hardly friends now. I don't plan on playing "Happy Families" with him.'

'Okay. You've got a partial decision. Would you consider an abortion?'

'Possibly. Probably. Part of me hates the idea. It's killing a viable being. But there are additional problems with a pregnancy at our age.'

Kate could not stop a small gasp at the word "our" and covered it with a cough.

'Genetic defects like Down's Syndrome. We have a

delightful little girl with Down's who comes into the pharmacy with her mother. She's a joy and I love talking to her. But that's part of my job. I don't want to bring one into the world. And there are further risks in such a late pregnancy, pre-eclampsia, delivery can be harder, there's even a higher chance of a multiple birth. Think of it, Kate. I'd never survive!'

Becky was panicking in a way Kate had never seen. Becky sailed on the waves of life and even if buffeted, took a deep breath and carried on. Where had this Becky gone?

'Even if nothing goes wrong, I don't want to bring a totally perfect child into the world. I cannot see myself as a mother. I'm too old. Too inflexible. I like the life I've got. Other parents at the school gate would think I was the grandmother. The kid would be teased. I'd be too old to join in the games. Grumpy, impatient, a fuddy-duddy. I'd be around seventy when the child went to university.'

'Older parents are far more common now than when we were small.'

'True. But not many as old as me. And I don't relish the idea of being a single mum. Not because of the stigma. It's accepted now. Just the sheer hard work on your own. You're the one who gets up when there's a cry in the night, you deal with all the illnesses, everything is on your shoulders. There's the cost of child care, as well, 'cos I'd have to continue working. The guilt of neither working properly nor mothering well enough. The list is endless.'

Becky wiped her sleeve across her eyes and suppressed a sob. 'I can't cope with this.'

'Of course you can. You're not the first woman to find herself in this situation. There is another option. You could have the baby and put it up for adoption.'

'No! No!' Becky looked around and put her hand over her mouth. An elderly lady eating a cream cake frowned at her. 'It's not an option for me.'

'Fine. I'm only laying out the possibilities. You've made

up your mind about something.'

They sat in silence. Kate fetched two more coffees and a chocolate brownie.

'I think you need an energy boost. Eat it.'

Kate looked at her watch ten minutes later. 'Sorry, Becky, but I need to go. Do you think talking has helped?'

'Not sure I'm nearer a decision. But, yes. It's been good to tell someone. No-one else knows. I can't tell my staff – it wouldn't do much for my credibility – and my family would be unsympathetic. Unbelieving and unsympathetic. You're someone I thought would understand. Thank you.'

'Call me if you want another chat.'

'I will, Kate. Yes, I expect I'll need to. And you'll keep this to yourself, won't you?'

Kate nodded.

'Don't even tell Neil.'

Kate left Becky finishing her coffee and looking at her face in her handbag mirror. Was this the woman Neil was involved with? No clues in today's conversation. But she did not want him to know. Understandable. No-one was to know. A pregnancy was not likely to endear her to him. It might kill any relationship they had. A nasty thought but Kate enjoyed it, nonetheless.

It seems to be my role in life to listen but not to share, she thought. Should I have said I'm in a similar situation? No. She might not have believed me. It is unbelievable. "Anything you can do, I can do better." It was not a competition; it would simply have made matters worse.

Chapter 7

A voice echoed around the pharmacy. It was an old, large building with a high ceiling and did echoes well.

'Hello, Kate – "the prettiest Kate in Christendom" or "Kate the curst". Which are you today?'

The dispenser, Monica, looked worried and one of the counter staff ran back into the dispensary.

'Kate, we have a strange guy in the shop. Not sure what he's up to or what he wants. Looks respectable but seems a bit wild. He might be drunk. Or on drugs. Can you come?'

Kate heard the voice and knew exactly who it was.

'Hello, Colin. Will you stop scaring the hell out of my staff? And why do you always greet me with quotations from "The Taming of the Shrew"? I bet you look them up specifically for me. I can't believe you know the play by heart.'

'Of course I look them up. You are the perfect target. Right name, shrewish character. Ideal opportunity. Can't resist. "Come on and kiss me, Kate!" Give me a hug.'

Fright now disappeared and the counter girls were amused. They gave each other looks that said, "What's Kate been up to with this guy?" and watched. Serving the few customers in the shop was an irritation they dealt with quickly as they waited for the next scene. A soap opera was unfolding before them.

Kate offered her cheek to Colin who gave her a hug anyway.

'Such compliments you offer me! I assume you haven't called in for some antiseptic cream or a shower gel?'

'Correct. I thought we agreed there was some unfinished business when we last spoke. And as I happened to be driving nearby it seemed rude not to come and see you.'

'I could have lived with your rudeness.' Kate turned and saw three pairs of eyes fixed on her. She did not need to say anything. Suddenly there were jobs to do although the whispering continued. Unruly customers who occasionally entered the pharmacy were never as entertaining as this. She guessed her staff speculated about her private life, a life outside her marriage. She once overheard, "Attractive woman – there must be a few stories there," and knew they were discussing her.

'Colin. Listen. If this visit is to harangue me and…' Kate lowered her voice '…get me into bed, you're wasting your time. I think I made my feelings for you clear at the reunion. You stalked me when we were students. Don't start it again. I thought I taught you a lesson.'

'You tantalised me, Kate.' They walked to the corner of the shop where the shelf display gave them some privacy. 'How do you think you can get rid of me by flaunting your body before me, implying you were willing to have sex and then walking out at the last minute? That's hardly teaching me a lesson. As I said at the reunion, if you aren't going to forget our earlier encounters, neither shall I.'

'If you recall, I also said I didn't go in for much sexual activity in my places of work.'

Colin laughed. 'And I said there are ways and means. But sex apart, how about a coffee? When are you free?'

'In thirty minutes. In case you hadn't noticed, it's a work day and I'm the only pharmacist on the premises. I'll come at closing time. Luckily for you it's not a late evening. Just wander off somewhere. You're too much of a distraction for my staff.'

She looked across to the counter where the required minimum was being done.

Colin waved to the girls as he left the shop, making the most of his temporary notoriety. They would not have guessed he was Chief Pharmacist at a major hospital.

Well, a coffee with Colin won't hurt, thought Kate. He's entertaining if you don't take him seriously.

An elderly gentleman wandered in carrying a bulging plastic bag. He greeted Kate by waving his stick in the air.

'Hello, Mr Jackson, how are you?'

'Not well, my darling. Not well. Sad. Olive passed away last week. Knew it was going to happen but never thought it would. The funeral's in two days' time.' Kate led him to a chair near the dispensary where he sank into his coat. She said how sorry she was. The couple had used the pharmacy for many years. She dispensed countless drugs for them, listened to their troubles and shared their small happinesses.

'Anyway, my darling…' He always called her his darling. Kate wasn't sure if it was old-fashioned affection or lack of memory for her name. 'Anyway, my darling, I've brought these for you.' He handed across his bag, full of packets and bottles of tablets, tubes of cream and ointment. 'She didn't use these so you can put them back on your shelves. They're all unopened. I threw away the part packs. A waste but I didn't think you'd want them.' He nodded, a weak smile of benevolence creasing his face.

Kate was about to say she couldn't use anything that had been out of the pharmacy but stopped herself. It was difficult getting the message across. The Jacksons wasted nothing. He wore jumpers darned badly by his wife until they fell apart; she used every scrap of food they bought whether it was strictly edible or not. They'd both had food poisoning, she remembered. But their medicines were different. The doctor prescribed them, the pharmacist dispensed them, they collected them. Then they forgot about them. Not totally. They took an assortment each day but the surplus accumulated.

Kate looked in the bag. Some of the labels were five years old, the medicines out of date. There were even controlled drugs in there.

'There are some empty bottles. I've washed them so you

can use them again.'

Kate wanted to explain to him empty bottles were no use, either. It was her duty. But how could she snub this kindly, old man in the depths of his grief?

So she patted his hand and took the bag with a smile. If it made him feel better, her actions were not wrong.

When he hobbled out of the door, bent by arthritis and the weight of his sorrow, she took the bag into the dispensary.

'Aren't we supposed to explain about returned drugs when folks bring them in?' Monica asked.

'Yes, I know, but it wasn't the moment. He's too old to change his ways. I've mentioned it before. He doesn't listen.' Monica went to take the bag for disposal but Kate stopped her.

'Don't worry. I'll do it before I leave.'

She deliberately took more than half an hour to finish off what she was doing and to sort Mr Jackson's drugs. A few items made their way into her handbag when Monica was well out of sight. She emerged to find Colin hovering outside the shop.

'Ah, here comes "Kate of Kate Hall". You're free!'

'Stop it, Colin, or I won't speak to you again.'

He shrugged and pointed to a pub along the road.

'Too late for coffee. Let's have a drink.'

They settled themselves in a corner and Kate asked for tonic water with ice and lemon.

'Not drinking, Kate? Unlike you. What is it, pregnancy? Or are you weight-watching to maintain your shapely figure?' He grinned.

Kate hoped her voice did not waver as she pointed out she was driving. Colin was prone to making random jokes.

'Do you know who I bumped into the other day?'

'No idea but I expect you'll tell me.'

'Jonathan. You know – Jonathan Carson. Your ex-boyfriend.'

'I know who Jonathan Carson is.'

'Never knew him well as a student. Thought he was too

full of himself, what with the modelling he did and all the girls ogling him. He didn't mix much with the guys.'

'You mean you were jealous?'

'Possibly.'

'You had your own fleet of followers, probably more than he had.'

'Anyway, we bumped into each other at a concert in Bristol and had a drink afterwards. Chatted a bit about the reunion. He's a sociable guy, good company. His ear looks okay now.'

Kate turned her head sharply. 'What do you mean?'

'Don't you remember? He fell down the stairs the first evening and cut it badly on a table on a half-landing. The odd drink too many. Had a big dressing on it. Someone suggested he should sue the hotel. Simon, it was. The guy who went on to study law after pharmacy so he knew what he was talking about. Unsafe position for the table. He said there was probably a case. But Jonathan didn't do anything.' Colin paused. 'I'm assuming what he said was true and it was a fall down the stairs that caused the damage.'

He gave Kate a questioning look but she ignored him.

'So what did the pair of you talk about?'

'This and that. He seemed keen to see you again. I suspect you might have relit an old flame. Never did understand why the two of you broke up. Seemed such a solid relationship. Everyone said you were suited. Much better than you and I would ever have been! Are you seeing him again?'

'Nothing to do with you, Colin. Things went wrong. Sometimes it happens. But at the reunion we patched up a few differences, talked to each other. Addressed a few wounds, you might say. That's all you need to know. And talking of old relationships, you and Becky picked up where you left off, didn't you?'

'Yeah. Won't deny it. We had a good time. Becky was always one for short-lived, passionate liaisons. Lots of them. Me, a guy from geography, another from chemistry, several from

Dramsoc. A few of your cast-offs, even Jonathan, I think.'

Kate opened her eyes wide and Colin covered his mouth with his hand.

'Well, not sure about that. Just speculation. Not while he was with you. Whoops, shouldn't have mentioned it. I may be wrong. Not that it's likely to bother you now, is it?'

'It's history, Colin. It doesn't matter. It's just she never mentioned it – and she told me about most of her affairs.'

'As I said, I could be wrong. Probably am. Do you see much of her?'

'We meet from time to time, sometimes in the course of our work, sometimes socially. She lives in the area. Saw her recently as it happens.'

'Does she ever talk about me?'

'What an odd question! Why do you ask?'

'She's single. I expected her to have a partner or a husband in tow and probably a flock of kids and grandkids. But it seems not. She's attractive, good fun, pleasant company. I'm on my own. I wouldn't mind getting together with her.'

'Another wine-fuelled romp?'

'You're a cynic, Kate. That wasn't what I meant. The sex was good but even I need more than physical relationships. Friendship is something I value. And perhaps Becky needs more than student thrills and frolics now. Maybe you could put in a good word for me.'

'What is this? Am I now a dating agency rather than a prospective fuck? Things have taken a turn for the better!'

'Don't know about that! Well, actually, I do. Much as I'd love to get you into bed, I may try to resist the temptation.' He could not help adding, 'For now.'

Kate wondered whether to mention Becky's pregnancy. Say there was something he should know but leave it hanging in the air? Blurt out the truth to revel in his reaction? Ask him how he felt about being a father again? All these ideas flew through her head like discarded paper blown by the wind from the gutter. They were tatters of inconsequential debris. What she could do and what she would do were different matters.

Kate knew she would say nothing. She kept her word.

'I'll see if you happen to come into the conversation next time I chat to Becky. But I'm not going out of my way for you.'

Colin had made his point and was satisfied.

'Funny coincidence – I bumped into an old university friend recently. Strangely, also at a concert. We knew each other through Dramsoc. She was in loads of productions, a good actress. Frances Mason. Doubt if you knew her.'

'No. Doesn't ring any bells. What did she study?'

'English. Anyway, her department had a thirty-year reunion a few months before ours. She met up with an old boyfriend there and is now pregnant. Not the souvenir she expected to bring away from a nostalgic weekend. Her husband believes it's his.'

'Stupid woman. I have no patience with anyone who can't look after their own fertility. Irresponsible, especially at a mature age. Anyway, should you be telling me this?' Colin, for all his bluster and clowning, felt his professional responsibility.

'If you'd recognised her name, I'd not have continued. It was a real shock to her. I think she needed to unload to someone about it. Someone not in her immediate circle. We talked for a long time. She thanked me afterwards. She'd kept it totally to herself until it was becoming apparent. Amazingly, her husband is pleased! They thought they couldn't have children on account of his low sperm count.'

'So I suppose it's not all bad news. Do you think your friend deliberately tried to get pregnant?'

'No. As I said, she was shocked. She thought she'd passed the menopause but was obviously wrong. Contemplated an abortion but it was against her principles.'

Kate wondered how far to go with this story. But she couldn't stop.

'Do you think she'll ever tell him the truth?' Colin asked.

'No. What is there to be gained? Living a lie with him is easier than leaving him in truth. She has a new lease of life, late in life.'

'Well, I wouldn't be pleased if I was in his shoes. The thought of paternity at this time of life leaves me cold. It's not going to happen.' Colin gave a dismissive snort and then turned serious. 'Is there a reason you're telling me this story?'

'No. None. Just that you mentioned bumping into Jonathan at a concert and it reminded me I'd done something similar.'

It was time to change the subject.

'I'm with you where babies are concerned. I can cope with infants in the pharmacy, even make nice noises to them, make the mothers feel proud, but that's the limit of my patience.'

Well, thought Kate, lucky Frances. She found a solution to her problems. She would live happily, if dishonestly, ever after in her unreal world. And in this unreal world, Kate helped her. Kind Kate who listened and advised. And made a useful discovery about Colin's views on children. It was neat and tidy. Imaginary predicaments are. I am not the imaginary Frances, thought Kate. I am real. I still need to find a solution.

Chapter 8

'How about Verona?'

'What did you say?'

'Verona. In Italy.'

'Jonathan, I've no idea what you're talking about. You phone me up out of the blue and start talking in riddles. I don't have time for silly games.'

'It's not a game. I said I wouldn't pester you for a while – and I haven't – but I also suggested we go away together. To get to know each other again, away from everyday distractions, our "to do" lists and other mundane responsibilities. My suggestion is a weekend in Verona.'

'You expect me to drop everything and agree? You're crazy.'

'I expect you to take me seriously. Because I've never been more serious. I promise you if we decide we have no future together, it will be the end. I'll disappear from your life. I'm flexible about timing. Choose the date. It has to be soon. I'll book the tickets and hotel.'

Kate was speechless.

'I'll phone tomorrow for your decision.'

Jonathan ended the call and Kate was left gazing at her phone. As the shock subsided, she took a piece of paper from the printer and picked up a pen. She put it back and chose another, a fine-liner. Maybe I need an Excel spreadsheet? No, I don't, paper will do. She took a ruler and divided the page accurately into two columns, heading them "Advantages" and "Disadvantages". Her need to analyse the situation was compelling. She needed data on which to base her decision. Scientific training kicked in: act on evidence, rely on facts. Her heart rate slowed and calmness, like the sedatives she often dispensed, spread through her body. She settled herself down, moved the few papers on her desk to one side, ensuring they were level with the edge of the laptop, put a glass paperweight on top of them and started to think.

She had never visited Verona but had heard good reports. Jonathan could have chosen a worse place. She would not encounter anyone she knew. Two positives. Do I need to go away with him? I don't know. It would surely help her to decide what to tell him, to gauge how he would react to her pregnancy. A step in the right direction? A move forward, anyway. It might help her to sort out her confused feelings about him. Or reinforce the toxic mixture of hatred and desire that accompanied any mention of his name. Clarity. It would provide clarity. Definitely a plus.

Then the realisation of the practicalities, the alibis she would need made her slump back into the chair, a sick sensation in her stomach. On the other hand, she knew Neil was going away soon for a week or more. He was constantly busy; they saw little of each other. She could tell him it was a last minute decision after he had gone. Or perhaps not tell him anything. If he phoned home, it would not be odd for her to be out. And he usually called her mobile. There were practical issues – that was a minus – but they were manageable. She still felt uneasy.

It might encourage Jonathan. He would think he was the winner if she went along with his suggestion. He might expect them to share a room. Big negative. Was he lying when he said he would leave her alone if it didn't work out? Could she trust him? If she refused to go to Verona, he would continue to pursue her with some other suggestion.

She compiled the list in her neat handwriting. The pendulum swung backwards and forwards. The piece of paper was now filled. She felt a sense of achievement. She was ready for Jonathan's phone call.

***

Making herself ugly and unappealing was an option. Not a pleasant one, but Kate was working on how to present herself in the most unfavourable light to Jonathan. She could leave her hair unwashed, abandon deodorant, wear no make-up and a frumpy outfit. No. She smirked at the impossible thought. Alternatively, she could use too much make-up and put it on badly. No. She was teasing herself; she was not a clown.

Jonathan would see through any silly ruse. She had to be confident and that meant looking her best. It had to be a more subtle approach.

And, anyway, she did not possess a frumpy outfit.

I'll have to behave badly, be rude, demanding, inconsiderate. Make him dislike me. See a side of me he's not seen before. She was a good actress but this was the type of challenge she'd never undertaken. And she didn't know if she wanted to become such a person. Play it by ear, Kate, she told herself. Think on your feet. You'll find a way.

***

They met at Heathrow, had a civilised drink, boarded the plane. Jonathan chatted inconsequentially and Kate listened, joining in from time to time. They were friends or perhaps work colleagues to the casual observer. A taxi took them to the hotel where they booked into separate rooms, arranging to meet before dinner in the foyer. Jonathan planned the evening; Kate did not know where they were going. She dressed with her usual care, smart, elegant, confident. No low-cut top, no revealing hemline, sex was not on offer tonight. But Kate knew she looked good. As she looked in the mirror, she tried to imagine how she would do "frumpy" and it amused her. She dressed for Verona.

Jonathan had taken her to an Italian restaurant on their

first date. She had not realised it was a date. They were not a couple; it was to celebrate the completion of a joint project in the final year of their degree. But it impressed her. And she impressed him. It was the start of their love affair. She had developed a love-hate relationship with Italian food as a result and rarely visited trattorias, osterias, pizzerias – any eating place with an Italian ending.

Was it a coincidence he chose a similar place now? The long, white aprons on the waiters, single roses on the tables, displays of wine and olive oil, an aroma of herbs in the air. Romantic, susceptible Kate said it was a clever ploy; practical, sensible Kate said this is Italy, what do you expect? Restaurants look like this. The barman asked them where they were from and chatted easily. Jonathan had more than a smattering of Italian.

'Where did you learn the language?' Kate asked.

'I travel. Travel photographers need to be able to get about and you are more welcome if you make an attempt at the language.' Jonathan presented his skills in a matter-of-fact way. I can't even accuse him of boasting, thought Kate.

They were sitting on stools at the bar ordering drinks when Jonathan's phone rang. He glanced at it, said he was sorry but he had to take the call and went outside into the narrow street. Kate raised her eyebrows as he left. She looked around at the other diners. A group of women, party-dressed and lively, were chatting at high volume in one corner. Two bottles of wine stood on the table and a waiter frequently topped up their glasses. There was laughter and much touching and nudging; it was a friends' night out. In contrast, a group of men sat at a long table. Their conversation was muted. It looked like dinner after a business meeting, a stiff obligation. An appealing spread of food was arriving as the wine waiter popped the corks on a couple of bottles of prosecco. Alcohol to soften the atmosphere and encourage them to relax. One of the men got up and wandered around. He started to chat to a waiter – a regular who was at ease here. Kate watched; there was nothing better to do.

'So your husband has abandoned you?'

Kate turned. A man with a strong Italian accent addressed her from an adjacent bar stool. He wore a tailored grey jacket over a black cashmere sweater, slim black trousers and elegant, polished shoes. His outfit had not been chosen at random. His hair was brushed back, silver streaking the black, and curled at his neck.

'He's not my husband and he'll be back.'

'Ah, if he's your boyfriend, he should behave better. Husbands may be excused.'

Slimy character. Thinks he's clever.

'We're just travelling companions.'

'A beautiful woman like you does not have a male travelling companion!'

You think I'm easy to pick up, do you? Kate glanced outside the restaurant and saw Jonathan watching her as he talked. She changed her expression and moved closer to her admirer.

'Well, maybe I'm the exception.'

'He does not seem like a polite man, whatever you call him. Leaving you here while he talks to someone else, probably another girlfriend. Now I am polite and courteous and know how to look after a woman, even an "exception". If you would like to leave your companion to his phone call, his *long* phone call, I would be happy to take care of you. There are many good restaurants near here. I know them all. We can choose one of those.'

'You are presumptuous. I don't dine with men I don't know.'

'You will know me soon. You are getting to know me now.'

Do Italian men all act like caricatures of themselves?

'I'll wait a little longer for him.' Kate glanced again towards the street. Jonathan was pacing around as he talked, his eyes fixed on Kate. 'Tell me about yourself. You speak good English.'

'I am Maurizio and I lived in London for two years. Therefore, my English is not bad. And I learned to love English women.'

I bet you did, thought Kate, smiling sweetly and casually touching his arm as Jonathan came through the restaurant door, frowning.

He looked from Kate to the Italian and back. 'Someone you know?'

'No. Just someone I was talking to in your absence.' She stressed the last word.

Jonathan barely nodded at him, suggested they took their drinks to the table, and guided Kate away from the bar. She turned to Maurizio, said she had enjoyed talking to him and offered him her hand. He took it, kissed it and shrugged.

'My God, Kate, how can you encourage the likes of him?' Jonathan did not care who heard him.

'I don't think you're in a position to criticise my behaviour. If I want to be sociable, I will.'

She wanted to touch Jonathan. She told herself not to be ridiculous. She had touched Maurizio instead.

'I'm sorry about the call. It was from my eldest daughter. She doesn't often ring me when I'm away but she knows I'll always answer. If it had been anyone other than one of my girls, I'd have ignored it.'

'If it had been your wife – your partner – would you have ignored it?'

'Yes.'

They sat in silence. Kate was not going to break it.

'She only calls if there's an issue of some sort. Good news can always wait.'

Kate still said nothing.

'I'll tell you. I can't sit here preoccupied with her problems. And I wanted to talk to you about my family. I want you to understand me, get to know the person I am now. I want you to become part of my life and that includes the girls.'

How she wanted to touch him! But she also wanted to hurt him, to scrape her nails down the suntan of his arm and leave red weals.

Jonathan took a hefty gulp of his wine. It was a good wine, a Barolo, one to be savoured, not quaffed. He had suggested a local wine, a Bardolino or a Valpolicella, but Kate was in expensive mode. It was wasted. He fidgeted in his seat and leaned towards Kate, ill at ease. She could reach across, take his hand and comfort him. But she would not.

'Right. It was Lara. She's just turned fourteen and is suffering teenage angst. A friend invited her to stay the night and Joanne, my partner, said she couldn't. They had an almighty row and I'm expected to sort it out.'

'I assume it's a girlfriend who's invited her?'

'That's the question. Lara says it's a girlfriend. I suspect Joanne isn't sure and is playing safe as I'm not there.'

'She's only fourteen. Surely she's not sleeping around?'

'I hope not. God, I hope not. She often has a sleepover with this friend. Not an unusual request. Joanne should trust her. It's difficult as a father. Girls confide better in a mother. Or someone in a mother's place. Joanne used to get on with them but it seems to be going wrong lately and she's not prepared to take decisions. You'd be much better at handling them, Kate.'

'I thought you wanted me because of who I am. Not because you need someone to help with your problem daughters.'

'This is going horribly wrong. I do want you. I want you for the relationship we'd have. I think we are well-matched, right for each other. Yes, you would be good for the girls but that was a throw-away line. One I should probably have thrown away before it crept out of my mouth.'

Jonathan smiled, the first since the phone call.

'Sorry, Kate. I'm getting uptight. Not like me. But I need to sort this out. One call to Joanne and the evening is ours.'

'I thought we were getting away from our everyday lives this weekend.'

'So did I.'

Kate made no comment. She did not need Jonathan. Much as she thought she wanted him, it was an unnecessary emotion. As he went outside again, she moved back to the bar, forcing herself to be pleasant to the distasteful Maurizio. But Jonathan was quick and she was soon ushered back to the table where she spent some time discussing the menu with the waiter, smiling sweetly at him, accepting his suggestions and thanking him excessively.

'Kate, what are you up to? You don't flirt with waiters. This isn't normal behaviour for you.'

'How do you know what my normal behaviour is?'

'You're right, I don't. You'll have to tell me more about yourself. But first, as the girls have intruded on our time together, let me tell you about them.'

He moved his chair closer to the table, closer to Kate.

'They're both bright, lively and sociable. I have a good relationship with them and I think they've come through the turbulent times we've experienced well. Of course, they miss their mother even though they were little when she died. She's still in their lives, a strong memory which I encourage. I've tried to blot out the experience of my second wife, for myself and them. And they accepted Joanne although it's getting more difficult. Especially since Lara turned fourteen. Sheena is nearly twelve, less complicated but I suppose that will come. I know we could be heading for an emotional and difficult time as they come to terms with their hormones, boyfriends and life in general. With us they'd have such a solid family to support them. Once they get to know and trust you. As they will.'

Jonathan was wound up in his monologue as he painted a picture for Kate. She drank more wine than she would usually do; she needed to. All the details of his wonderful girls, what they enjoyed doing, their prowess at netball and dance, their blond hair, pretty faces and charming personalities did nothing for Kate. If this was meant to draw her closer to him, it was a failure. She felt more and more alienated from this life-style. She had no wish to be a taxi service for after-school activities, to feel second-best to their much loved mother, to work at gaining their confidence and respect. What did she know about teenage girls? Little. She provided them with the "morning-after" pill in the pharmacy when emergency contraception was needed, and had short advisory talks with them. She had no nieces and few close friends with children in their teens. It's strange I don't, she thought, but childless couples often mix with like minds. Getting back with Jonathan was not reuniting with the lover of her youth. He was a different person with a raft of responsibilities now, not the light-hearted, attractive companion of student days.

'You're a caring father, Jonathan. Would you have been equally caring to our child?'

'It's not something I want to talk about.'

'You can't ignore what makes you uncomfortable.'

'Fatherhood was outside my world. I'd have been neglectful and self-centred. God knows what I'd have been. I don't think either of us can progress if we only talk about the past. There's nothing to be gained from it. The future is more important.'

'How would you feel if we had a baby now?'

Jonathan grimaced. 'Now we're getting into a fantasy world. I don't think either of us wants to go down that route, even if it were possible!'

I have no choice, thought Kate. She made a decision. She would tell him about the baby she was carrying – his baby. It would test him. She remembered the last time she had a similar conversation. He had not believed her. Or maybe he had but was in denial. Either way, their relationship ended on that day. What would it do now? It would shock him. He would probably not believe her – again. He might leave her alone. He might reject her. Or he might use it as a means of cementing their relationship. She did not know; she struggled to predict his reaction. And she could not decide which reaction was preferable. She composed what she would say. Jonathan's words droned in the background as he returned to tales of his family. Every so often, she listened and waited for a pause, for a lead that would allow her to begin her story. It had to be the right moment.

But the right moment to tell him was always a few sentences away.

Jonathan's phone rang again.

'You should turn it off.'

'I can't. I have to be available for the girls. It's Sheena this time.'

When Jonathan returned, Kate had her coat on.

'I cannot be third best, Jonathan. I'm going back to the hotel.' Kate turned her back on Jonathan and made a point of walking close to Maurizio who was still drinking at the bar. He followed her out of the restaurant and offered her his arm. Kate took it with a flourish, knowing Jonathan's eyes would be on her. She did not turn but put on her most animated face, laughing loudly at some inane comment. She felt reckless. I cannot be a pawn in anyone's life. I will do what I want. At that moment, she had a need to be with the smooth-talking, expensively dressed, smarmy Italian. She wanted to do something outrageous, something shocking, just to prove she could. She did not want a safe family life, a ready-made collection of duties, a weekly diary to which she had minimal input.

'I have an apartment five minutes from here. We must go there. We can be comfortable and I can give you limoncello and small Italian biscuits.'

'No.'

'No? Why not? Is a wonderful place. You will like it.'

'You don't know what I like. This is not the start of a romantic relationship, nor even the start of a romantic night.'

Kate's voice was gruff. No sweet words, no enticements. As they passed a small alleyway, a "vicolo", she turned, pulling Maurizio with her. Within a few metres, they were in darkness although she could see a church ahead. She walked quickly, cobble stones hurting her feet through the thin soles of her shoes,

Maurizio striding alongside her. They reached a small piazza and Kate continued down the side of the church.

'This is not a good place to be.'

'Shut up.'

Kate pushed her startled companion against the wall and started to undo his belt.

'Cara, we can go to my apartment, I told you. I can make beautiful love to you there.'

'You can do it here and it doesn't have to be beautiful. It just needs to be effective and satisfying. It can't be the first time you've fucked a woman against a wall.'

Maurizio did as he was told. The episode lasted several minutes. In that time, Kate clawed his back and bit his neck, drawing blood. He shouted. She climaxed before him. When he was done, he held her by the shoulders and looked in disbelief at her.

'You are an amazing lady. We must do this again. But I prefer not here. Not at a church.'

Kate pushed him away. She found tissues in her handbag and wiped herself. She pulled down her dress, removed her knickers from her left ankle and ran her fingers through her hair to tidy it.

'Maurizio, you are charming. Far too charming for me. And, I have to say, a rapid lover. I've had enough of this evening. Ciao.' She walked away, the first creases of a smile playing around her lips and the glow of satisfaction within her. Her heart began to pound as she realised what she had done and she stopped and leant against a wall. She was not a slut, she had told her mother as much. Well, she thought, there's a first time for everything. As she passed the restaurant, she could see Jonathan finishing the meal alone, a waiter topping up his glass.

***

They had another day to get through. Kate skipped

breakfast and Jonathan had his second, lonely meal. He phoned Kate and asked what she wanted to do.

'Jonathan, we're in Verona, we should see it. There is little point in simply booking an early ticket home.'

He bombarded her with questions, about her work, her free time, her opinions and views. She offered snippets of information in a desultory way, the weight of two prospective step-daughters heavy upon her. But it was impossible to remain unexcited in Verona. Jonathan knew where to go. They visited Saint Fermo's Church with its upper and lower levels and its roof built like the hull of a ship; they walked under the original Roman arches into the town; they sat in the Piazza Bra and had a drink, watching locals go by to shop at the stalls. The market was for everyone with fresh fruit and vegetables alongside cheap clothing and leather goods. It was early in the year for tourists and Kate preferred it that way. She forgot she intended to be a bitch.

'Come on, we have to go and see Juliet's statue,' Jonathan said.

'I prefer real history. Juliet is fiction.'

'Yes, but the statue is famous. It's important to Verona. It brings visitors. And you love Shakespeare so you've got to see it.'

They found the courtyard where the statue stood, outside the "Casa di Giulietta". A young man was vigorously rubbing her right breast and looking lustily at his girlfriend's anatomy which he went on to massage in a similar way.

'Touching her right breast is meant to bring true love,' Jonathan said.

Kate took one look at the now embracing couple and said, 'Don't even consider it.'

She declined to go into the house but, in spite of herself, enjoyed seeing the balcony. It was nothing but a tourist attraction. There were love letters pinned everywhere, many addressed to Juliet herself. The place was untidy with them.

'I can't believe people write such things,' she said. 'There's no point.'

'Not everyone is as practical and grounded as you. Sentiment takes over, folk get caught up in romance. Love is strange.'

'Don't get philosophical, Jonathan. Most of this is lust.'

Jonathan laughed and got his camera out of the leather satchel he was carrying. He started to take photographs.

'Don't tell me this is actually a work trip!' Kate exploded. 'Last night I was third best. I didn't consider I might sink to fourth, lower than the camera.'

'Don't be silly, Kate. Of course this isn't an assignment but I can't leave my photographer's eye behind. If there's an opportunity for an interesting photo, I have to take it.'

'Well be quick about it!' Kate was impatient. And something else – his words sounded familiar. Hadn't Neil said something similar recently? Something about observation being his business? How odd the two men she was most preoccupied with both happened to be photographers. She had wondered about this since the reunion when she discovered Jonathan had left pharmacy years ago for photography. Maybe it was their outlook she found attractive; they were both serious observers of life.

Her mood lightened. There were no more phone calls. Jonathan took a few photographs as they wandered around but did it unobtrusively; it did not intrude on their conversation. He was considerate, making sure Kate always had something to pique her interest, and amusing, his comments on the locals perceptive and witty. He would spot a busy "Nonna", fussily dressed and over-coiffed, escorting her talkative grandchildren; an elegant gentleman wearing ridiculously pointed Italian leather shoes. Details Kate might have half-seen but not registered, not noticed as Jonathan did. He was also a knowledgeable guide.

'You've been here before, haven't you?'

'Yes, briefly. I loved it and thought you would, too. It was an assignment. I've got some of those photos with me. Thought you might like to see them. Give you an idea of what I do for a living.'

They found a small bar, not a difficult task, and Kate relaxed over a second glass of wine. Jonathan produced a folder containing a dozen photographs.

'They were taken in summertime when the light was brighter than today but you'll recognise some of the subjects.'

Kate admired his compositions, not just beautiful frescoes and magnificent churches but the expressions on the faces of those gazing at them. She liked the amphitheatre, which they hadn't yet seen, with a group of children having a mock battle. She loved the Castelvecchio. It was not simply places that caught his eye; it was the interaction of places with people. He has much in common with Neil, she thought.

'We can go to the Roman Theatre – the Teatro Romano. If you're up for a big climb, we can walk above it to the Castel San Pietro for a fabulous view over the town.' Enthusiasm was bubbling through Jonathan and he could not sit still.

'And you can take yet more photographs!'

'I could, but it's not the point. I want to share these places with you. I want you to feel our sharing them. This is the sort of life we could have together.'

'It isn't, Jonathan. This is time-out from life. This isn't everyday.'

'Don't tell me you're not enjoying this. I can see you are.'

Kate did not reply. He changed the subject.

'What do you think of my photos?'

'They are clever and perceptive. Your level of observation is acute. Would you mind if I kept a few of these?'

'Please do.'

'Have you ever shown any of your work to Neil?'

'Neil? No. His line of work is different from mine. And our paths don't often cross.'

'I think he'd appreciate them. You have a similar way of looking at the world.'

'Do we have a similar way of looking at you?'

Silly of me to mention him, thought Kate.

'I expected you to ask about Neil. He's away a lot. Totally tied up with his next exhibition. He's got this idea about children with Down's Syndrome. Presenting them in different scenarios. All stimulated by meeting a young child with the Syndrome. He has huge sympathy with the condition and how people manage. I can't imagine how he'll do it. But I'm sure he'll make a success of it. You know how talented he is.'

'I do. I was impressed with his last exhibition. I recall you and I enjoyed a bit of banter there, in front of the famous "Love Bite" photograph'. Jonathan's laughter was forced; there was little humour shared. 'And is this clever husband of yours faithful? Seems he has opportunities not to be.'

'Maybe. Maybe not.' Telling Jonathan would not hurt. 'I think he's having an affair with Becky Whitehead.'

'Naughty boy! Shouldn't have chosen a friend of yours. She was always a live wire, Becky. Liked her men.'

'You know about that, don't you Jonathan?' The pleasantness of the day fell away as Kate's suspicion resurfaced.

'What are you suggesting?'

'Was it before we got together or afterwards?' Kate could not stop the question.

'I'm just saying what I've heard. Rumours. Men's chatter. She had lots of boyfriends.'

Lies. Kate could tell. He would have admitted to an early fling. Something that happened in the first or second year of their course. It was forgivable. One after he had rejected Kate would be a harder confession. And that was why he didn't make it. She hated him. She hated the world. Her relaxed mood disappeared. She wanted to scream, to say something hurtful, do something she would regret. She felt a fire within her that only malevolence could quench.

'I could tell you something interesting about Becky, Jonathan. Something that might surprise you.'

'You're not a gossip, Kate. I'm not sure I want to hear malicious stories about her. If Becky has told you something in

70

confidence, don't tell me.'

'Suit yourself.'

He was right, she was not a gossip. She did not understand herself nor what she was suggesting. Confusion filled her head. There was no point in telling him about Becky's pregnancy when she could not find the right moment to mention her own.

'By the way, did you enjoy the rest of the evening with your smooth Italian friend?' Jonathan's sarcasm was undisguised.

'It wasn't the rest of the evening. It was minutes. We had a rough fuck against the wall of a church and then I went back to the hotel and bed. On my own.'

'Sure. I guessed as much.'

What a perfect camouflage honesty is!

Chapter 9

'I need more information about kids with Down's Syndrome. Adults, too, for that matter. Do you think the mother of the child I was talking to in your shop – you remember – would be able to help?'

Neil called Becky for advice. He was wrapped up in his idea for the next exhibition but realised how short on hard facts he was. Organising venues and practical management he could do. But he needed contacts.

'I can ask her next time she comes in – it's usually Wednesday mornings. Her name's Karen, by the way. Why don't you contact the Down's Syndrome Association? I'm sure they'd help.'

'Yes, I thought of that. But I'm reluctant. I like to do things informally, unofficially. I get more truth in my photographs that way.'

'It would just be a start. Putting you in contact with the right people. Perhaps some self-help groups.'

'Mmm – maybe. Look, I'll pop round next Wednesday. It would fit in fine with other things I've got on. Perhaps we could have a bite of lunch? There's a legitimate reason if we're seen as you're advising me medically.'

'Getting super cautious? We've had lunch before.'

'Kate's been asking odd questions. Making comments about whether it's necessary to have an affair to keep a twenty-year marriage vibrant. And she noticed I'd got an old envelope with your name on. A silly slip on my part. I think I wriggled out of her accusations but I do wonder if she suspects.'

'If she does, we'll find out soon. Come round on Wednesday.'

Becky didn't seem bothered but Neil was plagued by the shadow that had settled on him. Luck runs out sometimes, he thought. And lately, he'd felt guilty. For years, his easy relationship had been just that. Becky was his comfort, his relaxation, his refuge. The relationship had happened; it had not been planned. He had never dwelt on potential consequences, never looked to the future. But Kate's recent comments had woken him up. Maybe it was time to evaluate. To straighten his life out. He was uncomfortable thinking of himself as a cheat. And he still loved Kate. Didn't he?

***

'You could come along to one of our regular meetings. There's a few of us with DS kids who get together each week. Sometimes you need the company of someone who understands the bad times. Can't promise folks will want to talk, but you can observe.'

Neil was keen, thanked Karen excessively and then wondered what faced him. He felt unusually nervous at the prospect of meeting these parents so he asked Becky to go along, too.

'You're more used to people suffering with health problems. You know what to say, how to deal with them. You can stop me if I set off along a wrong – or worse, inappropriate – track.'

'That's probably your first error, Neil. The kids who'll be at the meeting aren't ill. Well, many do have health issues, but you mustn't think of them as being sick or disabled. They're different, that's all.'

'You've just proved my point. I need to have you there.'

'Well, I'll come if I can but there's the problem of a

locum. It's short notice and locums are expensive.'

He rehearsed in his head the type of question to ask. This was not Neil. He got his results through spontaneity and started to doubt his own judgement in embarking on the project. For once, he needed to be prepared.

He was thinking about this over dinner that evening. Kate noticed his preoccupation.

'Something wrong with the casserole? You don't seem to be getting much pleasure out of it.'

'Sorry, Kate. It's lovely. I'm enjoying it. But my head is elsewhere, thinking about a visit I'm doing in a couple of days.'

He told her about the meeting and his apprehension. How he hoped it would lead to the photographs he needed. He decided not to say Becky was instrumental in setting it up.

'Super idea, Neil. You always have such depth to your photos. This'll give you just the right info. Tell you what, I'll work with you on the topics to raise. I do know a bit about Down's, as I said.'

They sat together and considered what he should ask. How the parents felt before the child was born – when did they find out they would be parents of a child with Down's? What were the issues after the birth? How did family and friends react? The list grew and Neil became more uncomfortable.

'I don't know if I can do this, Kate. It seems too intrusive. I'm not a medic. What right have I to ask these things? What benefit will the parents or the kids get from me?'

'Oh, Neil! Don't lose sight of your original aims! You wanted to show how "normal" these kids are, how they fit into society. You were full of it when you first had the concept. Don't let the difficult steps on the way distract you from your purpose. Of course the parents and the kids will gain benefit.'

'I wish I could be as focussed and single-minded as you are, Kate. I suppose it's your analytical mind. Once you make a decision, you don't deviate from it.'

'It's just how I am. I don't have your creativity. We're

different. Don't give up on this.'

'I don't want to give up. I'm still convinced about the concept. Just more worried than usual about how to carry it out.'

'When's the meeting?'

'Friday afternoon in St Andrew's church hall.'

'Let me come along. I'm intending to work at home on Friday. I could steer you if needed or provide the odd prompt. I could even chat to some of the parents and make some notes for you.' Kate saw the expression on Neil's face. 'Well, maybe that'd be wrong, too formal, not your style. But I could come as back-up. I may even know some of the families.'

Neil wondered why life was so complicated. He'd asked Becky to go along and now Kate was volunteering. He did not want both.

'I think it's probably better if you didn't come, Kate. As you say, you may know some of them. They might be in awe of you, a pharmacist. It might look like an onslaught, the pair of us there. Too official.'

'Oh.' Kate's disappointment was audible. 'Didn't expect you to turn me down. I wouldn't try to run everything, you know, Neil. It's your project. I can be diplomatic and tactful. That's also part of my job.'

'I know. The discussion we've just had has helped. It might be enough. And there could be further meetings. I'll get the sense from this one if it'd be right to take you along.'

'Well, the offer is there. You might change your mind over the next couple of days.'

I doubt it, Neil thought.

***

Seconds after Neil walked through the door, the little girl from Becky's pharmacy ran up to him with Karen following her.

'Where are your cameras? Can I see them again?'

'Hello, love. I haven't got them with me. I could bring

them another time. Would you like that?'

She nodded.

'Anyway, if I'm going to take a photo of you, I need to know your name. You haven't told me.'

'Elizabeth Rosemary Karen Mitchell. I'm named after my Grandma and my Nanna and my Mummy. '

'Well, Elizabeth Rosemary Karen Mitchell, aren't you lucky! They're nice names.'

She grinned and looked at her mother.

'Come in, Neil, and let me introduce you to some of the parents. I've mentioned to a few you'd be here.' She looked intently at him. 'You look worried. Don't be.'

Neil was welcomed, provided with a cup of coffee and biscuits and observed with kindly but curious and sometimes wary eyes. He explained the reason he was there, told them about his previous exhibitions and why he wanted to produce one about children with Down's Syndrome.

'I want to be accurate and fair to your kids. Anything you'd like to tell me would be useful. I'd rather you spoke about your "Ups and Downs" than me firing questions at you. And I'd like your permission to take photos at a later date if you're prepared to give it.' Neil knew he sounded far more formal than he intended to be. Nerves were controlling his words; he could not relax.

There was a general hubbub, comments thrown about randomly which Neil caught like precious stones. What lovely children they were, how the parents forgot much of the time they were different from other kids, how these meetings were helpful because everyone understood the common problems, how it was easy for strangers to underestimate what the kids were capable of. Neil absorbed it all, glad to get anything but aware of the superficiality. There were layers of stories beneath those he was hearing.

He glanced around the room at the children. It could be any playgroup. Some children were quiet, some were noisy, some sat and played, some rushed around. One small boy was making odd, whooping noises which overpowered the general conversation until his mother distracted him. Was that symptomatic of Down's Syndrome? Neil did not know. He realised he had no comparison; his knowledge of children in general was limited. And the children all looked different – well, variations on a theme. He had expected they would all look alike. A girl ran by making a noise like the squeaking of chalk on a blackboard. It was unpleasant but nobody seemed bothered by it.

The conversation petered out. He started to doubt the value of his visit as he wandered into the kitchen. He rinsed his cup and bit his lip. A young woman, maybe in her thirties, followed him. She stood silently for a few moments. Neil sensed she wanted to speak. He waited.

'I'm Sally. It hasn't been plain sailing, you know.'

'Do you want to tell me?'

'If you'd like to listen.'

Neil leaned on the wall and indicated he would listen to anything.

'I always thought it was only older women who had Down's Syndrome babies. I had the routine screening test when I was pregnant. I couldn't believe it when I discovered I was a high risk. I don't support abortion but I confess I thought about it seriously. I didn't think I'd be able to cope. I already had one child who was a handful. I didn't know how much special care such a baby would need. I wondered if it was fair to the family as a whole if I continued with the pregnancy.'

'But you clearly did continue with it.'

'I had to. I didn't even have the diagnostic test.'

Neil looked confused. 'Sorry, I thought you said the test showed you were high risk?'

'There are two types of test. The screening test is done routinely. It's a blood test, can't harm the foetus. The doctors combine that with a measurement they take at the base of the baby's neck, called the nuchal fold thickness.'

She smiled when Neil looked impressed at her medical knowledge.

'We all get to know the technical details. You learn as much as you can. Anyway, the measurements give a level of risk. If it's greater than one in a hundred, it means it's high. Mine was. You can then have an amniocentesis where the amniotic fluid is sampled if you choose to. It gives you a definite diagnosis.'

'Yes, I know about that. I just didn't realise there were two tests.'

'There's a small chance of miscarriage with amniocentesis. As I'd decided I couldn't bear to have an abortion, there was no point in going ahead with another test, especially a risky one. It wouldn't have altered my decision. I had three miscarriages after my first baby. It might've been my last chance. And I've been lucky. Petra has some medical issues, she's more prone to infections and her sight isn't great, but some kids – and some parents – have much more to cope with.'

'I noticed quite a few of the parents here are "older", in their forties, maybe.'

'Yes. I think they need the support these meetings provide. It's true the risk is higher in older parents, but as more young people have babies, there are actually more Down's Syndrome babies born to younger parents. Sorry, it sounds confusing. Do you understand what I'm getting at?'

'Yes, I do. And I gathered some facts before I came here, anyway.'

Sally gave him an appreciative glance.

'May I ask how difficult it was after Petra was born?'

'I had post-natal depression. Any new mum can get it. But it made life harder and it took me six months to get through it. And Petra had feeding difficulties. It's common – ask any of the parents here. I became neurotic, thinking folk were staring at me or Petra when they probably weren't. But people do stare. Total acceptance isn't there. We do get nasty looks and rude comments. You try to ignore them but you don't forget them. Petra is too young to notice. It's the parents who get hurt.'

'And what does the future hold for Petra?'

'She's going to the local primary school in September. They're understanding and have taken children with Down's Syndrome before. She's bright. Very friendly. I think she'll be fine.' Sally was as proud as any mother of a loving four-year-old could be. Petra ran in and pulled at her mother's hand, asking her to come and see what they were doing in the play-house.

'I appreciate your openness, Sally. I hope you understand the aim of my exhibition is not to poke fun at Petra – or any of the children. It's to show what these kids are really like, what they can achieve and do. It's also to show some of the problems and to get a wider understanding of them.'

'Yes, I do understand. That's why I came to talk to you.'

As Sally went to leave the kitchen, Neil noticed two other mothers hovering by the door.

'Can we talk to you, too?'

'Of course. That's why I'm here.'

The little kitchen, just a sink, a microwave, a kettle and the basics of coffee and tea making, seemed a more comfortable environment than the main hall. Personal feelings, struggles and joys would get lost in the lofty room, buried under the toys, hidden among the stacks of chairs. They could creep out among the mundane trappings of domesticity, the washing-up and the packets of biscuits.

'I didn't think I could have children. We tried for years and had given up when I fell pregnant at forty-five. I knew the risks. I'm a nurse. But I felt I had to be prepared. It's a big jump from being a couple to being parents at our age. So I had an amniocentesis. Not because I wanted to have an abortion because I didn't. I needed to get my head in the right place if it was positive. I actually waited until thirty-four weeks before having the test because of the risk. Had it triggered the birth, I'd simply have had an early baby. It would have lived.

'What happened? Was your baby born early?'

'No. He was actually born a week late. But you never know the effect an amniocentesis might have.'

Neil's head was buzzing. The level of knowledge of the parents impressed him. Then he scolded himself, knowing he would find out all he could in their situation. Once they started to talk, it seemed they needed to swamp him with information. He did not want all the medical details but was afraid to say "no" to anything in case the stories stopped. And they kept on coming, little snippets, sad situations, unexpected highs. He needed to make notes. But he felt the atmosphere of trust that was developing would be ruined by a pad of paper and a pen.

The air in the kitchen was saturated with words. As one mother finished her story, another started. The small space was now crowded, children were rushing in and out and concentration was getting harder. He heard about "a plethora of emotions", the thoughtlessness of doctors who gave a barrage of facts but little emotional support and "total devastation" on being given a diagnosis. One mother shocked him when she said she had been moved into a private room after the birth in case her baby upset the other new mums. But he heard about compassion and thoughtfulness, too. These were the undoubted survivors.

An Indian lady in a sari started to speak. Her voice was low and Neil leaned forward to catch her words.

'I didn't tell my family I knew my child would have Down's Syndrome. I didn't say anything until a month after she was born.'

Neil waited for the explanation.

'I wanted to make sure they all bonded with her first. My parents, my brother and sister, my aunts and uncles. I felt it best that way.'

'Do you think they may have rejected her if they'd known?'

'I don't know but the possibility worried me. Tiny babies with Down's Syndrome don't look so different from other babies. They didn't guess. And they all love her now. My plan worked.'

The noise in the kitchen had got to a point where people were moving out with their children to quieten them.

'Are you coming here again?'

A lady holding a small child approached him, speaking quietly. She looked ill at ease, and rubbed her fingers across her face as she spoke, shielding her words.

'If I can, I'd like to come next week with my camera.'

'Can I talk to you then?'

'Of course. But we can chat now if you want.'

'No. I'd prefer to do it without everyone around.' She looked across the room, her eyes darting from one person to another. Her movements were jerky as if her skin felt too tight. 'My story is a bit different. I'm Tina, by the way.'

'Finding a quiet moment might be a challenge.' Neil's voice was almost drowned by the shouts around him.

'Are you going out to your car?'

'Yes. Shall we talk outside?'

Neil went back into the main hall where several people were tidying up. He thanked Karen for the group's hospitality and openness and asked about the following meeting. It seemed they accepted him and would welcome him back with his camera.

As he left the building with Tina and her baby, Kate pulled up in her car. She leaned out and called Neil.

'I was passing. Just wondered how things are going. If I could help?'

'I'm just leaving, Kate. See you at home.'

Tina stopped. 'Maybe next week, Neil. You obviously need to get off. See you.' She walked away.

Neil got into his car and slammed his hand against the steering wheel.

'Shit! Shit! Shit! Just when I might have got a really interesting story, Kate has to barge in!'

He got out his notepad and scribbled furiously. He had a good memory and got the main points of his conversations down accurately. But the absence of the "different" story bugged him.

What was Tina going to tell him? Would she be there the following week? Would she change her mind and not share her story? He would have to say something to Kate. Well-meaning but clumsy and ill-timed, she had possibly lost him valuable information.

He looked through his notes and started to think how he could combine stories with photographs. This would work, it would! There was much that was positive. But he knew he would get positivity from such a meeting. These were people who were coping; able, knowledgeable parents who knew what to do. His researches told him a significant proportion of mothers decided to abort their babies when they received the diagnosis. Others put them up for adoption. Those were not the mothers he would meet here.

He turned on his phone and saw a text from Becky. "Sorry couldn't make it today, poss next fri xx". Well, he managed without her. Perhaps he could cope on his own.

Chapter 10

Neil arrived home with his anger barely under control. Kate had her back to him.

'How did it go? I thought about you.'

'It was going well until you arrived!'

'Until I arrived? What did I do?'

'A young mother wanted a private word with me. It could have been significant. You scared her off.'

'God, Neil! You're getting melodramatic. I simply asked if I could help. It's hardly a frightening thing to say.'

'Bad timing. She was nervous, wanted a private moment. You spoiled it.'

'Well, there's no point in shouting. I didn't know.'

'I did ask you not to come.'

'Okay, I won't do it again. Cool down.'

'She said her story was different. I have to find out what it is.'

'Everyone thinks they're different. They are. Whether or not Down's Syndrome is involved. Doesn't mean you'll get anything useful from it.'

'You're such a cynic, Kate. I think she was being truthful. She needed to say something to me. I must talk to this woman again.'

'She's probably attention-seeking. Clever. She's got you hooked already.'

Neil threw his jacket on a chair, his scarf on the table and an uncomprehending look at Kate. 'I don't know why I bother telling you anything. You knock down all my ideas.'

'I do not! This ridiculous conversation started because I tried to help. And I'm not a cloakroom attendant. Move your things.'

'Later. I've stuff to do.'

'Neil, you're a slob. Move them now. I'm continually tidying up after you – used coffee cups everywhere, dirty underwear on the bedroom floor, papers and files wherever you leave them. I'm sick of it.'

Kate's voice rose and her neck started to flush. 'I'm not your slave or your housekeeper. You need to pull your weight.'

'We've had this conversation a hundred times. I'm not as tidy as you. We both know that. But I try.' Kate started to speak but Neil interrupted her. 'You're obsessive, Kate. What you consider untidy most folk would regard as normal. This is our home, not a show house. Be realistic.'

'Why do I bother furnishing it beautifully and paying a cleaner to keep it looking good with you around? You'd be better off in a garden shed.'

Kate was screaming, her usual measured demeanour gone. This was not a Kate Neil had seen before and he stood and stared at her.

'Kate, Kate. This isn't you. Not the usual you. What's stressing you?'

'You are! Haven't I just said?'

'Then I'll keep out of your way.'

Neil marched off to the study to sort out his emotions and the scribbled notes he'd made. As he typed them up and got involved in creating the story he wanted to tell, planning the sequence of his photos, his anger abated. His temperament was occasionally stormy but, like a day in April, calm returned before long.

He was his usual self by dinner time, a smile on his face and the frown lines of annoyance smoothed out. Kate was quiet so he made no reference to her previous outburst.

'They are amazing people, Kate. The parents and the kids. You could sense the warmth between them, the optimism, joy even. I felt uncomfortable, an intruder at first, but they accepted me. A number of the mums volunteered info and I can go back to take photos.'

Kate gave him a questioning look.

'No, I don't need your assistance. It wouldn't be any help to introduce a new face now. I don't mean to be ungrateful.'

'What about this mother who was going to tell you something special?'

'I'll just wait and see. She said her story was different but I don't know in what way. I had a feeling it might give me a new angle on life with a child with Down's.'

***

Neil felt at home as he walked into the hall the following Friday. Elizabeth saw him and ran across asking what he had in his large bag. He opened it and said he was going to take some photographs, showing her the kit as he'd done in Becky's shop. She became excited and danced around, ran across to another girl and pulled her by the hand to come and see. Some of the children chatted to him, others were shy and ran back to their parents, watching from a distance. Neil had an old camera with him, one he could let the children handle, in addition to his main equipment. It was a technique he used when capturing children at play. He showed one of the older children how to hold the camera and what button to press. Who knows, he thought, maybe I can use a photo taken by one of the kids. It would be a new approach. Much of the afternoon was taken up in this way. The usual play equipment was abandoned; the best toys are articles you are not usually allowed to touch.

To his surprise, the parents kept away. They watched, vigilance always there, but allowed the children to mill around Neil. Like typical kids, Neil thought. Well, in many ways they are

85

typical kids. As the children tired of his attention, he got photos of them with their mothers. He captured a beautiful moment of a mum playing on a rug with a little one who had just learned to sit but was unstable. She called to him.

'Our kids have less muscle tone. They're a bit floppy so it takes them longer to learn to sit and walk. But they get there. They teach us patience.'

Neil was replying when he noticed Becky chatting to Karen. When he could, he excused himself.

'I've had a successful afternoon. Karen, you're a star letting me come along.'

'No problem. It's something different for us, too, an amusement for the kids. Will we get to see the photos?'

'Of course. They'll be part of my exhibition. I hope some of you will come along. But I can let you have personal copies of any you want. It's the least I can do.' He turned to Becky. 'Didn't see you arrive. Been here long?'

'About half an hour. You didn't need my help so I left you to it.'

He looked around to see where Tina was; he'd seen her earlier. Although Becky kept her distance, he worried that even her subtle approach might discourage Tina if she saw them together. When Tina headed for the kitchen, he followed, leaving Becky mid-sentence.

'Hi, Tina. Sorry about last week. I'd love to talk if it's okay with you.'

She bit a nail. 'I'm leaving early. In five minutes.'

'I'm going soon, too. Can we chat outside?'

She nodded, scooped up her little boy, balanced him on her hip and popped back into the main hall to collect her bag. Neil went over to Becky, thanked her for coming and said he had to leave unexpectedly. She gave him a confused look.

Outside, Tina was strapping her child into his car seat.

'He's adopted,' she said.

Neil was caught without words for a few seconds. Then he

said, 'What an amazing thing to do.'

They looked at each other. Neil took a deep breath, seeing the expression on Tina's face.

'Clearly, I shouldn't have said that. I didn't know what to say.'

'I get all sorts of reactions. Usually I don't tell people. Adopting a child, one you haven't conceived and carried yourself, is a brave and challenging move. But it applies to all adoptions. I guess you said it was amazing 'cos Adam has Down's.'

Neil nodded. 'But I did sense it wasn't the thing to say as I said it. I'm learning, Tina. Don't be too hard on me.'

'You are more honest than most.'

'Do your friends here know Adam is adopted?'

'Oh, yes. It's not a secret.'

There was more to come. There had to be an explanation why Tina would not talk with others around.

'There is a reason why we chose to adopt Adam.' She hesitated. 'Not something I normally talk about.'

Neil was silent. He was terrified anything he said would break the moment and the imminent confidence would be lost.

Before Tina could continue, they were interrupted by Sally rushing out waving a child's blanket.

'Tina, you left Adam's blanket. Thought there might be trouble at bedtime without it!'

'Oh, my God, thanks!' She grabbed the blanket and hugged it to her. 'Adam would never go to sleep without "fluffy blankey".' She tucked it round Adam in his seat and kissed his forehead. He grinned and rubbed the soft material against his face.

'But you'll tell me?'

'Sorry, what did you say?'

'You don't talk about why you adopted Adam. I just thought you might…'

But the moment was gone. Tina got into the car.

'Perhaps another time, Neil.' She looked around her in her jumpy fashion and pushed her hair off her face. Neil could see her stubby nails, bitten as low as they would go. 'It's difficult.'

She started the car and drove off.

'Shit.' Neil felt ambushed. Destined not to hear the one story he needed. His mood was disturbed by the arrival of Becky.

'You rushed off in a hurry. Why the grumpy face?'

'Sorry, I just needed to talk to one of the parents. 'She wanted a private chat.'

'Useful info?'

'Potentially. But something keeps interrupting us and she withdraws into herself. She's nervous. I'm sure there's a story waiting to be heard. I just can't get at it yet. But the whole visit here has really fired me up. I've got a load of photos to go through and plenty of other stories. There really are "Ups and Downs". I can feel the exhibition developing before me.'

'Want to tell me about it?'

'Yes, but not now. Need to sort it out in my head. And I need to talk to some older people with Down's Syndrome and their parents. I also need to have a chat with someone who's not coping well. Someone who doesn't come to a social group like this because it's too difficult. Do you have any contacts?'

'No, but Karen is bound to know a few folk who can help. Ask her.'

'Will do. Anyway, when can I see you?'

'Don't know. Give me a call.'

As they both walked to their cars, Neil saw Kate's red sports car disappearing round the corner, a screech of tyres as she took it too fast. Bugger! It was obvious Becky had been at the meeting. Luck was not with him today.

Chapter 11

Tina was on the phone. He had no idea who gave her his number but it didn't matter. She was talking to him.

'I don't know why I need to tell you this, Neil. There is something about you that inspires confidence. I feel you'll handle my story with sensitivity. Not spread it around, respect confidentiality.'

'Of course.' Neil whispered, not daring to stop the flow of words.

'I went to your last exhibition, the "Love Hurts" one. I like the way you express feelings and emotion in your photos.'

Neil thanked her; he was still sufficiently modest to enjoy compliments.

'There are few folk who know my story. You'll understand soon why I'm reluctant to talk. But there's a point I need to make. You might help me to make it.'

'Well, I'll try.' A shiver of apprehension went through him. I hope she's not expecting too much. I'm a photographer, he thought. Not a campaigner or a politician.

Tina was in her own world. Talking into an anonymous phone seemed to suit her. Neil preferred face-to-face contact; he gleaned information from the look in someone's eye, the unintended expression passing across a face. But the absence of eyes and faces freed Tina to speak.

'Around five years ago, I got pregnant. It was a mistake. We were on holiday, had too much to drink one evening and were careless. We had two children already, had decided that was it and Bob was about to have a vasectomy. It was a shock. We talked about an abortion but rejected the idea.'

Neil said a few words to show he was listening, reluctant to interrupt the monologue.

'I was thirty-eight, had the usual screening tests and came out as low risk for chromosome abnormalities. Then at my twenty-week scan, a heart problem was detected in the foetus. After much discussion with the doctors, we decided I'd have an amniocentesis.'

Neil wanted to know why but kept quiet, scared to speak.

'By the time the result of the amniocentesis came through, I was twenty-three weeks pregnant. The baby had Down's Syndrome.' Even on the phone Neil could feel the mood change. 'I can still feel the agony of trying to make a decision.'

The pause seemed to go on for ever. When Tina continued, her voice was barely audible and she struggled to get the words out.

'I wanted time to think but there was none. My head was a mess. I couldn't concentrate. I didn't eat. We talked about nothing else. I expect you know legal terminations have to be done by twenty-four weeks.'

Neil heard the sound of a nail being bitten.

'You don't know how ill a baby with Down's Syndrome will be. We looked at worst-case-scenarios. After two sleepless nights, we decided it would be unfair on the other children to go ahead with the pregnancy. I opted to terminate.'

She took a deep breath. Neil said nothing, confused. He could not see where the story was going or why Tina was telling him.

'This is the difficult bit.' There was another long gap. He could hear her breathing getting faster. 'I had a failed abortion.'

'I'm sorry, Tina, but you'll have to explain.'

'It means the baby, instead of being stillborn, was delivered alive. Babies can survive at just under twenty-four weeks, you know. It's rare but it happens.'

'I didn't know abortions could fail.'

'Nor did I. It was a tremendous shock.' There was a silence heavy with the weight of imminent disclosure.

'Our baby, Nicholas, lived nearly three weeks in the Intensive Care Unit. We were with him as much as we could be. Took shifts. I even prayed. I prayed to a god I don't believe in. Can you imagine that? Desperation makes you act strangely, do odd things. The doctors did all they could but he died. I was heartbroken. I wanted the baby I'd tried to get rid of more than anything in the world. And the whole thing was my fault. My guilt was enormous. It still is. It took me ages to come to terms with it. No, that's untrue. I'm still struggling.'

There was a gap in Tina's monologue and Neil could hear her gasping for breath. He searched for words of comfort but knew they would sound hollow. He turned to practicalities.

'How does this link with you adopting Adam?'

'We both knew we'd made a mistake. Our relationship took a nasty hit. We could barely speak to each other. We should not have opted for an abortion so late.'

Tina went quiet again. Neil could imagine her glancing around, the haunted, uneasy look in her eyes.

'We both blamed each other. Then we blamed ourselves. I worried about our other two; we weren't giving them the attention they needed. They became naughty and demanding. Bed-wetting started. Everything was going wrong.'

Neil had his story. His head was buzzing. How would he use it? Why did Tina confide in him? And where did Adam fit in? He wanted to encourage Tina, put a hand on her arm, hug her even, demonstrate her words mattered to him. How he hated telephone conversations! He listened as she continued.

'You can't replace a baby who dies but eventually, after some counselling, we knew what we had to do. We decided to adopt a baby with the condition. An unwanted, rejected child. A baby who chose the wrong parents.'

'I see.' The jigsaw fell into place. 'Do you know much about why Adam was put up for adoption?'

'No. We speculated. Perhaps his parents decided they wouldn't be able to cope. Perhaps they didn't have the tests, didn't know beforehand and the shock was too much.'

Neil heard the well-worn words. She mumbled them in a daze, not really talking to him. He guessed she and her husband had been over this ground many times.

'So what did you know about Adam when you decided to adopt him?'

'Not a lot. We were given full details of his medical condition but were told little else. His parents are white Caucasian academics. He has no brothers or sisters. That's about all we know.'

'How do your other children get on with Adam?'

'They adore him and he adores them. They come to the social group from time to time in the school holidays. We should never have said it wouldn't be fair on them.'

Neil was overwhelmed. He wanted to hug Tina. Would he get the chance? 'Thank you for being so honest. But tell me, what do you want me to do with the info you've given me?'

'I'd like to think my situation could help others just a bit. You know, help people understand the trials and the joys of living with a baby with Down's Syndrome. Understanding what we go through. And perhaps stop people from taking a late abortion option.'

Neil's brain was generating possibilities. 'I can preserve your anonymity. I can photograph you with Adam so you won't be recognisable. A side-on, partly shaded photo. I'll work on the wording to go with it. Don't worry, I'll check with you to make sure it's alright.'

Neil was left with a sense of elation. He put the niggle of uncertainty behind him; surely he would be able to do what he promised. As soon as he said goodbye to Tina, he called Becky.

'Quick question which I'm sure you can answer.'

'You want to know if I fancy you?'

'No – well, I hope you do but I wasn't going to ask. It's

technical.'

'Boring. But fire away.'

'If a routine chromosome abnormality screening test in pregnancy shows low risk, how come a mother can have a baby with Down's Syndrome? I've been told of a case like that. Is it possible?' Neil needed to know if Tina's scenario was credible.

'It is. "Low risk" isn't the same as "no risk". If, say, the risk is one in five hundred, which is low, there will be one baby in five hundred born with the condition. Folk don't always understand it. It's like the lottery. The chances of winning are remote but some people do win.'

'Hadn't thought about it like that. Interesting comparison. And, you know, I think some of the mums I met might consider a child with Down's Syndrome a prize. Thanks, Becky. Always there when I need you.'

Always there. The ache inside him was a reminder he had decisions to make.

Chapter 12

Blood. Not a significant amount. Not as much as a proper period. Not as much as when she lost the first baby. But it was there, a stain on her underwear, evidence in the lavatory. There was no pain, no stomach cramps, no backache. Kate poured herself a glass of red wine and contemplated the situation. She knew women who had lost blood during pregnancy and gone on to carry successfully to term. A word with the pharmacist was often their first thought. She advised them to see their doctor or midwife and to rest.

Well, she could rest. She swung her legs onto the sofa and positioned a cushion behind her back. But go to the doctor? No. No doctor visits yet. She had to be certain of her decision before she took that step. She was sure she was pregnant. She had felt small movements. And the cravings had started. One craving to be exact, for chocolate. Kate loved good quality, dark chocolate but concern for her figure always won. A small piece now and then or a praline from an expensive box, perhaps as a reward for a good week. Lately it had escalated to the type of confectionary she normally rejected – daily Mars bars or Snickers, calorie-ridden mid-morning treats, evening nibbles. She knew all the tales about "eating for two" were nonsense. It was a compulsion. And she gave in to it. Neil commented one evening as she opened a box of Belgian chocolates and ate three.

'What's this? Not like you to eat more than one at a time.'

'I know. Naughty of me.' She thought quickly. 'Someone bought me this box as a "Thank you" for advice I'd given,' she lied. 'And I felt tempted. Seems ungrateful not to eat them.'

'Kind person. What was the advice?'

Kate scanned her mind for any significant interactions at work and found none.

'It was a lady in her early fifties who found herself accidentally pregnant. She'd been to Italy on holiday and was swept away by an attractive Italian with an unexpected consequence.'

'Unusual to get pregnant at that age, isn't it?'

'Yes, but not unknown. '

'So what did she ask?'

'I think she needed someone to share her predicament with. I listened and explained the physical problems of a late pregnancy. But more importantly, I asked her to think about her situation – did she want the baby? Was she married? What would she tell friends and family? Was there support for her if she decided not to abort?'

'What was her decision?' The questions were becoming automatic.

'I don't know. She went away to think. A few days later she brought me the chocolates as she said I'd put it into perspective for her. I'd been a useful "Agony Aunt". She left without saying more. So there you are.'

'Mmm. Generous of her. Kate, have you seen a large, green folder? Can't remember if I brought it home or not.' Neil popped a truffle in his mouth, the topic of the pregnant lady already forgotten.

'It's in the kitchen by the coffee machine.'

The conversation was over. Kate knew Neil had lost interest minutes ago. But talking was therapeutic. She was her own imaginary customer. Eating another chocolate, she decided she still had weeks before decision time. Neil returned with his folder.

'By the way, Kate, thought you might like to know I saw Becky shopping in town a couple of Saturdays ago.'

'So?'

'It was the weekend you spent in London. With her.

Watching some Shakespeare play.'

'You're mistaken. It must have been someone else. She wears jeans and a sweater like most of the population. Thought you were away at a meeting that day, anyway. Is this some sort of trick?'

'No trick. The meeting was cancelled. I'm a photographer, Kate. Observation is my business. Think about it.'

Those words again.

***

There was a message on Kate's mobile. She phoned Becky back as requested.

'Oh, Kate, can we meet up again? I need to talk and as you're the only person who knows what I'm going through, I wondered if you'd come round?'

'Wouldn't it be easier to meet in town?'

'Maybe for you but not for me. I'm in such a state at the moment. I don't want to burst into tears in a café or restaurant. Come round for a coffee after work one day. Or would later in the evening be better? I can offer you a glass of Chablis and a nibble or two. Please, Kate. I've done a lot for you in the past.'

Kate felt pressurised. She didn't want to get involved with Becky's pregnancy even though she had told her to get in touch if she wanted to chat. She did not want to talk to her. Becky was an unnecessary complication. She hated the persistent thought she meant something to Neil. But there was an obligation. How many times had she called on Becky to cover for her, provide an alibi? At the reunion, she would have been stuck without Becky's help in her various schemes and intrigues. There was no alternative.

'I can come round tomorrow evening about eight.'

'You're a star, Kate. Thanks a million.'

Kate spent the following day wondering what the evening would bring. Had Becky made a decision and needed back-up? She could be positive and support her. She could simply listen, say little, drink a glass or two and escape as soon as she could. If Becky was still unsure, she might repeat her previous advice to reinforce the message. But there was nothing she could say that Becky did not already know.

She might mention her own pregnancy and point out she had enough to handle without Becky's problems as well. None of the options felt right. She didn't know why. I can't prepare for tonight, she thought. I'll have to wait and see.

A dishevelled Becky opened the door to Kate. She wore no make-up and what looked like yesterday's clothes. Kate followed her into the kitchen, glancing around as she went. She had visited Becky just once before when she held a charity evening in aid of the Tsunami in Thailand. There was a degree of randomness about her home, typical Becky décor. The colour scheme was far brighter than Kate would have chosen and an eclectic mix of pictures and ornaments littered the place. It was Becky. Exactly what Kate had expected.

But this evening it was the untidiness that surprised her. There were unwashed coffee cups and plates in the sink, a pile of dirty washing in a basket in the corner of the kitchen and a scattering of shoes on the floor. Some flowers were wilting in a vase in the hallway. Everywhere looked in need of a proper clean.

Becky noticed Kate's wandering eyes.

'Excuse the mess, Kate. I know I don't bother much with housework but it usually looks better than this.'

Kate shrugged. It was nothing to do with her.

'I couldn't go to work this week. Luckily Mary, my locum, was available and she's covering for me.'

'Are you sick?'

'Depends how you define sickness. I can't concentrate, I'm emotionally on edge the whole time and I feel wretched. Not really sick but too unwell to do my job. I would be a danger to our customers. And that's unacceptable.'

Becky sighed and got up, took the promised bottle of wine from the fridge and poured a glass for Kate, having a glass of tonic water herself. She tipped a packet of cashew nuts into a bowl and produced a plate with two pieces of cheese and some biscuits.

'Aren't you drinking? I though Chablis was a favourite of yours.'

'It is. That's why I've got this bottle. But I'm pregnant, Kate. Have you forgotten?'

So am I, thought Kate, but I'm damned if my life is going to be ruled by an unknown embryo. A parasite.

'Well, you're missing out on a good wine.'

'Glad you like it as you'll have to drink it or take it home. There won't be any other visitors this week. Help yourself to the nuts and cheese. You'd better tuck into the Brie. I bought it for you. I'll stick with the cheddar.'

'I can't believe this. I was more than half expecting you to tell me you were going to have an abortion. And here you are, being a totally neurotic first-time mother, afraid to breathe the air around you.'

'Don't be hard on me, Kate. I oscillate between desperately wanting to keep the baby and being one hundred percent sure I don't. The least I can do is care for the creature while I decide.'

Kate poured herself more wine and deliberately cut a large slice of Brie.

'You make it sound like a pet, a kitten or a puppy, a cute little thing to be pandered to. This is an unwanted child, Becky. A mistake. You didn't choose this situation. You need to be pragmatic. You have a life, a lot of future still to be enjoyed. Is a baby part of that?'

'I don't know, I don't know! I wish I did. You always see things clearly. I see a mess. I've even wondered if I should contact Colin. Who knows what his reaction would be if I told him the truth? It could be positive. And it might help my decision.'

'Funnily enough, he called into one of my pharmacies recently while I was there. We went out for a drink when I finished work.'

Becky looked horrified. 'You know I'm carrying his baby and you're trying to get off with him? I can't believe you'd be so disloyal to me. You always said he was a pain in the arse. What's his attraction now?'

'Don't jump to conclusions! I have no wish to attract Colin. He was being his usual annoying self but nevertheless quite amusing. He called in as he was passing and invited me for a drink. It's possible to be sociable without being sexual.'

'If you say so.'

'Anyway, it wasn't all about me. He mentioned you. I think he'd be interested in seeing you again. He made it clear it wasn't just sex he was after. Talked of a relationship. He's on his own. Even asked me to put in a good word for him.'

'Don't think I'm up to a relationship with anyone at the moment. But it does put him in a different light. I'll think about it. It's a factor in what I'll do next. Do you know if he has any children?'

'Yes. He has a daughter who's going to study pharmacy. She lived with him after his divorce and I got the impression they're close. No other kids as far as I know.'

'Just the one. Unusual. Maybe another would appeal?'

'I wouldn't know.'

Yes, I would, thought Kate, but I'll leave it to Becky to discover the true situation.

'I just need to pop to the loo, Becky, before I leave.'

'Go to the one upstairs. First door on the right. I think the mop and bucket are in the downstairs one. I was planning on washing the floor but never quite made it.'

Kate went upstairs and, although she was not intending to be nosy, could not help but glance through Becky's open bedroom door. The bed was unmade, the duvet dragging the floor. Clothes were scattered everywhere; Kate wondered how Becky knew if they were clean or dirty. A towel hung over the back of a chair. The wardrobe door was open as were two of the drawers in the chest revealing an imminent cascade of knickers and socks. She registered the mess in a glance but then something caught her eye. There was a framed black and white photograph on the dressing table. It was Becky. She was leaning on a wall in evening sunlight, a curly strand of hair blown across her face and the beginnings of a smile on her lips, a smile of contentment. A slight shadow rounded her face. Kate knew the style. There was one person who captured mood in that way. Turning away, she hurried to the bathroom, feeling intrusive and guilty. She trod on a flip-flop by the door and carefully placed it with its partner in a corner as she started to go back down the stairs.

'Kate, you need to eat more of this Brie before you go.'

'Okay, just a little.'

As she reached out to cut another piece of cheese, she said, 'By the way, Neil said he saw you in town on the Saturday we were supposed to be at the play in London. I said it couldn't have been you but he didn't believe me. Has he mentioned anything to you?'

'No. I haven't seen him lately. But I'm not prepared to start on a string of additional lies. I told you I wasn't intending on hiding away that weekend. You demand too much of a friend.'

'Are you a friend, Becky? A real friend?'

'After all I've done for you, you ask such a question?'

'Covering my tracks now and again or giving me an alibi becomes insignificant if you're having an affair with my husband.'

Kate had not planned on challenging Becky. It happened. The words formed themselves and became audible sentences. They were out before she realised she'd said them. She held her breath for the reaction. Becky sat still, her glass halfway to her mouth. She placed it carefully on the table and put her face in her hands. Kate could see tears wetting her fingers.

There was a long silence. No denial, no affirmation. No anger, no counter-attack.

Kate thought about the photograph in the bedroom. The silence lasted a long time.

'Well? I think you need to say something, Becky.'

'You've chosen a bad time. A few weeks ago I would have shrugged this off. Said we'd flirted a bit but it was insignificant. Just the natural interaction of two people who find each other attractive. I don't deny he's attractive. But you've caught me at my lowest point and I have no energy for lies. It has gone further. Yes, I've slept with your husband. But he's still your husband and he's remained with you. He's unlikely to be interested in a pregnant Becky.'

'So I can have him back because you think he won't want you now. How very generous of you! Your cast-off!'

'What about Jonathan? You're hardly the faithful wife yourself so why be self-righteous now?'

'I've not slept with a good friend's husband. It's different. And I'm sure Neil knows there've been affairs and accepts the situation.'

'Can't you be equally generous with him? He travels a lot. I'm sure I can't be the only one.'

'What I don't know, I can't worry about. But I do know about this now.'

Kate found herself overwhelmed with bitterness and anger. She wanted to feel like the photograph of Becky. She wanted to feel contented and for her face to be captured showing her emotion. She wanted whatever it was Becky had and she was lacking. An impossible wish. It made her ache; it made her body sore. But she would still be the winner here. She was not a person to make a scene. She walked across to Becky, pulled her to her feet and stared at her. Then she slapped her hard on the cheek.

'Thank you for the Chablis and the Brie. Keep the rest in case Neil calls. He enjoys both. But I expect you know that.'

Chapter 13

Finding out where Jonathan lived was not difficult. A couple of phone calls, an email, a quickly fabricated story and she had what she needed. About an hour's drive away, maybe a little more.

It was a large, modern house in a smart development called Merchant Close. The residents, having bought similar houses, were now trying to outdo each other in making them as individual as possible. Some had elaborate porches, most had different front doors. Extensions blossomed over garages, conservatories poked cornices and ironwork through gaps in the trees. The landscape gardeners had been busy with pergolas, rose beds and ornamental bushes. Kate imagined the proud occupants all considered they had won the competition for the most elegant and classy house, whereas no-one had.

It was four o'clock on a Friday afternoon. Would anyone be in? Deciding not to park on the drive, she pulled alongside the kerb and took a few deep breaths. Now she'd arrived, she felt nauseous. The visit had been an inspiration after several glasses of wine. She had been carried along by the force of her own ideas but now she had doubts. I do not give up when I've made a decision, she reminded herself. Turning around and driving back home was not an option.

She re-did her lipstick and fingered her hair. The vital folder was on the seat beside her. Picking it up, she walked confidently to the house. Before she reached the door, she could hear shouting inside. A young voice yelled, 'Don't come near me, Joanne. You're a bitch. I hate you.' There were footsteps running up the stairs and a door thudding shut. Should be interesting, she thought, and pressed the doorbell.

A fierce-faced woman opened the door.

'I hope I've come to the right house. Does Jonathan Carson live here?'

'Yes, but he's not here at the moment.' She glanced at the folder in Kate's hand. 'Is this a survey?' The reception was brusque.

'No. Nothing like that. I'm an old friend from university. We met up again at the thirty-year reunion last year. I was hoping to see him.'

'Is he expecting you?' There was more than a hint of hostility as she looked Kate up and down.

'Er…no. I should have called but it was a spur of the moment decision as I was in the area.' She tapped the folder. 'These are some of his photos. He left them with me to look through. I wanted to discuss having an enlargement done of one or two of them.'

'This really isn't a good time.' The two women looked at each other and Kate made no move to leave. 'Well, I suppose you'd better come in. He should be home in half an hour.'

Kate accepted the offer of a cup of tea and looked around the room. The styling was Scandinavian, sleek lines, no clutter. Modern paintings. A slim vase with a white rose in it. Vertical blinds in pale grey with a splash of orange. A darker grey carpet. Too minimalistic for Kate although she appreciated it. It was a thought-out, well-planned room, not one thrown together. Was it Jonathan's or Joanne's style? She couldn't tell.

Joanne closed the door but the sound of angry voices penetrated. There was a harsh exchange of words, too indistinct to make out, but the tone was obvious.

'I'm off!'

Kate saw a young girl striding down the path, a canvas bag slung over her shoulder, long hair tied untidily in a ponytail. She wiped her arm across her eyes, pushed her hands into her jacket pockets and kept her head down. I'm no good at guessing girls' ages, she realised. I've no idea which one it is.

Joanne brought in the tea. 'I'm sorry, I'll have to leave you on your own. As I said, a bad time.'

'Perhaps I can explain? My husband's a photographer, too. Actually, he and Jonathan know each other professionally although they're in different fields. I'm interested in Jonathan's work.'

Joanne nodded and made for the door. If she had told Kate to shut up the message could not have been clearer.

'Did Jonathan tell you about the reunion?'

'Not much.'

'Great fun. Good to restore old friendships, old ties. In some cases, old romances. I was surprised at some of the liaisons!'

Kate gave Joanne a look that said she could tell her a thing or two.

'Really? I do have work to do and I'll have to leave you. I work from home.'

'In fact, I learned the other day of an unexpected pregnancy. Can you imagine that?'

'No, I can't. And to be honest, it doesn't interest me.'

'At fifty! Unusual at that age. But it can happen. Poor woman. She's now in a real mess trying to decide what to do. What a decision to have to make! I'm glad it's not me. What would you do in such a situation, Joanne?'

'How do you know my name?'

'Jonathan must have told me. I have a good memory. Would you be able to cope with a baby at fifty?'

'How do I know? I'm way off that age. Why are you asking me such questions? Coping with these girls is quite enough for me.' She turned and left the room.

A little stirring, a few seeds planted. Kate was content. She did not know what she would gain from this visit but disturbing Jonathan's domesticity was a start. She got satisfaction from her brusque, almost rude, questioning.

She contemplated Joanne. An attractive woman when she was not frowning. Younger than expected, shapely, fine features, unblemished skin. Kate was unfamiliar with jealousy. Yet the uncomfortable feeling she was experiencing was akin to something like envy. She rebuked herself. If Jonathan had chosen a dowdy, unkempt, ugly woman she would have been astonished. Joanne was his type.

She imagined the pair of them making love. It hurt. She did not want his hands to stroke the smooth skin, his fingers to run through her well-cut hair. She did not want her to excite him, to raise his heart rate, to make him gasp with pleasure. She did not like the image of them wound together afterwards, her head on his chest, enjoying the glow of satisfying sex. She hated the thought he might tell her he loved her. She hated Joanne's youthfulness. She totally hated her youthfulness. She hated Joanne.

The door burst open and a young woman entered, presumably the other daughter, the one who had not stormed out of the house. Seemed to be the older one; she already had a shapely body. She stopped and stared at Kate who was trying to remember her name. Lara, that was it.

'Who are you?'

'A friend of Jonathan's. Your father, I guess.'

'What are you doing here?'

What a welcoming household, Kate thought. 'I was hoping to have a chat with your Dad. Joanne said I could wait.'

'Huh! Generous of her. She's a mean sod, doesn't like other women in the house.' She gave Kate a quick look up and down. 'Especially if they're attractive and well turned-out.'

'Thanks for the compliment.'

'Just a fact.' She rushed around the room looking for something. Kate's handbag was on the floor and she grabbed it.

'Ah, here it is!'

'Excuse me, but that's mine.'

'Damn, is it? Looks like Joanne's. Can you see another one anywhere?'

She darted around, looking behind chairs and in corners. She found the bag tucked beside some books on a shelf and immediately started to rummage in it.

'I don't usually search other people's belongings but I need to find her make-up. She confiscated mine after I'd "plastered it on with a trowel" the other day.' She mimicked Joanne's voice. 'I like Goth make-up. Of course, you have to use loads of black. Don't do it all the time. Might now, just to annoy her.'

She found a small pouch and looked in it. 'Huh! Pink lipsticks. Still, some of the stuff might be okay.' She tried a couple of the colours on the back of her hand and made an unpleasant noise.

'Got a tissue?'

Kate went to look in her bag but Lara found her own solution. She wiped the lipstick on the back of the nearest cushion, a pale grey, silk square with narrow, orange piping around its edge. She propped it back in its place, the dark pink scar invisible, the cushion perfect like all the others on the sofa.

'Nice surprise for Joanne! She loves these cushions. Very fussy about them. Me and Sheena got instructions about how careful we had to be when she bought them.'

Kate was watching this performance in silence, pleasure glowing within her. Lara confronted her.

'You can tell her if you like. I don't care! She'll probably guess, anyway.'

'It's nothing to do with me.'

'Didn't think you'd say anything.'

She put the make-up bag in her pocket.

'How do you know Dad?'

'We were students together, pharmacy students.'

'God, ages ago. Do you still fancy him?'

Kate ignored the question and hid her surprise in the story about the photographs and the enlargement she wanted.

'Well, it's an original excuse. Don't believe it, of course.'

Kate had no idea what to say to this provocative girl who had a response to everything.

'Do you smoke?'

'No.'

'Pity. I might have begged a few fags.'

Kate shook her head but decided against a lecture on smoking.

'You're Dad's type. He's fussy about his women.'

'His women?'

'Yeah. He's not the faithful type. Don't get Joanne on the subject!'

'Do you talk to your Dad about …' Kate wondered how to express herself to a fourteen-year-old.

'Not directly. But I'm not stupid. I can see what goes on. And what I don't know, I can guess.' She gazed out of the window while she spoke, glancing at Kate from time to time to see the reaction she was producing.

'And what do you think about "what goes on", Lara?'

'Fine by me. Enjoy life while you can.' She stopped her ambling and turned to face Kate, abandoning her flippant tone. 'Dad has never got over Mum's death. No-one will replace her, for any of us. If he wants to have a succession of women as compensation, it's up to him. Not my business.' Lara flicked her hair off her face; end of conversation.

What an innocent I was at fourteen, Kate reflected.

She half-watched as Lara wandered around the room in her own world. She fiddled with her hair, looked in the mirror and squeezed a spot on her chin, filed a nail with an emery board and gazed out of the window. She was herself, neither trying to impress nor shock.

Could I tolerate a teenager like this? I like her independence but I wouldn't want it daily. As she thought back to the conversations with Jonathan in Verona, she became angrier. She could feel her pulse rate soaring as fury built up inside her. She dug her long nails into her hands to retain control. Control is what matters. Then any situation is manageable. How dare Jonathan expect me to take on his problems? One daughter wild and wilful; the younger one heading in the same direction. As she forced her breathing to slow down, she noticed blood on her palms. A single droplet had fallen on to one of the cushions. It was tiny but it was a stain. She rubbed it gently and it spread out. Turning the cushion over, she replaced it beside its companions. Lara would probably get the blame for that, too. Tough.

A car pulled onto the drive. Lara said her Dad had arrived and left the room. No "Bye" or "Nice to have met you". Kate did not expect it; she had learned enough about this precocious young lady already.

Kate heard the front door open and Jonathan's voice saying he was home. She composed herself, burying her feelings of spite and acrimony towards Joanne, her anger against Jonathan and her amazement at Lara. There was a conversation, a briefing, going on in the kitchen. A couple of minutes later, Jonathan appeared.

'Hello, Jonathan. Good to see you again.'

She was pleased at his look of wary surprise. How well will he manage this situation?

'Kate! Well, I don't know what to say. What brings you here?'

Before Kate could reply, Joanne joined them. He asked the two women if they had introduced themselves and went through a few formalities. Gaining thinking time, crafty man.

'You remember the photos you left with me, Jonathan?' Kate indicated the folder with his name on it.

She knew he remembered. He gave them to her in Verona. He looked uncomfortable, clearly worried what Kate might say next. She hoped Joanne was too preoccupied to sense the electricity running between the pair of them.

'You said at the reunion you could do an enlargement for me and frame it if I wanted one. Well, I do. Then I realised I'd be near here today – I've been to visit a friend a few miles away – so

I decided to pop in. Sorry, I should have let you know. I think I've inconvenienced Joanne.'

Joanne shrugged. Jonathan relaxed.

'I've been telling Joanne about the reunion.'

'I don't suppose you're interested, are you, Jo? Other people's reunions are tedious. That's why I didn't bore you with it.'

'Oh, I agree,' Kate said. 'The details are dreadful. But sometimes the consequences are interesting. As social comments. Observations on how people behave, especially when they feel they are detached from the real world. Reunions can feel like that.'

Kate caught Jonathan's eye. His look was impassive.

'Did you know, Jonathan, a few "old flames" were relit? With unexpected outcomes.'

'I saw one or two heads bent together but didn't think much of it.'

'Ah, it takes a woman to notice these things. I have to admit to being tempted myself.'

'I thought you said you were married, Kate?' Joanne was being drawn into the conversation, an obligation rather than a choice.

'I am. I only said I was tempted.'

'Were you also tempted, Jonathan?' Joanne showed more interest now, sarcasm tainting her words.

'I spoke to an old girlfriend and reminisced a bit but we are different people now.'

'You didn't answer my question.'

'What is this? The Spanish Inquisition?' He laughed loudly, the Jonathan trademark. 'Of course I was tempted. I slept with a different woman each night. And one in the afternoon.'

'You probably don't know a pregnancy resulted from that weekend, Jonathan. I was telling Joanne.' She was not letting him escape so easily.

'Well, more fool her. At her age she should have more sense. I don't want to know who it is as it's got nothing to do with me.'

He got up, the topic over in his eyes and got some glasses out of a cabinet.

'A glass of wine before you go, Kate? Joanne and I are meeting friends at the pub this evening so I'm afraid I'll have to evict you soon.'

'How kind. I'm driving, just a very small glass.' She noticed the look Joanne gave him following the lie.

They filled the following half hour with awkward pleasantries and Kate discussed which photos she was interested in. It was civilised and uncomfortable. Joanne pulled Jonathan to one side and said she needed to talk to him about the girls. The conversation in the hallway was short. Joanne was the second person to slam the front door and march out. She got into Jonathan's car, reversed out rapidly and clipped Kate's wing mirror as she drove off.

'Shit! That's all I need!' Jonathan rushed outside to look at the damage. 'Bloody woman! Needs to control her temper. I'll pay for the damage.'

Kate suppressed her amusement. Who had the upper hand now? 'It's only a scratch.'

He placed his hand on her shoulder and the inevitable pulse ran along her arm. 'You shouldn't have come here.'

Why does he always touch me and send me back into the past?

'I know. But I needed to. I wanted to see for myself.'

'See what?'

'The truth of the situation. I never know when to believe you.'

'I didn't lie to you in Verona.'

'I can judge for myself.'

'Sorry about the car.'

'It's repairable, Jonathan. Rather more so than your relationship with that woman, I think.'

Chapter 14

Neil ate a ham and cheese sandwich from the motorway services washed down with a bottle of water as he drove home. My life is a mess, he thought. Constant meals on the move, poor diet, no time for any exercise, little sleep, no time for Kate, no time for Becky. Work, work, work. So why do I feel elated?

He loved it. Life was a constant adrenaline rush. He had the world's most interesting job, he reported to himself, money was coming in and he was a minor celebrity. This must be better than drugs, he thought. It's my choice, I'm not complaining. But I can't expect others around me to see everything with my eyes. I need to pause and decide where I'm going.

After he left the motorway, he looked for a lay-by and phoned Becky.

'I'm about forty minutes away. Are you free this evening?'

'I don't want you to come, Neil.'

'Why not? Haven't seen you for ages. I know it's my fault. Been so bloody tied up with the next exhibition. Got loads to tell you. We could have a precious evening together. I could stay the night. Kate isn't expecting me until tomorrow.'

'I feel dreadful. Have been off work. I'm completely anti-social. And Kate's been here.' Becky stopped suddenly. 'She knows about us. She challenged me and I admitted it. I probably should have lied but suddenly it was too much. I had no strength to resist her.'

Becky cut off without saying any more. Neil sensed rather

than heard her tears.

He rang her doorbell thirty-five minutes later but there was no answer. She has to be here, he thought. She's ignoring me. He walked round the side of the house, climbed a bolted gate and fought the holly bushes growing across the path. The back door was unlocked. He looked at the bedraggled Becky and the chaos that was the kitchen in amazement.

'Whatever has happened?'

'I'm not well.'

'Have you seen a doctor?'

'No. I don't want to. I just need time on my own to sort my head out and I'll be alright.'

'Don't be stupid, Becky. I know you enjoy a bit of a mess but this is ridiculous. Yours is a happy, carefree untidiness. This is verging on squalor.'

'I don't want your opinion. I don't want your rudeness. I told you not to come. I don't want you here.'

She walked to the front door and opened it. 'Go.'

'I don't understand. What do you need to sort out in your head? Can't I help with whatever the problem is?'

'I can't discuss it. Just leave me alone.'

'Why were you talking to Kate about us? I need to know what's going on.'

'Go home to Kate. She'll no doubt be thrilled to tell you.'

Becky stood at the door until Neil left. He walked backwards down the path with his hands held out, hoping to be called back, but the door shut firmly before he was halfway to the road.

He did not relish an encounter with Kate. He thought back to her comments about Becky and how he wriggled out of the situation. The inevitable is going to happen. Luck does not last. I've been so wrapped up in my own life I've been unaware of the carnage around me. Oh, Hell!

He drove home, opened the front door and called out he had managed to get back earlier than expected. There was no reply. Relieved, he wandered into the kitchen and made himself a cup of tea. The contrast with Becky's house was striking. It was immaculate. It was how it always was, how he expected it to be. He loved Becky's topsy-turvy house because it was different, without rules about toilet seats and linen-baskets, but realised he also enjoyed the tranquillity and order of his own home. He took a biscuit from a packet on the second shelf in the cupboard next to the microwave – where biscuits lived – and ambled about, knowing he was dropping crumbs but ignoring them. He started to sort out his belongings.

His bag was bulging and he pulled a few folders from it and took them to the study. He stopped abruptly at the door. The sight appalled him. Scattered across the desk and floor were hundreds of his photographs. Empty folders and boxes littered the room. His immediate thought was a break-in but it was clear nowhere else was in disarray. Then he noticed four black and white photos propped up on the middle of the desk, Kate's silver paper knife in front of them. They were all of Becky. He had taken them several years ago. They had been away together and gone for a walk in the early evening. The light was perfect. She put her folded arms on an old, stone wall and gazed into the distance. The wind tousled her hair, blowing strands across her face. He had taken several photos before she realised she was the subject. He took more but the first ones were the best. He framed one for her.

It must have been difficult to find them; he had hidden them well. How did she know about them? Kate was diligent and determined. She never gave up. My God, what has got into her? He knew she had a bitter, vengeful side which appeared if she felt wronged, the result of her strong sense of justice. But it rarely made an appearance. He remembered once when she came out badly in a carefully planned business deal and again when she had a fierce row with her mother. But neither occasion was as violent as this.

He picked up one of the photos of Becky and looked closely at it. There was a hole through her left eye. He looked at

113

the other three. There were similar holes in all of them. He could not remember ever having pinned them up. And anyway, he would never put a pin through her eye. The holes were small, made by a fine needle, all in the same precise position. His confusion was replaced by realisation. He licked dry lips and muttered, 'Christ!' This was not a random, unthinking act of anger. What was it? What was Kate planning?

He abandoned his cup of tea and poured himself a whisky. He now had more to deal with than his own disorganised life. Becky not wanting him for no reason and now Kate unhinged. Was she mentally unstable? Surely not. She was the most sensible and ordered person he knew. How had this happened without there being a clue?

In automatic mode, he gathered up his photographs, sorting them as he went and putting them back in their boxes and folders. None of them was damaged apart from those of Becky which he placed in an envelope and laid on the desk. It took him an hour. He could not pretend everything was normal. He and Kate needed to have a serious discussion.

He heard a car arrive and the key in the door. He stood up, feeling his pulse race and braced himself for an explosion. There was activity in the hallway as Kate removed her coat. He knew she would hang it in the cupboard, always on the left side, with her scarf on the shelf. Her footsteps, the familiar click of her stiletto heels on the wooden floor, approached. She was her usual, immaculate self. Her face was as unmoved and precise as the line of the jacket she wore.

'Back early, I see. Good job I had the foresight to rearrange the study last night.'

'What are you up to, Kate?'

'Isn't it obvious?'

'Obvious? No. I understand you are upset with me. There are things we need to talk about. But these photographs are my life. This is how I earn my living. Many are irreplaceable. They're not a hobby or holiday snaps. You may want to get at me but you should never attack my work. It's like me going into one of your pharmacies and emptying all the bottles of tablets on the floor.'

'That would be different. It would be annoying. Very annoying. But it would be a police matter and not a personal attack on me. Don't bother considering it.'

'It was an example. I would never do such a thing. Why have you done this?'

'You've hurt me badly. I needed to do the same to you. It's called revenge. Personal revenge. You should have thought about my vengeful side before you decided to have an affair with Becky.'

She turned and went upstairs. Neil could hear her moving around the bedroom, getting changed, putting her smart work clothes away in the wardrobe. She returned in jeans and a T-shirt but with the same fixed expression on her face.

Neil topped up his whisky, his third or fourth? He poured one for Kate and gave it to her without a word. She took it, muttering something about preferring brandy. They sat at the kitchen table.

'Where would you like to start?' Kate asked the question without emotion.

Neil felt he was already at a disadvantage. Kate had created havoc in the study and horribly defaced his photos of Becky. He should have the upper hand. Morally, he should. Yet he was the one feeling guilty. He could not tell what she felt, her mask implacable. He had to say something.

'What did Becky tell you?' He wished he had found out more from her. He wished they had agreed a strategy.

'I know you've slept together. How long has this been going on?'

'A while.' How many years was it? He would not admit to the length of their relationship. 'But it's just a release. I've never considered leaving you. She's fun, friendly and undemanding.'

'And, no doubt, readily available.'

'You know as well as I do she's single. And I expect I'm

not the only man she has.' Neil realised he had no idea about Becky's other sexual activities. Were there any? They had never discussed the topic. Kate had commented that Becky relit an old flame at the pharmacy reunion. It shocked him at the time. But he didn't challenge Becky; he did not own her. 'You demand a lot of a man, Kate. Sometimes it's just too much.'

'I could accept the odd casual fling. You travel a lot and have a healthy sexual appetite. But Becky is my friend. Couldn't you have looked elsewhere?'

'I didn't plan it, Kate. I honestly didn't. It was one of those things that happened. You were distant at the time, unresponsive in bed, your mind elsewhere. I thought you were having an affair. I bumped into Becky by chance in town. We chatted over coffee, got to know each other. I suppose it was a natural development. An uncomplicated, undemanding relationship. But nothing that would damage my relationship with you.'

Kate thought back to when that might have been. There were a number of occasions matching Neil's description. She neither acknowledged or denied his implied question.

'And you say Becky is your friend. Is she really? You aren't close. You do things together from time to time but I don't see real friendship. I get the feeling you use her. Anyway, I expect you've had more affairs in the last twenty years than I have. Becky is the only one. And it's the truth.'

Neil needed to fight back.

'Of course I've had affairs. I assumed you either didn't mind or didn't notice. But they were short-lived, of no significance and did not impinge on our marriage. When I asked you recently about whether I should be worried, whether marriages went wrong after so many years, you wriggled out of it. I even mentioned Becky, asked why you were in her pharmacy. I gave you the chance to come clean.'

She should have been a barrister, not a pharmacist, thought Neil. She could get anyone stuck in a corner. So much for my attack.

'Another matter, Kate. Why did you pierce the photos of Becky through the eye? That isn't just anger, it's evil. I went cold when I saw what you'd done.' With some reticence, he added, 'You aren't intending to damage her in any way, are you?'

'I'm not a common criminal, Neil. You know that. I don't intend to attack her personally with a needle. I just needed to spoil her beauty for you.'

They sat and looked at each other. Nothing was resolved.

'So what happens now?' Neil asked the question.

'Do you intend to leave me for Becky?'

'No. If I'd intended to do that, it would have already happened.'

'Do we still have a relationship worth rescuing?'

'I thought we had. But after what you've just done, I don't know. If you can attempt to ruin my career, how can you still care for me?'

'Don't be melodramatic, Neil. I haven't ruined your career. Nor do I want to. You've already put the photographs away. I was making a point, teaching you a lesson. Showing you I'm not a person to be messed around with.'

Neil nodded. He already knew that. 'I'll have to talk to Becky.'

'You'll do more than that. I don't want you here. You can move in with her. Not permanently. Just long enough for the pair of you to sort yourselves out. And long enough for us to decide on our future relationship, our marriage. A thinking time. A break from each other is needed. It needs to happen soon.'

Living with Becky for a while will cure him of her. Kate was sure of that. He won't survive her chaos for more than a week or two. Then I'll have him back on my terms. If it's what I want.

Chapter 15

Annie Shaw defined herself through others. When asked about her life, she would say she was Kate's mother, Brian's wife. She liked to fit in. She fitted in with Brian – he was the organiser. He always made their plans. When they travelled, he would write down every detail on a lined sheet of paper with dates and times. There was a column called "Notes" with useful, additional information. Looking at the list gave him pleasure. A grin would spread across his usually inexpressive face as his sheet got more complete. Gave him a sense of power, of being the man in the house, she thought. Good for a person who was essentially timid. He would organise their holidays down to the minute, over-organise them she sometimes felt, but that was his way. 'Well done, Brian,' she would say, 'You've triumphed again.'

But since he died she had to learn to look after herself. Her world shrank to the limits of her comfort. Kate suggested she sold his car and bought a smaller one, a Ford Fiesta, one she could handle. So she did. She drove to the shops and the hairdresser's, even the doctor's surgery; she could find her way to the friends who lived near. Once she drove fifteen miles to see an amateur production of "Guys and Dolls" on the other side of town. It was a challenge, especially the return journey in the dark. It was lucky Marilyn, one of her neighbours, needed a lift and could help with the navigation.

She liked to go to bed at the end of the day – around ten o'clock, not too late – and reflect on what she had achieved. She got a warm feeling from venturing a little further, like a child allowed to go shopping alone for the first time. There were other milestones. It was usually something to do with technology: mastering the remote for the television, changing the message on the answerphone. She liked to relate her successes to Marilyn. One step at a time, she would say to herself, just one step.

It was a difficult decision to make. The idea of driving a hundred miles to visit Kate had never occurred to her. Kate came to her. When Brian was alive, they sometimes went for a visit, for a night or the weekend, but even then it was usually Kate and sometimes Neil, if he was free, who travelled. They had slipped into a pattern. An irregular one. They did not see a huge amount of each other, not like many of her friends and their families. But with them it was the grandchildren who acted as a magnet. When she thought of what she missed, her spirits sank. Kate did not know how much; there was no way she could tell her.

Lately, Kate had been on her mind. She was unhappy about the pregnancy discussion. It felt unfinished; she could do more. The idea of a visit began to form. She phoned Kate as she often did on a Sunday evening.

'What are you up to this week, love?'

'Nothing special. Just work as usual. Quiet weekend ahead. Neil's away on Saturday and Sunday. I might go shopping for some new shoes. How about you?'

'Haven't decided. Maybe clear out the airing cupboard. Perhaps call in on someone on Saturday.'

'The airing cupboard doesn't sound very exciting!'

'It isn't but it needs doing.'

A few more mundane comments and the call was over. She had found out Kate would be at home the following weekend but Neil would be away. Perfect.

With considerable trepidation, she embarked on the journey to Kate's. No point in saying she was coming. Kate would do everything she could to stop her. She had contacted the AA and asked them what the best route would be. They sent her details which she studied at every free moment. She still felt anxious when she set off, a trembling in her stomach like visiting the dentist. There was minor panic when she missed a junction but she turned at the next roundabout and got back on her route. She talked to herself for most of the journey. In ten minutes, I'll allow myself a peppermint for doing so well. At the next service station, I'll get petrol and buy a bar of chocolate. I fancy a Bounty. Regular encouragement, especially if it was edible, worked. At four o'clock, she pulled onto Kate's drive, elated if fatigued by her success.

'God, Mum, whatever's wrong?' Kate saw her arrive and came running out of the house in alarm. Her mother's cheerfulness showed everything was fine.

'What are you doing here?'

'I thought it was time I visited you.'

'But without telling me? I might have been out or away for the weekend.'

'You said on the phone you'd be here but Neil was away. So I decided to come.'

'I could still have gone somewhere, to have coffee with a friend or to the shops. In fact, I've only just got back.' Her mother's face crumpled with disappointment. 'Oh, never mind. I'm here. You'd better come in.'

'Who'd have thought it, Kate, when we took you to university all those years ago, you'd achieve so much and end up living in a place like this! Of course, we didn't think you'd fail or anything. But such success!'

Like a prospective tenant, she went around noting all the features, the chandelier over the stairs, the new curtains.

'How long is it since I last came? Well, I don't know. Well before your Dad left us. That was eighteen months ago. Eighteen months and five days, actually. A year or two before that. Lots of things have changed. Is the coffee table new as well?'

'Probably. Can't remember when we bought it.'

'This is a palace, Kate. And it looks immaculate. Such a lot of work for you.'

'You know I have a cleaning lady, Mum. You know I dislike housework and you also know I need the place to be spotless and tidy. We've talked about it before. You may think I waste my money but we don't have to go over it again.'

'Just saying.' She was saying a lot and nothing.

'Sit down, Mum, and tell me why you're here.'

'Alright. But could I have a cup of tea? It was a long journey.'

'Yes. Sorry. Of course. I wasn't thinking.'

Annie's mind was blank. The carefully thought-out phrases, rehearsed all week, disappeared into a tangle of nerves. Now she sat and waited for Kate to prise them out but silence was unbearable.

'The curtains look lovely. I like the colour.'

'Mum, stop it. You haven't come all this way to make comments about the décor. You don't drive long distances so there has to be a reason. Tell me.'

Kate had the knack of staying quiet and waiting. Annie could not survive the silence. After a false start it came out in a rush.

'It's the baby. I've thought of nothing else.' She was breathless with the effort of forcing out the words. 'I know I said I couldn't advise you. I know I said you shouldn't have shared your problems with me. But I've changed my mind.'

'Why?'

'It just happened. I could see the little one in my arms. What I always wanted. I could help you. Mind the baby when you were at work. I'd have a renewed purpose to my life.'

'I don't believe this.'

'I mean it, really I do. Now I've driven here once, I know I can do it. I could come for a couple of days each week. And I'll go along with whatever you choose to tell Neil. Don't like lies but I won't let you down.'

Annie's face glowed with grandmotherly anticipation. She reached out to touch her daughter.

Kate ignored her mother's hand, stood up and took her by the shoulders. 'I am not in the business of providing you with "a purpose in life". This baby is inside *me*. I must decide what's right for my life, my future. Whether or not you want to be a childminder is irrelevant.'

She gave her mother a push, more vigorous than intended, which rocked her into the back of the armchair. Kate barely noticed her own actions. Her eyes narrowed and her normally soft mouth turned into a hard red line. There was a break in her voice as she struggled to control it.

'I cannot comprehend such selfishness. I fail to understand how you think your words could help me. We agreed to forget that conversation. It never happened.'

'But Kate – you came to me and I turned you away. I felt really bad about it afterwards. I'm your mother. It was wrong. I was being narrow-minded. I'm making amends now.'

'No, you're not! You are absolutely, fucking not!'

'Language, Kate, language! I didn't know you used words like that.'

'For God's sake, Mum, what does it matter? I only swear in extreme circumstances. Can't you see how you've upset me?'

Annie pulled a tissue from her pocket and rubbed her eyes, smudging her eyeshadow. 'I can't for the life of me understand what I've said wrong.'

'You never could. Everything I've ever done, everything I've achieved you looked at as a tick in the box for you. I went to university. That made you better than your neighbours. You bored them to death with it.'

'We were proud of you.'

'Because I was your daughter – weren't you clever parents!'

Her mother opened her mouth but Kate would not let her speak.

'When I opened my first shop, you took photos to boast about. When we bought this house, you told your friends what it cost. Much more than their kids could afford. What a feather in your cap!'

'Everything we did was for you. You were our life. We loved you so much and wanted the best for you.'

'You overwhelmed me when I was little. I had to be an image of you, like what you liked, behave like you behaved. Any spark of independence was quickly snuffed out. You probably won't believe this but sometimes I lack confidence. I have to work at appearing not to be nervous and afraid. And it's totally due to my upbringing.'

Annie was now sobbing, gulping air and struggling to say the simplest thing. The two women looked away from each other. A newspaper landed with a soft thud in the hall and the paper boy whistled down the path. Kate's phone rang. She looked at it but did not answer. Outside, a young lad shouted, 'See you later!' to his friend. Kate got up and stood with her back to her mother.

'You're fifty-one, Kate.' Annie had to speak. 'You've had enough time to make your own way in life, to get over anything I did wrong. Do you have to blame me still? I never said I was a perfect parent but I did my best. I didn't know I was misguided. '

Annie heaved herself out of her chair and rushed to the toilet where she vomited violently. Kate remained silent. She swallowed two tablets from a pack in her handbag, then unlocked the back door, walked along the path to the end of the garden and sat down on a bench, oblivious to the cold.

Half an hour later, Annie was back in the sitting room. She wanted to go home. Oh, how she wanted to click her fingers and be whisked back by magic into the comfort of her semi! But the thought of driving back terrified her. She could not do it in the dark, the second long drive of the day. She sat upright in her chair, stiff and tense, afraid to bring her overnight bag in from the car in case Kate did not want her but yet more terrified of asking Kate if she could stay. Surely she won't turn me out? She may not love me but she must have some care for my safety. Perhaps I could find a local B and B? Do they have them in posh areas like this?

'Mum, give me your keys and I'll get your bag from the car.'

'It's alright for me to stay?'

'Do you think I'd throw you on to the street? Come on! I may be an ungrateful daughter but I have some compassion.'

The atmosphere became less charged. They spoke in considered sentences, watching their words and each other's reactions. Kate was detached, in her own world. She took several doses of her tablets.

A weird kind of peace settled on them. They ate chicken salad for supper with cheese and biscuits to follow. Annie asked for instant coffee and Kate, to her shame, found some out-of-date Nescafé at the back of the cupboard. No matter, it would do, Annie said. They each ate a chocolate. Annie went to bed early.

'I'll just watch the news.'

'Fine. You know I'm not a night owl.'

Annie was a good sleeper. Brian used to envy her. 'You could sleep for Britain!' he would say. But it was elusive that night. She knew Kate did not want her help now. She could accept that. Well, almost. Knowing she had been a bad parent all along was what really hurt. Brian would have comforted her. He would have said the right words. She fell asleep hugging a pillow, a poor substitute for the man she missed.

She left after a light breakfast, just tea, toast and marmalade.

'Are you sure you know the way back?'

'Of course. I've got it all worked out from the AA instructions.'

'Give me a call when you arrive.'

'I will.'

Kate carried her mother's bag to the car while Annie got into the driver's seat. It avoided the necessity of either kissing or hugging each other. Annie reversed the car on to the road. When she turned to wave, Kate had already gone back into the house.

Chapter 16

Kate played with her phone, swapping it from one hand to the other. Then she decided.

'Would you like to come round for a drink on Friday evening?'

'Kate, are you mad? You've extracted a confession from me and hit me actually and metaphorically when I was at my lowest. And you now invite me for a drink?'

'Why not? There's been enough secrecy. Let's get things out in the open. Be civilised, twenty-first century people even if friendship is a step too far.'

'This is crazy. I can't come.'

'Suit yourself. Just turn up if you change your mind. Think about it, Becky.'

'Will Neil be there?'

'I expect so. So may Colin.'

***

'Would you like to come round for a drink on Friday evening?'

'Great fun. Of course I would. Just you and me, Kate?'

'Do you think I'd invite you to a cosy, romantic evening for two, Colin?'

'No.'

'Correct. But Becky is invited. I'm not going out of my way to promote you as a suitor – you can speak for yourself if you come.'

'Try stopping me. You're a star.'

***

'Would you like to come round for a drink on Friday evening?'

'What is your ulterior motive this time?'

'How suspicious you are, Jonathan. I've decided to be less objectionable to you. There'll be a group of us. You won't be obliged to give me all your attention.'

'I might want to.'

'Including Neil.'

'Well, I could bring the framed photo. An excuse to be there.'

'You'll come, then?'

'Probably.'

'If you want, you can bring Joanne.'

***

Annie stood and looked at the phone for some minutes. Twice she picked it up and put it down again. She walked around the room, her heart racing. Finally, she dialled.

'I know I don't usually do this. In fact, I think it's the first time. It's Annie.'

'Who? Oh, Annie! It is a first – is something wrong? Are you ill?'

'No, I'm well. Well, I'm well in a way. I mean, I'm not ill, not needing a doctor. I'm not explaining myself very well, am I? There's a problem. I'm worried.'

'Go on.'

'It's Kate. I think there's something wrong with her. Oh, dear, maybe I shouldn't say. Maybe you know and I'm interfering. Maybe you'd rather not discuss it.'

'What sort of wrong?'

126

'She's behaving strangely. I saw her last weekend. She was horribly rude to me. I know we aren't particularly close but she really upset me.' There were some sniffs and the sound of tissues rustling.

'Last weekend?'

'Yes. I drove to your house.' Annie blew her nose and coughed to give herself time to compose herself.

'She can be fiery. You've had arguments before. They usually blow over, don't they?'

'I expect you to defend her. You're her husband. It's what husbands do. But it's never been like this before. It was as if she was in a different world, had taken on a different personality. She told me what a dreadful parent I'd been. It hurt. So much. She didn't kiss me goodbye.'

'She probably didn't mean anything by it. A bad day at work. I bet if you call her, she'll be back to her usual self. Probably apologise.'

'Oh, Neil, I don't think she will! Believe me! I'm not just a silly, fussy, old woman. I thought you'd listen. I'm really worried.'

'Shall I have a word with her?'

'No! Don't! Everything will be worse if she knows I've spoken to you. Going behind her back, she'll say. Just keep an eye on her.'

'Did you say you'd driven here last weekend?'

'Yes.'

'Why ever did you do that? You never drive so far.'

'I needed to, Neil. Please don't ask any more. And please don't make me wish I hadn't phoned you.'

'I don't want to do that. I *am* listening. I appreciate your call.'

There was a pause, the conversation hanging unfinished in the air.

'There's just one other thing, Neil. She's taking pills, tablets, quite a lot. I've never known her take anything in the past.

Except perhaps a couple of paracetamol for a headache. But this was often. She didn't talk about them. I don't know what they're for.'

'Okay, Annie. I'll keep my eyes open. You look after yourself. And don't fret. You did the right thing in talking to me.'

Annie put down the phone with shaking hands and took a gulp of her cold tea. She dared not mention the pregnancy but she had done everything she could. Neil probably did think she was a neurotic, stupid, old fusspot. If only Brian were there to confide in. He would'nt have known what to do either, but at least they could have talked.

***

'Will you be back before eight o'clock on Friday?'

'I expect so. Why?'

'I've invited some people round for drinks.'

'Shit, Kate, you might give me more notice.'

'I didn't decide until yesterday. Just thought it was time we were sociable. We owe Gwen and Barry some hospitality. They made us very welcome at their Christmas party.'

'Who are Gwen and Barry?'

'God, Neil! Our neighbours. The old-fashioned couple two doors away. Don't you remember anything? You are so tied up in your bloody exhibition, I could parade up and down the street naked and you wouldn't notice. Probably mutter, "That's nice". Just join the real world for a bit, will you?'

'But why now? You've told me to move out and go to Becky's. Temporarily, anyway. I can't get my head around your moods.'

'And I've invited the folks next door plus a few others. A random assortment. Mix and match.'

'I'm not feeling sociable.'

'Then pretend. You're still living here so join in.'

'Who exactly have you invited?'

It was too late; Kate had cut off.

***

She knew Gwen and Barry would be there on time. They were the sort who were ready ten minutes early and would wait until the precise moment to emerge from their front door. He would wear his beige trousers with the finely pressed creases, shiny slip-on shoes and a striped shirt. Would he wear a tie? He did at Christmas, naturally; he always did as a host. She could imagine him discussing it with Gwen. He would look smart in the unfashionable way her father had looked smart, even though sixty was still a few years away. He resembled her father in many ways. An upright man, in morals and views if not in stature. There was a forward lean to his stance as if his body was trying to catch up with his head but never making it.

Gwen, on the other hand, looked ruffled whatever she wore. It was mainly down to her hair. It was the wiry sort with a will of its own. She liked flowery skirts which ended just above her ankles and loose blouses. Her clothes appeared to wander around her plump body as she moved, not knowing quite where they were meant to rest. She had large eyes that looked surprised. It was her main expression whatever the topic of conversation. They came with a large bunch of flowers, no tie and their daughter.

Gwen had called in a flap an hour before.

'Oh, Kate, we've got a problem. Louise has just turned up. We didn't know she was coming. We don't want to miss your "do" so would you mind if she came, too?'

'No problem. Of course, she can come.' Louise was their eighteen-year-old daughter; they called her a "late-in-life bonus".

'I ought to mention...' Gwen stopped to find the right words. 'You know she can be, well, unpredictable. We never know quite what mood to expect. At the moment she's a bit...excitable. Just to warn you. Like she was at our Christmas party.'

'Don't worry. Just come.'

Kate did not want Louise there. She was noisy and exuberant at Christmas; she overwhelmed everyone with her chatter and excitement. She was exhausting. Gwen's brother called her "Loopy Lou" and Kate gave him one of her frowns.

'I wish folk wouldn't use such expressions,' she whispered to Neil. 'I think she's got real problems. I don't think she's just larking about. She might have mental issues, a personality disorder of some sort, not necessarily diagnosed.'

'Have you talked to Gwen about her?'

'I don't know her well enough.'

'Poor mother. Poor parents. Poor Louise.'

Whatever he thought of Louise, he liked Gwen and Barry. They were pleasant, no-trouble neighbours.

So were David and Grace from next door. They would appear fifteen minutes late, would bring several bottles of wine with them and consume large quantities. They were casual and loud, their clothes would be quirky and loud, David's jokes would be rude and loud and Grace's response would match. Kate liked them. They arrived with Angela, who lived opposite. Recently widowed, she was slowly regaining her social life and was gushingly grateful for Kate's invitation.

Louise threw her arms around Kate and said how wonderful it was to see her again. She presented a bottle of wine, saying it was the best the corner shop sold and she had no idea if it was drinkable. She just rushed round there when her parents told her about the party – no way was she coming empty-handed. She offered to help Kate with the drinks and followed her into the kitchen, talking non-stop.

'Honestly, Louise, there's not much to do. Go and enjoy yourself. I'll follow you in.'

Barry was getting heated about the amount of dog poo on the pavements. He called it his "pet hate" with a clever grin. He was going strong when Colin arrived. Kate was glad to remove herself, having heard it all before. Colin glanced around the room.

'Becky not here yet?'

'No. I've a feeling she may be late.'

'A problem?'

Kate shrugged, knowing Becky may not turn up at all, placed Colin in the dog poo discussion and disappeared into the kitchen. She looked at the various cocktails she had made. Four different ones, four vibrant colours, all based on well-known recipes but with a planned twist. She had given them special names, made a menu card with descriptions and intended to offer them later in the evening. She was checking everything was ready when Neil came in.

'Had to have a quick shower and change. Who's here?'

'Both sets of neighbours, plus Angela – and Louise. She turned up unexpectedly at her parents' house and Gwen asked if she could come. What could I say? She's dominating the room at the moment. Oh – and Colin is here. You haven't met him. We were students together and he's now Chief Pharmacist at the Royal Hospital.'

Neil raised his eyebrows. 'Sounds dull. He's not going to talk shop all evening, is he?'

'He's a clown. You'd barely guess he was intelligent at times. But he can be fun. Let's go in.'

Kate escaped as soon as she could to collect dishes of nuts and various other delicacies acquired from Waitrose, having neither the time nor the inclination to make anything. She topped up the wine glasses. David, it seemed, had prepared for the party with a few apéritifs at home and was raucously into his latest bawdy joke. Neil was sorting out the music when the doorbell rang.

'Jonathan. What a surprise!'

'Weren't you expecting me?'

'Sorry, that sounds dreadful. Kate organised this while I was away. Only got back an hour ago and haven't had time to ask who she invited.'

'A stranger in your own home, eh?'

'Something like that. Anyway, come in.'

'I'll just wait for Joanne. My partner. She's gone back to the car to get the chocolates.'

Kate heard most of the conversation from the kitchen. Should be an interesting evening. I wonder why Jonathan has brought his woman?

People split into small groups. The hum of voices rose above the music or huddled beneath it. Louise could always be heard. There was rumour exchange and gossip between those who knew each other and more mundane conversation elsewhere.

'I'm glad you came, Joanne.' Untrue. 'I doubted you would after my recent intrusion.' Kate sat beside the woman she disliked.

'It wasn't a good moment as you obviously saw. I wanted to apologise for hitting your car.' Joanna took several sips of wine. Her hand with its elegantly painted nails was unsteady.

'Don't worry about it. It's already booked in to be repaired.'

The conversation stalled. Kate wondered what to talk about.

'Seems like Jonathan's girls are a bit of a handful.'

'Understatement.' She looked around the room. Jonathan was talking to Neil, out of earshot.

'We used to get on well but it's all gone wrong lately. Their age, I suppose. I think they now see me as competition for their father's love.'

Kate felt her body tense but she disguised it by crossing her legs and turning towards her guest. A more confidential position. She refilled Joanne's glass.

'We'd talked about getting married. To be honest, Jonathan wasn't happy but I felt we'd be more a family if we did. Now I wonder.'

She gave the glass an "I shouldn't really" glance and continued to drink.

'I'm in a difficult position. You probably don't know the story. The girls' mother died. Subsequently, there was a bad marriage which ended in divorce. Jonathan still misses his first wife. I can never replace her, I know. But there was someone else, too.'

'Seems he likes his women.'

'He does. He's not a man to be on his own. There was an earlier relationship that haunts Jonathan. He started to tell me about it several months ago when our relationship was closer. Suddenly, he stopped. It was as if he'd said too much. I can't get any more out of him.'

'When was this relationship?'

'While he was a student. Something happened that he regrets. It scarred him. He said part of the sum-total of the love he is capable of giving was left behind with that woman. How odd is that? And how wounding to me! I can't get my head around it. But he clammed up. He just wouldn't say any more and got angry if I asked.'

Kate wanted her to repeat all she said. Over and over again. She needed to hear the words about the left-behind love. She wanted to drown in it, to feel the lost emotion and relive her memories. But Joanne would think she hadn't been listening; it would be foolish to ask. And she had most definitely heard every word.

'How strange! I suppose we all have episodes in our past that pursue us. You just have to put them behind you.' Words, words. Words she did not believe.

'Part of me agrees with you. But I want all his love.' Joanna was now tripping over her words. Not badly but the alcohol was noticeable. 'Does mean I have more competition for Jonathan than I can cope with. Competition I can't do anything about.'

Kate glowed with satisfaction, revelled in her power. This beautiful, perfumed, young woman in her classy, well-cut dress, her diamond earrings and red-soled shoes was being rejected for a memory.

'We even talked about a baby.'

'What?' Kate returned to the conversation with a start. 'But Jonathan's over fifty.'

'I'm only thirty-eight. The age many career woman start a family these days. Not a ridiculous idea. But Jonathan thought it was. To be honest, it was my suggestion. A mistake. I think the relationship went downhill from then on. Although I still have hopes.'

Kate had to get out of this conversation. 'Think I'd better go and get another bottle. Seems the Sauvignon Blanc is popular.'

'Sorry, Kate. I've monopolised you. I suddenly needed to talk but I've probably said too much. Thanks for listening. Bloody alcohol!' She looked guilty. Was this because of the drinking or her words? Kate could not tell.

***

'I hear from Neil there's a new exhibition planned. Not sure we can contribute to this one as well as the last.' Jonathan leaned on the kitchen wall and watched Kate, a sleek animal in her accustomed habitat.

'Why did you bring Joanne?'

'You invited her. I asked her and she said she'd like to apologise to you. Simple.'

'You're not a happy couple, are you?'

'No. What has she told you?'

'Probably more than is sensible. But observation is enough. There wasn't much I hadn't already guessed.' Apart from one valuable piece of information.

'What are we going to do, Kate?' Jonathan sounded like a small boy.

Instead of her usual rebuff or a cutting, sarcastic remark, Kate looked at him and shrugged her shoulders. She could not get Joanne's words out of her head. She took a pace towards Jonathan.

'Ah, caught you!' Colin bounced in, shedding tact and discretion along with his jacket. 'Naughty, naughty! Can't get off with the hostess while her husband's around.'

'Not everyone thinks like you, Colin. Go and talk to Angela. You'll make her day. She needs a comedian in her life.' Colin refilled his glass, left the kitchen, returned immediately and took the bottle with him.

'Remind me, which one is Angela...'

***

Becky looked at Kate and shook her head. 'I must be crazy. I shouldn't be here. But I am.'

'You have a choice of men. Past lovers, present lovers, non-lovers, potential lovers.'

'Shut up, Kate. I don't want to listen to you. I know it's rude and I'm in your home. But it's nothing like how you treated me in mine.'

Kate laughed too loudly. 'A drink? I'm bringing cocktails out soon.'

'A tonic water will do.'

'Might have guessed.'

Colin saw Becky and called her across. He excused himself from Angela and the conversation about their various pets.

'Remind me I haven't told you the rat story!' He was adept at recounting – and inventing – anecdotes and Angela was relaxed and enjoying herself.

'Becky, come over here.' He lowered his voice. 'I've done my good deed. Now I can focus on you.'

Becky pretended to be the person he knew and flicked her hair back, smiling.

'You look happier to see me than I expected,' he said. 'We parted on less than the best of terms, I recall.'

'True. I left you because you were drunk and disgusting. You'd gone way past merry and amusing, which I enjoyed. I'm sure the following day's headache must have given you a clue as to why I left.'

'You're right. It was a paracetamol job. But before I made an idiot of myself, we had a good time.' He looked questioningly at Becky, his head tipped sideways, a grin trying to emerge. 'We did, didn't we?'

Colin was a skilled lover. Becky nodded at the recollection but its consequences rather than the pleasure were uppermost in her mind.

Colin topped up his glass, emptying the bottle. 'What are you drinking?'

'Tonic water.'

'Not like you, Becky. Come on, have a glass of wine. You can have a small one even if you're driving. Or do like me, leave the car and take a taxi home. Hey, you can share my taxi!'

'No, it's not driving that's the problem. I'm taking metronidazole – some dental problems.'

'Fair enough. Well, not fair at all, but it can't be helped. Poor you! I'll drink your share!'

Becky had planned her story and her antibiotic. She knew there would be no questions. Kate would not believe it but she knew the truth, anyway. Louise sat beside them with a bounce and introduced herself.

'Hey, you guys need a top up. I told Kate I'd help. I'll go get a bottle.'

'Nothing for me,' Becky said. 'On antibiotics.'

'It's rubbish, you know, the business about not being able to drink with antibiotics. I drank when I was on them. Nothing happened.'

'Depends which one it is. You can drink with many of them but not the one I'm on.'

'You sure? I'd try.'

'Louise, stop being stupid. This place is full of pharmacists. You're talking to one.' Barry threw the remark to his daughter as he walked past, rolled his eyes and headed for the kitchen.

'You a pharmacist?'

'Yes.'

'Whoops! Bad choice of medicine!' She rushed off to harangue someone else.

'Who was that?' Becky asked.

'Daughter of one of the neighbours. Complicated girl, it seems. A few problems. It may not be simply alcohol that's giving her a high.'

Colin sat and looked at Becky; he was unusually quiet. She wriggled in her seat, disliking the inspection, wondering what he could see, what he might guess.

'Stop it, Colin. I'm not an exhibit.'

'Didn't think there were rules about looking.' He put both hands in the air. 'No touching! I'm behaving myself.'

'You rarely behave yourself. There's always an ulterior motive.'

'Actually, ulterior or not, there is a motive. You're an attractive woman, Becky. We get on well together.' Becky looked wary. 'I'm not just talking about physical compatibility. We have a similar sense of humour, both a bit wacky. We don't have to be people who bump into each other occasionally at this event or that. We could see more of each other.'

Becky said nothing.

'Unless, of course, you're in a relationship.'

'My life is complicated, Colin. There's been someone but it's not a relationship that's going to last. I'm sorry but I can't go into details.'

'Does that mean you will or you won't see me again? Where do I stand?'

'Give me a little breathing space. Then I'll see you. I'll call you soon.'

Colin beamed. Becky was afraid he was going to make an announcement to the room. He was still grinning when Neil came over.

'Feeling any better, Becky? Didn't expect you'd be here.'

'I'm on the mend, Neil, thanks.'

'Bloody horrible, dental problems!' Colin joined in. 'Especially when it means you can't drink!'

Neil looked confused. Becky did not explain.

'I need to talk to you about a contact Karen gave me regarding adults with Down's Syndrome,' Neil said to Becky. 'You might know her. Sorry, Colin, talking shop.'

Colin realised he had lost Becky's attention and made a few random comments before returning to Angela and the rat.

'Who are you talking about?'

'Nobody. It was a means of getting rid of Colin. I need to talk to you.'

'It's not the best place.'

'It's the only place at the moment. You won't let me visit you. You don't answer your phone. You haven't been at work. I'm gobsmacked you're here.'

'I shouldn't be. But I needed to speak to Colin. Kate told me he was invited.'

'Colin? Why?'

They were interrupted by Kate who made an entrance with a laden tray. Indoor fireworks were spraying sparkly fountains over four jugs containing different coloured liquids. In small dishes were strawberries, cranberries, cucumber, slices of orange and other garnishes.

'Ta-dah! This is my...party-piece! I've always enjoyed making potions and lotions, mixing and blending – I'm a pharmacist, after all. It's not a big step to turn that skill into inventing cocktails. So it's what I've done.'

There was a cheer. Kate had the glow of alcoholic confidence and revelled in everyone's attention. She handed out cards with the names of the cocktails on them.

'I'll go through the menu and you can choose. There's plenty so you can try them all if you want.'

'This one, "Singing the Blues", has a gin base and the

138

colour is from blue curaçao.'

'I'll have one of those!' shouted Louise. 'Not that I'm feeling blue.'

'Shh, Louise. Wait till Kate's finished telling us about them,' her mother said.

'The green one uses absinthe which used to have a reputation for encouraging loose morals and illicit behaviour. It was even banned in the early 1900s. I've named it "The Hallucinogen".

'I'll have this one instead!" Louise could not keep quiet and her father frowned at her.

'The yellow one is tequila-based, like a margarita. This one's especially for Neil. It's called "Love Bite" after his famous photograph.'

Neil gave a half smile and shook his head.

Grace whispered to David, 'What a lovely couple they are, but she might've embarrassed him.'

'Finally, the red one is made from vodka and cranberries. Red is a dangerous colour so I've called this one 'Kate's Revenge'. She laughed and most people joined in. She noticed out of the corner of her eye neither Neil nor Jonathan were smiling.

'Wow, revenge! Do you think Kate has a grudge against us and the red one will poison everyone?' Louise thought her comment hilarious and hooted with delight. Her parents gave each other anxious looks.

'Only joking! Kate is lovely. But it could be an Agatha Christie!'

'I'll do an official tasting, if you like, and you can see if I drop dead on the spot!'

'No need, Kate. I'll have the red one!'

'Those are the main ingredients. There are various other flavourings in the cocktails as well, and you can choose your own garnish. Before you get started, there's one other important thing – I have a secret ingredient to add to each. I'm not telling you what it is.'

'Why are you doing that?'

'To make them all unique.'

Kate poured her coloured liquids into elegant glasses, added fruit, straws and ice and handed them round. With panache, she produced a small, antique medicine bottle with a dropper in it. It was from her collection of old medicine and pharmacy containers. There were many around the house on display. This one was ideal for her special ingredient.

'Magic drops, anyone?'

She added a few drops to each glass as people offered them.

'Great theatre, Kate,' Colin said. 'You were always one for a bit of drama.'

***

Gwen and Barry went home. They tried to persuade Louise to go with them but it was in vain. Angela said it was lucky she only lived over the road as any further would be a challenge. She giggled and hiccupped her thanks, hugging anyone she could get her arms around. David and Grace stayed until the cocktails had gone, knowing it was rude to leave any. Colin and Becky were chatting. Neil was talking to Louise about his exhibition and she was full of enthusiasm as only she could be. She promised she would be there. Joanne was pale and quiet. She had spent the past half-hour in the bathroom.

'Bloody hell, Joanne. At your age you should know better. Getting drunk is for students.'

'Don't be such a preacher. You were drunk after that stag "do" a couple of months ago.'

'Yes, but I didn't throw up.'

'Don't make it a public announcement.'

'And another thing, Joanne – I assume you forgot it was your turn to drive.'

'Oh, shit!'

'I can't drive. I'm over the limit. I'll speak to Kate.'

He found Kate tidying up in the kitchen and explained the situation.

'Stay the night. No problem. Beds are made up in all the rooms. You can go home in the morning.'

'I'd better tell Joanne.'

'Tell her later. I can see her from here – she's got her eyes closed. She's not with us.'

She took Jonathan's hand and led him out of the kitchen, through the utility room into the garage, shutting the door behind her. There was an earthy smell, soil left on garden tools, and a shiver of cold air leaking under the garage door. She leaned against the wall and pulled Jonathan towards her.

'What's happened to the Kate who kept her distance? The one who met me with reluctance, who did her best to be rude to me as often as possible?'

'It's her night off.'

'How much have you had to drink, Kate?'

'Enough to make me adventurous. But not too much.'

'Your husband's within shouting distance. My partner's equally near. There are guests who might come in at any moment. Louise wouldn't think twice about going anywhere in the house. Someone might look for you.'

'I know. It's what makes it exciting.'

'Neil might come out here to get something.'

'Unlikely. Why would he want his toolbox?'

'He has a toolbox?'

'A little-used one, yes.'

'Well, something else out here he might need?'

'His bike? Spare light bulbs? I don't think so.'

They were talking in whispers. Kate enjoyed the nearness, the conversation about nothing in particular, the daring silliness. This was how they were, in the heady days of their relationship. Hearing his voice, breathing his air. Jonathan's face was close to Kate's. He sighed and the warmth touched her lips. He kissed her.

141

'We'd better be quick.' Jonathan was tense. He glanced towards the door, a thin barrier between them and the party.

'No rush. Sex shouldn't be rushed.'

Kate thought about the love he had left with her, thought about Joanne's words. But mostly she thought about the physical pleasure ahead. She undid his jeans and slid down until she was on her knees in front of him. Jonathan moaned quietly and ran his hands through Kate's hair.

Suddenly, he jumped back. 'No! Don't!'

In the semi-darkness, Kate could see the look of horror on his face. For a moment, she didn't understand. Then she threw her head back in a silent gasp.

'Oh Jonathan, you fool! Not even I would bite the end off your penis!' She gave it a tweak and he lost his erection. 'In spite of my record.' With difficulty she contained her mirth. She was choking into her hand. It would not be a good moment to alert anyone to their presence in the garage.

The atmosphere was ruined. Kate got up, said she should go back to the remaining guests and left Jonathan with his jeans around his ankles and a bemused expression on his face.

Chapter 17

Joanne was unwell the following morning. Jonathan came down to breakfast with a stony face, saying little. Kate resisted the temptation to mention the previous evening although she was bubbling with amusement inside. When Neil returned from buying a newspaper, he was unusually quiet. Communication between the three of them barely lifted above a request for the marmalade.

An ashen face peered round the kitchen door, a sad-faced clown, a contrast to the stylish woman of the evening before. The dark rings under Joanne's eyes had more to do with the dregs of make-up than lack of sleep as she had slept as only the inebriated can do.

'Can we go now, Jonathan?'

'Sure.'

They gave their thanks and left immediately, Jonathan raising his eyebrows at Kate as he kissed her on both cheeks. She couldn't interpret what he meant but he meant something.

'I bumped into Barry at the newsagent's,' Neil said. 'Louise has been throwing up.'

'There's a surprise. I'd throw up if I drank half what she consumed.'

'He was worried. Said he'd not see her so bad before.'

'I suspect it wasn't just the alcohol she drank here. God knows what she was under the influence of. I'm nobody's nurse-maid. Adults should control their own drinking. She is an adult, you know.'

'Only just.'

'She's eighteen. Old enough.'

'I also saw Angela looking a bit peaky. She said she thought she'd had a drink too many.'

'It was a party, Neil. People drink at parties. Often too much. It's fun until the following morning. We've all been there. What's your problem?'

'Those cocktails were strong. And there was a bitter aftertaste. I thought there was, anyway.'

'No-one complained last night. You didn't either. Are you accusing me of something?'

'What was your "secret ingredient", Kate?'

'If I told you, it wouldn't be a secret any longer.'

'I'm serious. You weren't deliberately trying to make people sick, were you?'

'I was just being inventive. You know, if you create a brand new cocktail, you can register it. I could do that.'

'Stop being flippant.'

'So you think I'm in the business of poisoning our friends. That's a first! Good to have the confidence of my husband.' She spat the words at him. 'There were several pharmacists here, folk who know about such things. No-one else was suspicious.'

'They might be this morning.'

'Do you think I'll make the evening news, then?'

Kate tipped her head back and sniffed. She was finished with the discussion. Neil shook his head and took his newspaper into the sitting room. Kate turned her back on him. 'What?' she muttered under her breath. 'A poisoner?' There was a certain appeal with such a reputation.

***

'Do you think the cocktails Kate made on Friday tasted okay?'

'I've no idea – I wasn't drinking.'

'Shit, I'd forgotten. Something about dental problems and

144

antibiotics?'

Becky was back at work and could not avoid Neil in the pharmacy.

'It's a funny question. Why do you ask?'

'I thought they were bitter. There was a pleasant flavour to start with but bitterness lingered. I tried some of the cocktails left in the kitchen without Kate's "secret ingredient". They tasted far better. What might Kate have added?'

'No idea. I don't make cocktails.'

'I'm not talking about normal cocktail ingredients. What might she have access to that's bitter?'

'You're asking me to dredge up some pharmaceutical chemistry? Not an easy task. Alkaloids are bitter. Many drugs are alkaloids. But without some research, I couldn't guess what she might've used. Anyway, why would she do something like that?'

'She's behaving oddly. Everyone in my world is behaving oddly. I wonder if she'd tried to make folk ill. Just to show she could. She likes to dominate. You know that.'

Becky nodded. 'But it would be dangerous behaviour, unethical behaviour. She would be struck off the Register.'

'It would have to be proved first.'

'Aren't you making a ridiculous leap here? Just because the drinks tasted bitter doesn't mean there was something bad in them. Maybe they just weren't to your taste.'

'Several people were ill either that evening or the next day.'

'Surprise, surprise! Have you never felt sick after a party?'

'Barry said Louise was worse than he'd ever seen her.'

'I think Louise has problems. I bet Barry is unaware how bad they are. He dotes on her. I expect he wouldn't imagine she could do anything seriously wrong.'

'Angela wasn't well. And both David and Grace told me they had horrendous hangovers. Said they had too many cocktails.'

'They probably had. Mixing their drinks big time.'

'I really thought you'd take me seriously.'

'Kate is not my favourite person. But I don't think she's a poisoner.'

Becky excused herself to deal with a customer. When she was free Neil said, 'I'm coming round this evening. I'll be there at half seven. I expect you to let me in.'

***

He arrived exactly as he said. Becky was a different person from his last visit. She was dressed in jeans and a freshly washed, if unironed, shirt with a hint of make-up on her face. And the house was clean and tidy – relatively tidy, Becky's tidy. She allowed Neil to hug her, turning her face to avoid anything more intimate.

'You look better. Not your usual self, but better. And this place does, too. Are you going to tell me what happened?'

He put a bottle of wine on the table and got two glasses from the cupboard.

'A glass of Chablis should brighten you up, put a bit of colour in your cheeks.'

Becky shook her head.

'You're not still on the dodgy antibiotics, are you?'

'I was never on antibiotics at all.'

'Come here.' Neil put out both hands to take Becky's. She stood before him and tears slid silently down her cheeks.

'I'm at a loss to know what's going on. You behave in a way I've never seen, your home turns into a tip, you avoid me, shun me. Now you're inventing stories – dental problems, antibiotics that stop you drinking. Why? You have to tell me, Becky. What's wrong?' He spoke gently. 'I want to understand.'

'It's complicated, Neil. Not what you're expecting to hear. I think this is the end of our relationship.'

'I realise things have changed now Kate knows. Although I still don't know why you confessed. She's more or less evicted me. Sent me to live with you for a while. We have decisions to make.'

'Are you here because you've nowhere else to go?'

'No, Becky, no! I'm here because I want to talk to you. To get to the bottom of what's happening.'

Becky let go of his hands and sat down facing him. She took a deep breath.

'I'm pregnant.'

Neil did not move. The silence was absolute. His eyes locked on Becky's, searching. He turned away, snatching his face from her gaze, got up and stared out of the window. Anything other than sit looking at Becky's face. He watched a cat pad across the grass, its tail held high. He focussed on the flapping branches of a tree, a dirty mark on the patio, a rose that should have been pruned. These were familiar, part of the world he recognised and knew. Turning away from them took him into a strange land.

'You're right. I wasn't expecting that.'

'I'm over four months. It will start to show soon.' She wiped her eyes on her arm.

'I didn't know there was someone else. How long has this been going on?'

'There isn't someone else.'

'Really? Don't tell me the Angel Gabriel visited you! Or do you have your own special incubus?' Neil could not help bitterness colouring his words.

Becky winced. 'I'm not having an affair. That's what I meant. It was a one-off.'

'Do you often do that? Go out looking for one-night stands? I suppose I'm lucky it hasn't happened before. Or maybe it would have been better if it had.' Neil paced around the room. 'I'd have known sooner what you're like.'

'I don't have random sex. I said it was a one-off and I meant it.'

'So you know who the father is?'

'Yes.'

'I'm not sure I want to know this. But I have to ask. Do I know him?'

'It's Colin. The guy at your party. The pharmacist.'

'The buffoon?'

'He isn't actually a buffoon. He's a decent bloke.'

'That makes it alright then. Go to him. It's what you're intending, isn't it? Now I understand why you turned up at the party. You said at the time it was to see Colin. But I didn't twig. Why should I?'

'Colin doesn't know.'

'Really? I'm supposed to believe that?'

'Neil, I'll explain everything if you give me a chance. Go outside for ten minutes, a walk or something. Then come back. Please.'

Neil shrugged dismissively but went out, anyway. When he returned, he looked more composed, his face less flushed and his breathing normal. He opened the Chablis, poured a large glass and drank half of it.

'Okay. I'm listening.'

'It was at the pharmacy reunion. At the end of September last year. Colin was there and we both had too much to drink. We had a wild affair as students. It didn't last – Colin always moved on and that was fine by me. But we both remembered those few months and revisited the past. It didn't cross my mind I might get pregnant.'

'No, of course not. You're used to me. Me with my inadequate sperm count. I'm no risk. Obviously not sufficiently a man for you.'

'Don't be ridiculous. I never thought of you as anything but a wonderful man, a great lover. And a good friend.'

'You didn't think all that much about me. You wouldn't have jumped into bed with Colin if you had.'

'It wasn't planned. It happened. He's divorced, I'm single. It's probably happened to you, too, on your travels.'

'I can't remember the last time it did. I don't get into those situations.'

'Remember, Neil, although we've had an affair for years, I have to accept you and Kate still have sex. You're still living with her, still have a relationship. You have two women. It's not so different.'

Neil didn't answer. He did not know if Becky was trying to score points but she silenced him with truth.

'So what are you intending to do?'

'Making a decision has been killing me. It's why I was in such a mess. I haven't even been to the doctor's – I did the test myself. I was worried a rumour might spread and ruin my credibility as a pharmacist.'

'Have you made a decision?'

'Yes. I'm keeping the baby.'

'So what about the reputation?'

'I think most people will understand. If they don't, I'll cope with it.'

'And what about Colin?'

'I've told him I'll see him. He actually wants to start a relationship. Not just a physical one, so don't look at me like that.'

'So he does know about the baby?'

'No. I told you he didn't. I wanted to tell him but couldn't. But I shall have to do it. It might turn him away. But he has a right to know and decide.'

'So you move in with Colin. I get thrown out by Kate because of you. Looks like I'm the loser all round.'

'I don't have the energy to feel sorry for you, Neil. Whether or not I have any sort of future with Colin, you won't want me now I'm pregnant with another man's child. I'm not stupid.'

Neil had an urge to take Becky in his arms. To tell her how much she meant to him. To bury his face in her hair, to feel the warmth of her body, to relax against her. To tell her everything would be alright. But he got up stiffly, picked up the Chablis, commenting there was little point in leaving it to go to waste, and

149

left.

***

'Colin, can I come and see you?'

'Of course. Yes, yes, of course. I wasn't expecting you to call me so soon.'

'On Saturday?'

'You mean in two days' time?'

'Yes. I'll drive to your place if you give me the address.'

Colin suggested they meet in a restaurant near Becky's, but she was insistent.

'Don't argue, Colin. I may change my mind.'

Chapter 18

It has to happen quickly before I lose my nerve. Then I'll know where I stand. I can start to plan properly. My life won't stop while I dither. And the baby continues to grow. Becky was preparing herself for the ordeal to come. Colin had to know before they started on any sort of relationship. The longer she left it, the harder it would be.

Her hands felt clammy and she ran her tongue over her lips. She wondered if her carefully applied make-up was smudging everywhere, dribbles of sweat and mascara making her look like a ghoul. The quick glance in her handbag mirror told her she looked okay. Just okay. Not the lively, sparkly person she once thought herself to be. As she rang the doorbell she had an immense desire to turn and run. The intercom crackled and the door opened. His flat was on the first floor and he was standing by the open door when she reached the top of the stairs. The keenness in his eye and his pleasure at her presence made her swallow hard. She wished he had disguised his feelings better. But that was not Colin; it never had been. She caught a glimpse of someone behind him, a woman. Colin noticed her puzzled expression.

'Sorry, I assumed you knew. My daughter lives here.'

Damn. It could make things difficult. She did not want an audience. Perhaps this daughter would find them boringly old and disappear.

'No, I didn't realise.' What had Kate said? Something about his daughter living with him after the divorce but she hadn't taken it in. She certainly did not expect to find her still there.

'I'll miss her when she goes to university in the autumn. Going to be a pharmacist – I tried to put her off but she's determined!' Colin put his arm around his daughter and pulled her towards him, showing her off to Becky, a prize specimen.

She was graceful. Not a model's grace but the result of natural posture, a long neck, short hair that knew where it should lie and a clear, light skin. It was the look millions of women spend thousands of pounds to achieve, and usually fail.

Becky tried to focus on being pleasant to the teenager. She made a few inane comments about her pharmacy which entertained Colin. He was in the mood to find the slightest quip amusing; Helena was a serious girl and smiled in a stiff, wooden way. As if the topic of pharmacy was too important for humour. When Becky sat down, she joined her, sitting slightly too close, fixing her eyes on her.

'Tell me about retail pharmacy. Dad only knows about hospital and I've heard all that loads of times.'

'What do you want to know?' Go away, girl. This is not what I'm here for.

'Why did you decide on retail? Is it satisfying? Do you feel you contribute to the local community? Aren't parts of it boring? Is it better than working in a hospital?' Her eyes widened with each question. 'Tell me anything you think I should know.'

Perhaps if I do, she'll go away. 'I love it because I like people contact. I know my customers. Some have been coming to me for years. I know their families and their problems. They value my advice. As you know, hospital pharmacy is different, a changing population. It depends what you want from your career and also where your talents lie.'

'Yes, but does it mean you have to stay in one place, one position, for ever?'

'No. If you're ambitious, you have to move on. You won't build up relationships straight away. Sometimes folk clam up if they don't know you. Time builds trust. It's your choice. I've had several jobs but I've stayed in the latest one for fifteen years. It suits me.'

'Did you get any training in counselling?'

'Our course didn't cover that. I suppose I learned on the job and from more senior pharmacists. You'll probably get training now. I really don't know what the syllabus contains these days.' Go away, go away!

'I don't know how sympathetic I am. Could I really comfort anyone? Would I be a good listener? I'm sure I can learn all the technical stuff but beyond that…' Helena stared hard at Becky, then at her hands.

'You don't have to choose your career path yet. Do the course. Enjoy it. Your way forward might become obvious.'

'Yeah. I don't like uncertainty, though. When did you actually decide what was best for you?'

'You know, I don't remember. The jobs chose me rather than the other way round. I seemed simply to end up in them. I worked in retail and hospital in the long vacs to gain experience and I suppose it helped. It's good to do that.'

'Could I work in your shop with you?' Helena jumped up, animated, elated to have found the answer to one of her problems.

'When you're ready, come and see me. I'll see what I can do.' Shit. Who knows what the situation will be by then?

Colin hugged Helena and kissed her forehead. 'Don't monopolise Becky. You've hardly stopped talking since she arrived. I thought you were going out this evening, anyway.'

'I am.' She looked at her watch. 'Paul's calling for me in ten minutes. Okay, I'll leave you two to reminisce. Thanks, Becky. Hope we can talk again, I really do.'

Becky was relieved to see her go. She felt wrung out, exhausted by the inquisition, drained of energy. What an unworldly girl I must have been! I never debated much about my future. A few decisions then I let life happen. Perhaps I should have planned more. The irony of it – too late now.

Colin was beaming with pride.

'She's an intense young lady, your daughter.'

'She is. It's her mother in her. You probably noticed it isn't one of my traits!'

'I didn't see a lot of laid-back Colin, that's for sure.'

'It was one of our problems. We were totally unalike, her mother, Alice, and me. I still wonder sometimes why we married. It can work, opposites, but it didn't for us. It should have stayed a wild affair – she was a beautiful woman and the sex was bloody amazing. But you need more than that to keep going.'

'Not rocket science, Colin.'

'Yeah, yeah, I know. Funny, really. Helena's intensity is fine. I can cope with it. Well, mostly. We have the odd clash. But her mother got on my nerves big time.'

'So that's why you divorced?'

'Partly. Also because Alice wanted more children. Two more at least. God knows when she'd have stopped. I didn't want any at all. We argued about it until there was little else we spoke about. Then Helena came along. I suspect the "pill-forgetting" was deliberate though Alice denied it. Start of the end.'

'But you seem close to your daughter.'

'I adore Helena. Always have. Strange how it works out. You can't fight parental love even if you didn't want the baby in the first place. But it didn't make me want more.' Colin stopped suddenly. 'Sorry, Becky, selfish of me. Going on about parenthood.'

'No, not selfish. Just natural.'

She liked the paternal Colin. A new side to him. Even so, it was hard to imagine him with a baby in his arms, holding a dummy where there was usually a wine glass. Hard to see him changing a nappy, cooing at a giggling infant. Would he get up at two in the morning to soothe a screaming child? She remembered him waking her at two or three or four during their passionate affair, rolling against her, stroking her back, unable to wait until morning, the previous evening's pleasures insufficient to keep him going. Difference circumstances, a different decade, a previous life.

'Were children ever part of your grand plan, Becky?'

'Not sure I ever had a grand plan. I suppose there was a time when I assumed I'd marry and have a family. My friends and colleagues were doing it.'

'So what happened?'

'Nothing. That was the problem. I had plenty of relationships but they were like fireworks that fizzled out. I never found myself a slow burner.' Until Neil. Straightforward, down-to-earth Neil who brought the biggest complication of her life with him.

'It sounds dismal and my life is anything but that. I've always enjoyed my freedom. Who knows? I may still find the right man!'

Colin went to get glasses and a bottle of wine. He returned with an odd expression on his face. Becky could not interpret it.

'So, tell me – did your ex-wife have the large family she wanted with someone else?'

'Alice remarried and has two other children. She got her way.'

'How long did your marriage last?'

'Four years. I told Alice I was going to have a vasectomy. I couldn't trust her to take the pill and there were constant arguments about contraception. She thought she could make me change my mind. I objected to her trying. We're far better apart. Even friendly on the occasions we meet – admittedly, not often. Helena goes backwards and forwards although mostly lives here. Suits us all.'

Colin popped in and out of the kitchen, tipping nuts into a bowl, opening a jar of olives and some crisps.

'You okay with Riesling?' Colin stopped suddenly, about to pour her a glass. 'Are you alright? You look pale.'

'I feel rather light-headed. Sorry. Don't know why. Where's the loo?'

Becky disappeared. She knew exactly why she was pale. A vasectomy? Had he really had a vasectomy? It was impossible.

155

She was carrying his child. It was rare for vasectomies to fail. Perhaps he simply talked about it to make a point to his wife. Yes, that was it. It was a threat. It made sense. All the same, she had to find out. She needed a definitive answer.

The doorbell rang and she could hear Helena talking to someone. A minute later, the door closed and it was quiet. Good. They had gone. She put on a little more blusher, ran her fingers through her hair and took a few deep breaths. She emerged, her unruffled exterior hiding a lingering nausea.

The bedroom doors were open and she glanced in as she passed. Helena's was neat and functional. A plain cream duvet cover with an old teddy bear sitting on it, his limp head flopped against the pillows. Lines of books on a bookcase. Some looked like text books, their spines dull and bent, the titles unreadable. Others showed a flash of colour, maybe a best-seller or two. She was tempted to look, to find out more about this strange girl. There was a poster on the wall, some kind of map and a couple of pictures. A hockey stick rested against a wooden box. Had it been her toy box?

Colin's room interested her more. It was a man's room. A similar cream duvet cover on a less well-made bed. A suit on a hanger hooked on an open wardrobe door, a couple of sweaters cast aside on a chair, a sock like a ball on the floor. The open door into a shower room showed a bright red towel cast lazily aside. A light room, a movement of the curtain showing the window was open. A room to breathe in. A room with enough space for a cot. This man was the father of her child. This was his home. Everything in the room was marked by him, touched by him. His presence lay on the curled pages of a thriller by the bed, on the shoes and trainers tumbled into a corner.

If we begin a relationship, I will spend time here. Is this a room I would be comfortable in? Not tidy but nothing like my level of messiness. Would he want me to live his type of life? To slot in like an unresisting shadow? Becky had never been anyone's shadow. Could I settle here? Could I live so close to a teenage daughter? She knew in an instant it could not be her home. Her home was where she lived now. But perhaps she could cope with this room, if it was required.

'That looks better!' Colin greeted her with a glass of wine in his outstretched hand.

'Sorry to be a misery but I'm not drinking tonight.'

'You're being super cautious. One glass will be alright even though you're driving. I said we should meet somewhere closer to you or near the train. It would have solved the drinking problem.' A frisson of irritation roughened his words. 'Come on, Becky. This isn't like you. Where's the party girl?'

'It's nothing to do with driving. Nor is it metronidazole. This will no doubt surprise you. It astonished me.'

There was a burst of noise as the front door opened and feet clattered on the tiled floor. Colin went to look.

'Nor has it anything to do with the fact I don't particularly like Riesling,' Becky muttered.

Helena rushed into the room pulling her boyfriend behind her.

'So glad you haven't gone out. I've been telling Paul about you, Becky. About how helpful you've been. Then I thought it would be far better if we came back so he could hear what you've been telling me.'

Becky felt flattened, exhausted, her mental effort and preparation thrown away. Just on the point of telling Colin she was pregnant, this had to happen.

'Is Paul going to be a pharmacist?'

'No, he's going to study psychology. Wants to be an academic. But you could try to make him change his mind!' Helena did her approximation of a laugh and gave Paul a small push.

'So why does he need to listen to me?' They were talking about him as if he were somewhere else.

'To help me make up my mind. We discuss our careers all the time. Tell him what you told me about retail pharmacy. About your relationship with your customers, their trust. All that stuff.'

It was a replay of their previous conversation, only longer. Becky tried to be lively, an effort needing more energy than she possessed. Paul listened and sought answers. He seemed to find nothing strange in asking multiple questions about a career he had no intention of following. He was a reflection of Helena, a more studious version of a seriously studious girl.

Colin lay back in an armchair with his wine and sipped. He had no need to listen to the young pair. He watched Becky's face, studied her body, her movements, how she fingered her hair, how she frowned, how she rubbed a finger by the side of her mouth. The way she forced a laugh but smiled little. By the time the conversation was done, he was on his third glass.

Back on their own, neither knew the next step.

'Okay, Becky. Before the rude intrusion, I think you were about to tell me something.'

'I was.' She composed herself. 'I'm pregnant.'

Colin stopped moving. He slowly opened his mouth and blew out a long breath. Putting the glass down, he ran his hands through his hair.

'I wasn't expecting it although the thought did cross my mind just a couple of minutes ago. I was watching you. It was the only piece of news I could imagine needing such a build-up. Are you going to tell me about it? What you are going to do?'

'I've decided to keep the baby.'

'What the fuck…are you mad?'

'No, I'm not mad. At least, I don't think so. There are lots of reasons why a termination would be the best and simplest route. You could reel them all off but I don't need you to. Ultimately, it's an emotional decision. I can't bring myself to get rid of a living being however many problems it might bring.'

'Probably shouldn't ask, not my business, but d'you know who the father is?'

'Yes.'

'Does he know about the pregnancy?'

'I've recently told him.'

'And...'

'I suspect he doesn't think it's his baby.'

'There's always DNA testing.'

'I'm not going there. This isn't a conflict situation.'

'However did you get yourself into this mess, Becky?' Colin was unsettled and tense. He refilled his glass and paced around the room, drinking without noticing, swallowing handfuls of nuts. 'Contraception isn't difficult. You're sexually active – why aren't you on the pill? Why take chances?'

'A complex situation, Colin. One I don't intend to explain. But there was a sensible reason for my choices.'

'Are you prepared to bring up the child on your own?'

'Yes, if I have to. I'd hoped the father might play a role. But I might be wrong there.'

'A child at your age – our age – is no small undertaking. Yes, yes, I know.' Colin put his hand up when he saw the expression on Becky's face. 'You've been through it all. I was just thinking about it from the guy's perspective.'

'How would you cope, Colin?'

'Me? Christ, I wouldn't. I couldn't. Already told you it's one of the reasons my marriage failed.'

She had to ask him but the words would not form into sentences.

'You're a good dad. I can see that from the short time I've seen you with Helena.'

'I do my best. It's never been a natural role. I just hope my shortcomings are compensated for by the love I feel for her. She knows I love her. Maybe one day I'll be presented with a grandchild and I'll have to cope with a baby again.'

He laughed, trying to escape from the troubled cloud he'd created around himself. 'Hopefully, it'll be a long way away.' He left the room muttering about needing a wee.

When they planned this evening, Colin suggested they ate nearby at a bistro he liked. But the thought of finding conversation

159

for a further couple of hours was too much for Becky.

'Becky, are you still up for a meal round the corner?'

'You know what, Colin? I think I might just go home. My revelation has put a damper on our mood. I'd planned to tell you but didn't anticipate the effect it would have. Thanks for the offer.'

'Maybe another time? Always good to see you.'

Becky got her coat, gave Colin a hug and headed for the door.

'Just one thing, Colin, before I go. Did you threaten your wife you'd have a vasectomy or did you actually have one?'

'I had one, of course. Why wouldn't I?'

As Becky disappeared down the stairs, realisation struck him like a hammer.

Chapter 19

Becky drove home in a trance, her thoughts a tangled knot in her brain. When the traffic lights changed, the driver behind had to lean on his horn for several seconds before she realised she should move. She waved an apology but he glared and mouthed some insult. Concentrate, concentrate, she told herself, or you won't get home at all. But within minutes she had to brake violently when the car in front stopped at a pedestrian crossing. As she screeched to a standstill, she was only a couple of centimetres from an accident. Turning into her drive, relieved to be back without further incident, she nearly ran into a child chasing a ball. She heard the screaming of an adult and the child was scooped up. She burst into tears.

In the previous week, the week before her visit to Colin, her world had settled down. She'd made decisions. Her home was looking normal – as normal as it ever was; she was functioning at work. There was the build-up to the conversation with Colin. She ran through the most positive scenario where Colin was amazed but thought he could manage with a baby on the scene. She spent more time on the likelier situation of his wanting no further relationship with her, in spite of the baby. She rehearsed the arguments, had a series of proposals to put forward, foresaw the pros and cons and even planned their next meeting. She felt she could handle the outcome of their discussion and getting her thoughts sorted out soothed her.

But none of it helped; none had been necessary. The possibility he was not the father had never occurred to her. There was simply no-one else who could be. Her sex life was not rampant. She struggled to think who her last partner, other than Neil and Colin, had been. There was no wild party where drink and euphoria had taken her along dodgy paths; no sun, sand and sex holiday she enjoyed in her younger days. And, she thought wryly, no alien had visited as far as she knew.

Her mind strayed to Neil. He made her feel good; the constant positive in her life. Theirs was a carefree, happy relationship. Passionate and comforting, it gave her all she needed. Well, it used to, she reflected. But it had changed. Thoughts of him now caused a hollow ache inside her. Guilt had started to trouble her. It was one thing to have a fling with a married man, quite another to have a prolonged affair with a friend's husband. It wasn't planned that way, she told herself. But it had happened. Initially, she thought Kate was an uncaring, unfaithful wife and wasn't worried about her. But they saw more of each other these days. Hell – Kate had even sent her flowers as a friendly gesture when she'd provided an alibi. Her conscience had made her consider parting from Neil. Then the pregnancy washed everything else from her mind.

Maybe I'm not actually pregnant! She felt pregnant. There was a possibility she had done something wrong in the test but it was unlikely. If a pharmacist performs a pregnancy test incorrectly, what hope for an inept fifteen-year-old? Easy to check. She repeated the test with utmost precision and got the same result.

A cup of tea, a large piece of cheese and some pickles, a handful of nuts and she knew the next step.

***

She booked the appointment with Neelam Patel as soon as the surgery opened. She knew her on a professional basis and liked her. But she rarely needed to visit her GP so their relationship had not developed. Going to someone outside the area, booking a private consultation, was a possibility. But she decided against it. It might have been the best option for a termination, but keeping the baby meant it would not be a secret for long. And, anyway, GPs do not divulge information about patients. She knew that; she also knew how quickly local gossip spread.

Sitting on the edge of a chair in the doctor's office, she went through the pleasantries without noticing what she was saying. She had to get to the point.

'Neelam, I believe I'm pregnant.'

'You believe…?'

'Stupid thing to say. I am pregnant. I've done two tests so I know.'

If Neelam's eyebrow lifted a millimetre, it was hardly noticeable.

'Okay, let's have your dates.'

'This is a problem. It sounds ridiculous at my age – getting pregnant at my age is ridiculous – but I don't know for sure who the father is.'

Becky wriggled in her seat and paused a while. Neelam did not interrupt or rush her.

'Okay. Let me tell you the story. I'll make it the short version.'

She related, as unemotionally as possible, how she and Colin reconnected at the reunion. Then about his vasectomy.

'Vasectomies don't suddenly fail, years after they're done, do they?'

'No. This man is not the father.'

Again, there was a pause.

'I've been in a long-term relationship. With a married man. We only meet from time to time. He has a low sperm count.'

'How long have the two of you been together?'

'Ten years or so.'

'Regular sex?'

'As often as circumstances allow. But yes. Pretty regular.'

'Have you ever used contraception with him?'

163

'In our early days I was on the pill. But I never liked it so came off. There was no need for it as I don't sleep around. It's the truth. The incident at the reunion was unusual, trust me.'

'You say this man is married. Without children?'

'Yes. He and his wife tried for a baby years ago and failed.'

'Men with low sperm counts do conceive. There are sperm there.'

Becky looked disbelieving.

'From what you've told me, it seems the most likely explanation. Anyway, let's get you a scan, find out how far you are and do all the tests.'

'I should mention I intend to keep the baby. I know all about the hazards of a pregnancy at my age. I've done the sleepless nights, the agonising over the decision already. Even if I have to do it alone, I intend to keep the baby and bring it up.' Becky was fierce in her determination.

Neelam smiled. 'You know as well as I do my role is to help you with whatever your choice is, to provide information where required so all decisions are made in full knowledge and never to judge.'

'Yes, of course, I know. Sorry if I sounded defensive. I suppose I'm already building my protective armour against the unforgiving world. But it doesn't include you.'

Becky went home. She sat in her familiar kitchen and looked at it as if it were new to her eyes. The world was new. She now admitted she was going to have a baby and keep it. Telling Neelam her decision had taken her to a new stage in her life. She would have someone other than herself to think about, a being to care for and love. Her relationships, even the relationship with Neil, had been essentially selfish. There was a longing that filled her as she thought of him. She pushed him from her mind.

She picked up a frying pan sitting by the sink, the remains of her breakfast spotting the base with burnt, yellow flakes. One day, I will make scrambled egg for my son or daughter. A daughter. She placed her hands on her abdomen, as if she could tell by touching. Yes, I think it will be a daughter. She will sit at this table and look out of this window at the very trees I can see now. She looked at the floor and could see a crawling child. She looked at the washing basket with a scattering of her clothes in it, a sock hanging over the edge, a tangle of bra straps. There will be Babygros and…

She shook her head. For a person who let life happen and barely reflected on anything, this was momentous. Restlessness prodded her. Yet she also felt at ease. How could the two co-exist? She didn't know. This was new territory, a sensory baptism. She decided she should do something, anything, to get her world back to normal. Normal? Maybe she was in the new normal.

She went upstairs to change her clothes, take off the outfit she had worn to the doctor's and put her jeans on. She didn't know why she had felt the need to be smart. Folk wear what they like when they go to their GP. But it had helped, given her the extra confidence she needed. She stopped by the door to the small bedroom. This was her "study". She decided she needed one when she bought the house and put an old desk in there with a computer. She no longer used it. Had barely ever used it. And what had she studied in there? Nothing. She kept up to date with what she needed to know but serious studying stopped when she graduated.

Now the room was simply a cupboard, a depository for junk, a home for items that lived nowhere else but which resisted being dumped. Right. This will be the nursery. She could see the curtains with animals on them, lined to keep the light out. The cot would fit in the corner and there was space for a chest of drawers. It would need redecorating. Maybe pale yellow walls. She was not a girly-pink, boyish-blue person. Some pictures. She was good at DIY. She could get going on that soon. But first, she needed a good sort-out. Most of the stuff would end up at the tip.

She was starting to sort through a cardboard box of papers when her phone rang.

'Becky, can I come round?'

'I didn't think you wanted anything to do with me. You were pretty resentful last time we spoke.' She kept her voice level, fighting emotion.

'I know. But I've been thinking. Can't explain on the phone. Please can I see you?'

Where did he fit in now? Did he fit in at all? Becky waited but Neil remained silent.

'Alright,' she agreed. 'When?'

'Tonight.'

***

'I want you to tell me again what you told me last time. I can listen rationally now. The shock element won't be there.'

'I'm pregnant. You know that. Why will repeating it make a difference?'

'I'm testing myself.'

Becky frowned. Testing himself for what? 'I don't sleep around. The fling at the reunion was simply a fling – a one-off.'

'Are you certain you want to keep the baby?'

'Yes. I wouldn't have told you if there'd been any doubt in my mind. A termination would have remained my secret.'

'And Colin doesn't know?' A hint of derision tinged his words.

'He does now. I've been to see him.'

'And…?'

'There will be no relationship with him.'

Becky told the truth but could not manage the whole story. She omitted to say she had not told Colin she thought he was the father. She left out her shock at the vasectomy. Nor could she bring herself to suggest to Neil he might be the father. He would not believe her. He would assume there had been yet another lover. There would be a further argument, more fierce words. Another time, perhaps. Another time when she felt stronger. She had to sort it out in her own head. She had to feel able to face that

166

battle.

'So you will be alone.'

'No. I'll be with my baby.'

'You know what I mean. You intend to raise the child on your own. You'll be a single mother.'

'Yes.'

'What about work?'

'There are other single mothers in the world, you know. It's been done before. I'll take my maternity leave. When I have to, I'll return to work. There'll be locum cover while I'm off.'

'What about us?'

'I hope you don't despise me. I hope after you've got over the shock we could remain friends. I don't know what that would look or feel like. But you've been in my life for so long, it would be hard to imagine never seeing you again.'

Becky had not intended to say that. She *had* imagined breaking up with Neil when guilt got the better of her, when she felt ashamed of being a husband-stealer. But that was when Kate was a friend. Now it was an unbearable thought. She cursed herself for loose talking. She had decided before Neil arrived to make everything factual and precise. Feelings were dangerous; they were elephant traps. And she had just gone and fallen into one. Her voice sounded strange, a higher pitch than normal; she could not rely on it.

'I'll make some coffee.' She turned her back on Neil and fussed round the kitchen. She wished they had sat in the lounge so she could have escaped. Could have breathed air not shared with him. Left him to think. But they always sat in the kitchen. When they were together. Old habits, she thought. She avoided his eyes as she found the mugs and a packet of biscuits.

Neil coughed. It was a pre-speech cough. A clearing of his throat. It made Becky's heart beat faster as she steadied herself against whatever he was going to say, whatever rebuke or challenge was coming her way. She grasped the edge of the work surface with both hands.

167

'I said some horrible things to you last time.' Becky nodded. 'It was the shock. There was no way I could have anticipated that conversation. My reaction was spontaneous.' He paused and looked at Becky. Their eyes met briefly but she turned away.

'Becky, look at me.' He waited until she did. 'I'm sorry.'

'You don't have to apologise. I doubt you are sorry. You hated the fact I had sex with someone else and I don't expect you've changed your mind.'

'That's true. But I've come to terms with it. You made me appreciate how self-centred I'd been. Always expecting you to welcome me, never asking about my life with Kate – or only superficially. I don't know if you've been faithful to me – until now – but I always thought you were.' He raised his eyebrows in question and Becky nodded. 'I've expected you to give more to me than I gave to you.'

Neil took a sip of his coffee, a break to assemble his thoughts.

'If I'd not reacted as I did to your news, it would have told me you were unimportant. That I could manage without you, move on. Move back to Kate…' He sneered. 'Not that she needs or wants me.' He drank more coffee. 'Or to someone else.'

'This is the result of sleepless nights. Of hours of pondering and self-exploration. I've thought more about my life and what I want from it in the last few days than I have over the last ten years.'

Becky listened. The words mirrored her own situation. Hadn't she spent more time reflecting on her life than ever before?

'I love you, Becky.'

The words drummed on Becky's ears. She put a hand up to her head, she rubbed her brow. Neil was waiting for her to speak.

'Is this misplaced pity, Neil? Is it guilt driving you to this? What do you intend to do? Pay for a nursery place for the child?'

'I can't blame you for your cynicism. You haven't been in

my brain. No, I mean what I say. I would rather be with you than with anyone else. My marriage to Kate is hollow.'

'You would say that if she's thrown you out.'

'Throwing me out could make me want her more. She actually threw me out temporarily. She might expect me to return.'

'So you've got options! I can't run into your arms, Neil. This isn't like making up after a lover's tiff.'

'I know. I also know I had to tell you. I'll give you time to think about what I've said. I'll stand by you and the baby. Colin's baby.'

Neil finished his coffee and said he thought he should go. Becky could see him debating whether he should hug her, kiss her on the cheek or make any other gesture. His arms flapped up and down, not knowing where they should be. He touched her lightly on the back of her neck – his compromise.

Chapter 20

'No, I'm not shocked. Not even surprised. It doesn't change anything.'

'It's not too late to reassess, you know. There's no shame.' Neelam spoke gently, making the often-repeated words personal.

'I'd been through every scenario before I first visited you.'

'Sometimes actually getting a test result causes an unexpected reaction. I've seen it before. If you do feel differently now, differently from how you thought you'd feel, that's normal, acceptable.'

Becky was simply being Becky. She knew her age placed her at the risky end of the spectrum for congenital abnormalities. Had she not discussed all this with Kate? Had she not tossed and turned her body and brain through many sleep-troubled nights? This was behind her now. That the tests showed her to be at high risk of having a Down's Syndrome child was unsurprising. But she understood Neelam was being her professional self, making sure her patient understood the options and was making considered choices

'I can't say I thought this would happen. But I can accept it has.'

Neelam continued to explain. 'And "high risk" means one percent or more. There is still a much greater chance the baby won't have Down's Syndrome than it will. Many people struggle with the stats, think the risk is higher than it is, so I have to go over this. Forgive me if I'm telling you what you know already.'

'It's okay. But I do know.'

'And there's something else. You said you thought you became pregnant at the end of last September. The scan indicates you are around twelve weeks, not sixteen. A September conception seems unlikely even if there wasn't the question of the vasectomy.'

Becky nodded slowly. She had to accept this was not Colin's baby. Everything pointed that way.

'Do you want an amniocentesis to confirm the situation?'

'I think I'd prefer not to risk miscarriage. It wouldn't alter my decision.'

'You could defer the decision. An amniocentesis can be done at any time. We can leave it until a few weeks from your due date.'

'Why would I need to know with the birth so close, anyway?'

'Some people do. They can prepare themselves. Even if they know they'll keep the baby whatever the outcome of the test, they want certainty. It's a personal thing.'

Becky shrugged. Everyone had their coping mechanisms.

On the way home, she wondered what Neil's were.

Neil, Neil, Neil. Having decided he was part of her past – a memorable, exciting, warm, loving, comfortable past – but her past, nonetheless, she had no idea how to handle this latest announcement. He said he would stand by her. What did it mean? Perhaps he would defend her against the inevitable slurs and insults of the unthinking. A shoulder to cry on. Maybe he was proposing financial help. Perhaps he intended to visit often, to become a kindly uncle. They were all possible; they should comfort her. How much better than rebuff and antagonism! But they only left her feeling unsatisfied.

Could she accept having part of Neil? A friend where once there was a lover as well. A new, strange relationship, like an ill-fitting coat. Would she be better off without him in her new life?

He turned up, unannounced, early evening.

'I called this morning but couldn't get through'

'Sorry, forgot to charge my phone last night. Always forgetting.'

'No probs. You're here. Need to talk to you about Down's Syndrome.'

Becky turned quickly towards him. Was he psychic?

'Do you remember I said Karen gave me a contact so I could talk to adults with Down's Syndrome? Well, I've been invited by a couple of parents to meet their daughter. She's twenty, has Down's Syndrome but holds down a job and is apparently living a good, successful life.'

'Excellent. Perfect person for you to photograph.'

Neil hesitated. 'I just wondered if you'd come along?'

'You don't need me, Neil. You were brilliant with the kids and their parents. I could see them falling over each other to give you their stories and their views. Once they'd accepted you, there was no stopping them. It'll be the same.'

'I don't know. It feels more intrusive this time. It's one family. What benefit will I be to them? You have such an easy manner with people. It would help to have you there.'

'Let me know when you're going. I'll see if I'm free.'

'No. I'll make an appointment with them that fits with you, too. If you'll agree.'

***

Daisy-Lee led the conversation. She was in no way inhibited by her condition. She wore Down's Syndrome like a bright badge. She understood her limitations, knew she learned more slowly and sometimes worked more slowly than others. She explained she was no different from her friend, Amy, the one who had no left hand. Amy took longer over tasks as well. Everyone in the office accepted them equally. She put Neil and Becky at ease and her parents let her talk, rarely interrupting, rarely adding anything. Occasionally, they contributed.

'We chose an unusual name for her because she's a different person. We weren't disguising that. She was going to be called Catherine. But we decided it was too … I don't know. Traditional. Standard. Conventional. We'd never heard of anyone called Daisy-Lee. I suppose we invented it. What you don't hide, you celebrate!'

'Do you want to know about my boyfriend?'

Daisy-Lee continued, not waiting for a reply. It was a story she loved to tell.

'He's called Frank and he's twenty-two and he has Down's Syndrome, too. He's been my boyfriend for two years. A month ago, he asked me to marry him and I said yes!'

Her wide grin made everyone smile. Both Becky and Neil looked towards her parents. Was this marriage going to happen? It would. The date was not fixed but they said they had confidence the pair would be happy.

'I love him. I feel warm inside when I'm with him. He's kind. He says nice things to me. I like holding his hand.'

'Maybe I could take a photo of you together?' Neil repeated his earlier explanation about his exhibition, how he needed photos and a story to go with them. This would exactly fit the bill, he said. Becky knew he was already seeing his pictures on the wall, his fingers itching for his camera. She loved the animated, dynamic Neil. A charge of desire passed through her and she sighed. Don't go there. Don't hurt yourself.

Daisy-Lee rushed around the room with excitement. She could not stop talking. She asked if she would be famous and if people would want to go and look at her photograph with Frank.

As always, after a piece of successful research, Neil was on a high. He talked non-stop, just like Daisy-Lee, as they drove away.

'Wonderful girl, amazingly eloquent! And I should get some good photos. What a story to go with them! In reality, Daisy-Lee isn't so different from any other excited girl who's fallen in love. I think it's a lesson I've learned.' Becky said nothing. This was a Neil she knew; one she was happy to listen to.

'You're quiet.' Neil sounded apologetic. Becky had barely spoken. 'Don't you agree?'

'Of course, I do. I was just thinking.' Becky selected her words. 'I could be the mother of a girl like Daisy-Lee. The tests came back. I'm high risk for Down's.'

Neil glanced in dismay, almost horror, at Becky. His face was more eloquent than words.

'Oh, Neil! How can you react like that? You've just been expounding the normality and resourcefulness of Daisy-Lee, yet you look at me as if a disaster is about to happen.'

'It's a shock. You're becoming expert at delivering those.'

'You've talked to lots of the parents. I assume you've learned about the risks for older mothers. You could have anticipated this. I did.'

Neil pulled the car into a lay-by and stopped. 'You're amazing, Becky. Unbelievably cool and sensible. You're normally the wild one, the unpredictable firecracker. Well, you're still unpredictable, I suppose, but in a different way.'

'You looked at me as if it'd be dreadful to have a child with Down's. Do you believe that?'

Neil leaned back and rested his head, closing his eyes. He stayed like that for a long time. Becky felt it was minutes but afterwards knew it was perhaps thirty seconds. Long enough for him to consider the situation; an age when waiting for a reply.

He ran his hands through his hair and turned to face Becky, taking one of her hands in both of his.

'No, it isn't dreadful. But it takes some getting used to. I hadn't anticipated the possibility. I hadn't thought about it. You being pregnant gave me enough to occupy my mind.' He patted her hand. 'I honestly believe in all the Down's kids I've met. But it's bound to be hard work for you.'

'I know. Emotionally and physically.'

'I'm not a cynic. I'm not using these kids just to promote my photography. This is a test in a way. A test of my belief in them.'

'And have you passed the test?'

'I hope so. I'm sorry for my initial reaction. But it's a warning. I might not be the only one who reacts badly. There are still people around who expect such kids to be hidden away, to be kept apart from "normal" people.'

Becky sighed; she guessed what was to come.

'I've learned something about the Syndrome from the parents. Are you going to have the amnio test?'

Becky explained why she was not going along that route and Neil accepted everything she said. She explained what "high risk" meant, gave him the statistics, reassuring herself as well as him. Stillness developed between them. She wanted to ask him whether he would still stand by her and what it meant. But she was afraid of the answer.

As if he realised, he said they needed to talk about the future. Becky felt her heart bouncing like a ball in her chest. The conflict of wanting to know what he was about to say and the preference for ignorance tormented her. While she did not know, she could hope.

'Talking in the car doesn't work. I can't concentrate. Let's get back to your place.'

***

'I will leave Kate permanently.'

'Do you have a choice?'

'What I mean is, I will leave Kate for you.'

'This sounds like expediency.'

She wanted him to leave Kate; she had wished for it many times. Looking back, before the pregnancy, she would have welcomed the news. But such thoughts had always been pushed to one side. Such a suggestion might have driven him away. It was clear now, much clearer than before. Yet she still needed to defend herself with tough words.

'You could have left her before. How many years have we been together? There's never been a hint of this.'

'Don't make it hard for me, Becky. I've admitted I've been selfish. Things ticked along so easily. We were happy. Why change something that's working?'

'Exactly. It's not working now. I've come in useful, haven't I?'

Why am I saying this, Becky asked herself, when she simply wanted to put her arms around Neil. Why don't I accept what he's saying and be glad he's saying it? Why so hostile? I'm torturing both of us.

'If you could forget the complexity of the current situation and recognise I've just woken up to reality. Okay – Kate discovering our relationship was the trigger but it's made me evaluate my feelings. It's made me assess what I feel – something I should have done ages ago.'

He stopped for Becky to speak but she remained silent.

'I need to be with you. Not because Kate doesn't want me. Not out of pity because of your pregnancy. Nothing to do with Down's. Just because I do. Because I've come to realise how much you mean to me.' He took a deep breath. 'I now know how much I love you.'

Was now the time to tell Neil he was the father of her baby? Everything said it was. But the words would not be formed. She could not think how to say it. She was too scared he would think there was another lover, that he would not be able to accept what she knew to be the truth. But it would have to happen. And soon.

Chapter 21

'I'm not sure why you're telling me all this,' Kate said. 'I can't do anything.'

'You're listening. I knew you would.'

Not much choice, Kate thought. Louise had turned up on the doorstep, exploded into the kitchen and poured out a tirade of abuse against her parents. They sounded totally unlike the gentle neighbours Kate knew.

Louise had been crying. Her carefully smudged eye make-up was now streaked in dirty patches on her cheeks. She tugged at her creased cut-off top and rubbed her hands down her tight, stained jeans. The whole outfit was in need of a wash; Louise needed one, too. When she stretched to run her hands through her hair, she displayed a ring in her navel.

She picked at her purple nail varnish as she spoke, small flakes peeling off and falling on the floor. Kate stopped herself from commenting on the mess. But her eyes kept returning to the purple confetti and she needed to go and get a pan and brush. It was an effort to focus on what Louise was saying.

'Every now and then they have a real go at me. They *can* be nice but that's when I behave like the little girl they think I am. I'm eighteen for fuck's sake! If I do my own thing they never approve. They hate my belly-button piercing. Said it made me look cheap. I haven't told them about the tattoo on my bum. They'd go into orbit!'

'You're an adult, Louise. You don't need their permission for tattoos or piercings. Or anything else.'

'Try telling *them* that!'

'They speak of you with huge affection.'

'They love an image of me, a younger version of themselves, not the real person. They want someone to show off to their friends.'

It sounded a familiar situation to Kate.

Barry and Gwen were old-fashioned, traditional people. She could see potential conflict with this scruffy, headstrong, wayward daughter they had produced.

'So what caused the problem this time?'

Louise stuck out her tongue. A small, silver ball shone from near the tip of it.

Kate disliked piercings. She particularly disliked tongue piercing and had seen some unpleasant infections resulting from them. She did not want to argue and it was nothing to do with her. She hesitated, debating what to say, trying to keep her face impassive.

'Why have you had it done?'

'One of my friends had hers done a few weeks ago. Her boyfriend loves it. Says it's great when she sucks his prick.'

'So that's why you've got it?'

'Yes. Well, sort of…well, no. Oh, I don't know.' She shrugged her shoulders.

'Have you got a boyfriend?'

Louise glared at Kate, flicked her hair back and walked across the kitchen. She stood scratching her head. Kate waited and wondered about head lice.

'You were meant to be listening to me. Not asking questions.'

'I've listened. But if you want me to understand, I need to ask as well. Especially if you want any advice.'

'I just want to talk. I like you. You're not a huge amount different from Mum's age but you seem loads younger. More on my wavelength.'

Louise moved closer and the absence of a recent shower

became more apparent.

Kate made a decision. She stepped back and held Louise at arm's length.

'Right. We'll have a proper talk. You can tell me what you like. I won't be shocked. I won't tell tales to your parents. And if you want my opinion, I'll offer it. Honestly. In return, you'll pull yourself together. Go home. Have a shower and wash your hair. Put some clean clothes on. Have a good think. Then come back and we'll talk.'

'You cheeky bitch! Telling me what to do!' She stamped her foot like a petulant child, raised her shoulders and scowled. 'You're as bad as my parents. And I thought you were different. Wrong again! Why should I do what you say?'

'Up to you. It's all the same to me whatever you do. Those are my terms. Take them or leave them.' Kate turned her back on Louise and went to get the pan and brush. Louise spat on the floor and left.

***

It was less than an hour later when she returned.

'Don't know why I've come back. You were fucking rude to me.'

'You came in the first place. I didn't ask you to come. I think I'm entitled to lay down some conditions. And it includes not spitting on the floor again.'

'You always talk fancy. "Lay down some conditions" isn't what normal people say. Are you trying to piss me off?'

Louise was on edge. Her words were darting out like arrows. But she looked cleaner. Her hair smelt of shampoo and she had changed her clothes.

'Right. Sit down. We'll have a glass of wine.' Louise's face brightened.

'Just one glass. It's a civilised thing to do. We're not boozing.'

'Are you saying I'm not civilised?'

'Louise, don't misinterpret everything I say. You've come back. I assume you want to talk.'

Louise started to speak but changed her mind. She got up and sat on another chair. She started to speak again but turned it into a sigh. Tears filled her eyes. She wiped the back of her hand across her face. Indecision surrounded her like a mist, almost palpable. Kate remained silent.

'I don't know why I came back. When my parents shout at me, I run away. Usually to do more of whatever they complained about. You shouted at me. Well, not really. You gave me your "conditions". Somehow it was different.'

'Glad you understood.'

'You're different. I can't talk to them. It gets too emotional and I end up screaming. I think I can talk to you.'

'Go on.'

'They say they love me. Maybe they do in their own way. But it's a possessive love. They can't let me go and be myself.'

Kate felt another shiver of familiarity. 'What does "being yourself" mean?'

Louise started to sob. 'I don't know. That's the trouble.' In between wiping her eyes, blowing her nose and wailing like a child, Kate heard about "leaving home", "wanting to move in with her boyfriend", "being independent", "finding her real identity" and a random selection of other phrases gathered from teenage magazines.

'In practice, which of these things have you done?'

'I've left home and share a flat with a workmate, a girlfriend.'

'And the boyfriend?'

In a small voice, she admitted she did not have one.

'So the tongue piercing…?'

'I thought it might make me more attractive. Especially after what my friend said.'

'And the tattoo and belly-button piercing?'

'It was to show my independence. To show I'm an individual. Not just a goody-goody daughter. And I know loads of girls with bigger tattoos than mine and lots of piercings.'

'What I'm hearing is a rebellion from one set of rules just to fit in with another.'

Louise stopped crying and stared at Kate.

'I'm not fitting in with anyone's rules.'

'Everyone wants to belong. You want to belong with your mates and the world they live in.'

'What's wrong with that?' Louise tensed her body, a cat about to pounce.

'Nothing if it's what you really want. But don't just follow the crowd. It's no better than blindly following your parents. You have to decide for yourself. That's independence.'

Louise scratched a bit more nail varnish off and gnawed at the surface of her thumbnail. She took a mouthful of wine, then another. The glass was nearly empty.

'I can't get used to this thing in my tongue.'

'So remove it. A boy who went with you just because of it wouldn't be worth having.'

Louise glared at Kate. She suddenly stood up, her eyes wild.

'You're back to being like my parents again. I don't know why I bothered coming back.'

She slammed the door on the way out.

***

The following morning she was back. Kate frowned and sighed.

'What now, Louise?'

'I've decided you're better than my parents. You say what you think, for my sake, not yours.'

Louise pushed past Kate and headed for the kitchen. Her eyes darted around and she could not stay still, touching the

181

toaster, moving the kettle, stroking fruit in the bowl on the table. She was a child's toy hoping its battery would never run out.

'If you're busy, just carry on. I can sit here while we talk.' She perched herself on a stool.

'What are we talking about?' Kate continued emptying the dishwasher.

'Oh, things.' She got up and wandered around.

'I thought you said you'd sit while we talked?'

'I can talk and walk. I like this kitchen. Mum's is too cluttered. Can I have a banana?' She took one.

'You're a nuisance, Louise. Go home.'

'Huh! Fucking rude again. I know you now. You won't upset me this time.'

'You're hyper this morning. What have you taken?'

Louise giggled, a high-pitched squeal and jumped up and down. 'A little blue pill, a little white pill, a little pink pill, who knows?' She started to dance around the kitchen, singing a made-up song. 'Have you got any drugs here? You're a pharmacist. Must be easy for you.'

She aimed her banana peel at the sink and missed.

'Pick it up.'

'In a minute.'

'Now.'

'In a min, I said.'

Kate turned towards her and tried to stop her antics. They crashed. The knife in Kate's hand cut Louise's arm.

'Ow! You've cut me, you bitch. You stabbed me!'

'Your own fault for being an idiot. It's a scratch.'

Louise's face was pale as she watched a dribble of blood run down her arm and drip on the floor. Kate was unmoved. She had made her mark.

'Wash it in the sink and press a piece of kitchen roll on it.' She picked up the banana skin, washed the spot of blood off the tiles, carried on with her tasks and ignored Louise.

'I think you like hurting people.'

Louise waited for a reply. There was none.

'You do. You put something evil in our drinks at the party. You tried to poison us.'

Kate remained silent.

'You know about drugs. You made us all ill. Mum told Uncle Mike about those drinks. He's a police sergeant. He was very interested. Mum said not to tell you. But I have, so there! She and Dad had a row about it. He said she was ungrateful 'cos we all had a good time. Hey, Kate – you never know – he might come and arrest you. Wow! Imagine that! Give us all a bit of excitement.'

Kate shook her head.

'I bet *you* weren't ill. I bet you didn't drink your own cocktails.' She shook Kate by the shoulders. 'Talk to me! I hate this silence. Argue!' As her volume rose, she grabbed the knife that had cut her arm and slashed at Kate. The point went into Kate's upper arm. Both women screamed as the weapon hit the floor. Louise ran out of the kitchen and out of the house.

***

'You've got a cheek coming back here.'

Louise stood sadly at the door with a bunch of flowers in her hand. They had the look of the local garage about them, the day's leftovers, leaves curling.

'I'm sorry.'

'I don't think we have any more to say to each other.'

'I didn't mean what I did with the knife.' She pushed the flowers against Kate who turned away. They fell to the floor. 'Please can we be friends?'

Kate ignored her. She would have closed the door on her but Louise was too quick and was already in the kitchen.

'I'll behave.'

'Seem to think you said that once before. Or something like it.'

'I mean it this time. Look, I'll do something useful.'

She opened cupboards randomly as if there was a job waiting to be done in one of them. She found an iron.

'Let me do some ironing for you. It would help, wouldn't it?'

'Stop being an idiot. I don't need you to iron.'

'Where's the vacuum cleaner?'

'I have a cleaning lady who does a good job. Look at the house. Do you think it needs a clean?'

Kate grabbed Louise's wrist and dragged her to the table.

'Ow, you're hurting me.'

'I can hurt you a lot more if you don't leave me alone. You don't listen to me. So stop visiting me. Now go.'

Louise sat still, her eyes wide. The two women stared at each other.

'What would you do? What would you do to me, Kate? I want to know.'

Louise's breathing got faster. 'Would you attack me with a knife? Would you drug me? You aren't like anyone I know. I want to be powerful, like you.'

'This isn't about power. And I've told you to be yourself. Stop this nonsense and go home.'

Louise got up slowly and walked to the door. She stood there for some seconds, opened it and walked away, looking backwards over her shoulder.

Seems I have a follower, Kate thought to herself. Nothing she had planned and a situation she could do without.

Yet…wasn't there was something exciting about the whole scenario?

Chapter 22

Kate looked at her Excel spreadsheet. Column one: 'Reasons for termination'. Column two: 'Reasons to continue pregnancy'. She felt the reassuring influence of a list; it helped her focus and make decisions. The first column was easy. "Life will continue as normal" was the obvious first point. Well, not exactly. She had thrown out Neil. She changed it to: "Work life will continue as normal". Next she needed something about her mood. She felt unsettled and reckless. There was a compulsion to cram in as much as possible before the life-changing, imminent event. She debated what to call it and settled on "Restored mental state".

There were points to do with her feelings towards children. She knew only superficial facts about babies. There was nothing endearing about the bawling and unwell infants she saw in her pharmacies, nothing that made her feel broody or want to hold them. The pleasant sounds she made were a well-rehearsed act. Once a tired and upset mother asked if there was anywhere she could change her baby's nappy as there had just been an "explosion". The stock room smelt disgusting for days afterwards.

She could not stand the noise and mess of youngsters – her visit to Pauline proved that. Teenagers tested her patience. They were either wilful and angry like Jonathan's girls or overly demanding like Louise. Maybe it would be a boy? She could not imagine boys being any easier.

There was the problem of her mother. She would wriggle like a worm into all things infantile. She would pester her with calls and visits, advice and recommendations. There would be tears when Kate ignored her. How much better the distant, unemotional relationship they had maintained for years! The child would be surrounded by elderly women as it grew up. She winced to describe herself like that but knew it would become true. The first column was filling up.

Kate was feeling hot and clammy. Discomfort was sticking to her, down her back and under her arms. She needed to wash away the sweat and her mood. She looked down at her abdomen. Was it starting to expand? She had maintained her shape with gym visits and careful diet all her adult life – this would ruin everything. At her age, getting her muscle tone back would be a challenge. And how would she find time for exercise with a baby to care for? What about sagging breasts? She involuntarily cupped them with both hands to feel their shape. They were getting larger and were sore. It all went on the list.

Fifty-one. Soon to be fifty-two. Too old in her eyes for pregnancy. Would she survive if the child suffered from a genetic disorder? She thought of the stories about Down's Syndrome children Neil had told her. How the little ones were amazing, how the parents adored them. Could she see herself being one of those parents? What if there was a more serious genetic abnormality? She prided herself on her ability to manage whatever came her way – staff problems, financial decisions, business matters – but this was outside her world. Did she want to test herself with a disabled or ill baby? "No, no, no," rang in her head like a sonorous church bell. And what if she ended up on her own? The words "single mother" produced a dull heaviness inside her.

Kate walked around to clear her head. She found herself in the study, now littered with Neil's material for the exhibition. Bloody man! Always untidy, always taking up more than his share of the space. When he moves out, his mess will go with him. Wonderful!

She picked up some papers from the floor, cursing, and went to look at the desk. There were several large photographs awaiting mounting. Beautiful ones, his best. They would be his centrepiece. One was of a young girl with her mother. The child had a camera in her hand and was showing it off; lying next to it was a crooked photograph taken by the youngster. They were a pair. She remembered Neil talking about the situation, how the child asked to use the camera and he let her. She wanted to photograph her mummy, a woman engulfed with explosive pride. A wave of animosity passed through Kate. She could not tolerate the smile, the love, the delight on the woman's face. She could not bear it because it would never be her. Yes, she could look at the infant. She could accept her pleasure in the camera. But not the mother. No! She picked up a black marker pen and obliterated her smile. Satisfaction washed over her. She let out a long breath. Time to return to the list.

Instead of her planned coffee, she poured a glass of wine. A good Sancerre. Six o'clock, not too early. She sat with it for a few minutes, closed her eyes, rested her head on the back of the armchair and ran the pale yellow liquid around her mouth. Forget about the disadvantages for a while, she told herself. Focus on the positives. The obvious one was saving a life. She supported the right of any woman to an abortion, yet still felt an uncomfortable pang when she knew one had happened. Yes, a definite pro-pregnancy point. She stalled, searching for the next advantage. "Jonathan would be a good father" – should she add that? He was not keen on the idea of fatherhood in Verona when she tested him. But he was unaware of her pregnancy; a few facts might change things.

Her musings were interrupted by her phone ringing. She was glad to be disturbed.

'Kate, it's Jonathan. We haven't spoken since your party and Joanne's stupidity. We're not getting anywhere. I'm no closer to knowing what will happen to us than I was months ago. I must see you.' His words tumbled out as if he had stored them until there was no longer space and he had to let them go.

The call surprised Kate. Thinking about him had conjured up his presence. His voice raised her spirits.

'Hi Jonathan. You know what? I'm pleased you've called.'

It was an escape from the list, a reason to defer the decision making and, she realised, the chance to be with someone who cared about her. She heard the amazement in Jonathan's voice as she agreed to meet him in a pub later that evening. She had no idea where Neil was, where he now considered "home" and had not prepared a meal. She needed no excuse for being out.

***

Jonathan was stressed. There was a greyness about his face, his eyes looked heavy and he frowned as he spoke. He greeted Kate with a hug, a brotherly, absent-minded expression of affection that bothered her. She wanted a glint in his eye, at least a kiss on the cheek and some sign that she appealed to him, that the sexy Jonathan was there.

'What's up, Jonathan?'

He sighed, said he would explain and went to order drinks. Kate watched him. Was she to be used as his advisor, his sorter-out of problems? Was there yet another family issue? This was supposed to be about the two of them, not a counselling session.

'Bloody Joanne. I was getting ready – said I was meeting a magazine editor for a drink – when she rushed into the bedroom crying. Apparently her period was three weeks late so she'd done a pregnancy test. She was crying because it was negative. She thought she was about to make an announcement to me. Well, she did but not the one she'd hoped for.'

'Were you trying for a baby?' Kate struggled with the words.

'Christ, no. It's the last thing I want. But Joanne's keen. We've been through it all before – several times – and I made it as clear as I possibly could a further child was not on the agenda. She knows the score. She's on the pill. I trusted her to take it. Now I don't know what she's up to.'

Jonathan put his head in his hands then wiped them down his cheeks. He made his face age. Kate reached out and touched his arm.

'Have you never considered a vasectomy?'

'Of course, I have. But the moment was never right or it didn't seem necessary. And…' He paused. 'I'm a bit of a coward. I don't like the idea of it. I'm worried I'll feel less of a man.'

If only you *had* liked the idea, mused Kate, life would be a lot simpler.

'Our relationship is faltering. Maybe she thought a baby would set things back on track. It won't! It's a stupid, crazy idea. Add to that her increasingly poor rapport with the girls and I think we're over. If she wants a child, she'll need a different man.'

Jonathan took a large swig of his beer. 'Sorry, Kate. This wasn't meant to be like this. When I phoned, I'd no idea there was an imminent clash with Joanne. I wanted to talk about us.'

They sat in silence. Kate debated whether she should go home. Her meetings with Jonathan were plagued by family intrusions, unexpected interruptions that ruined the mood. Two noisy guys distracted her as they tried to pick up a couple of girls sitting nearby. The simplicity of their evening – whether they get off with the girls or not – contrasted with her own muddled brain. She hoped the girls were prepared, that they had condoms in their handbags. Ever the pharmacist, she said to herself. They may need the "morning-after" pill tomorrow.

Jonathan suddenly roused himself. He relaxed and a little of his sparkle returned.

'Maybe this happened at the right time. Maybe it's better you see the truth of my life. I'm not just wandering from woman to woman although I know you don't believe me. I've tried to make this relationship work. But I can't agree to a situation that's wrong. I don't want to be a father again, not at my age, and I dislike Joanne trying to trick me into it.'

If I want to be with Jonathan, I need to add that as another reason on the 'Termination' list, Kate told herself. And she needed to remove her positive point about how good a father he would be.

'Kate, Kate. Tell me honestly about you and Neil. I didn't see much affection between you at your drinks evening. But it was a party and you were busy. How are things between the pair of you?'

'I've thrown him out. I told you when we were in Verona I suspected him of an affair with Becky Whitehead. Well, I discovered it's been going on for years. I feel an idiot for ignoring the obvious. I challenged her and she admitted it.'

'God! Why did she do that?'

'I caught her at a weak moment. Something else that will surprise you. She's pregnant.'

'Is the world going mad? I assume an accident? Is it Neil's?'

'No. He has a low sperm count. We tried years ago and failed. It was hard for a while. Then we realised neither of us was bothered if we didn't have children.'

'Does she know whose it is?'

'She says it's Colin's. Probably shouldn't have told you but I don't feel obliged to keep her secrets any more. They had a fling at the reunion, re-igniting the embers of their student affair. She must have been more careful the first time around.'

'Does he know?'

'No idea. Perhaps she told him at our party. He was keen to pick up threads with her. Told me they had a lot in common, similar sense of humour, that sort of thing. Doubt if a baby on the way will thrill him. Could be the end of that relationship – or stop it restarting.'

'Why are we all being plagued with questions of pregnancy at our age? Joanne, me, Becky, Colin. Lucky you, Kate. Ever the planner, ever the sensible one.'

'Not everything has gone my way. As you know.' Kate thought back to her first pregnancy, the baby she lost. Jonathan's baby. And to more recent events.

'Yes, okay. But it was a long time ago. I thought we'd

dealt with it. Neither of us lives in the past.'

If only you knew, Jonathan, Kate thought. But this is one secret I'm going to keep. I've seen your reaction to one pregnancy; I don't need to see another.

'I accepted – decided – long ago children weren't going to be in my life. This makes a relationship with you difficult. I've seen your daughters, spoken to one of them. They're not little kids but they are your responsibility and they will impact us.'

'Lara said you were okay. Unusual for her.' He showed Kate a text on his phone, a few words from Lara. 'See, she says you're "cool". It's high praise.'

'She probably liked Joanne to begin with.'

'True. But she was younger and easier to please. I don't think there'll be a problem. You'll survive. We could take it gently. Maybe a weekend together. See how it goes.'

Jonathan let his words sink in. He went to get more drinks and chatted to the barman, turning his back on Kate. She knew he was giving her time to think. She looked at the phone on the table, read Lara's text again and jotted down her phone number. Never know when it might come in handy. When he returned, he reached out and took Kate's hand. She tensed and knew he felt her reaction.

'Good to know I still have an effect.'

Kate turned her head. She could not hold his scrutiny.

'Tell me why we can't try. Neil isn't a problem and I'm planning a serious discussion with Joanne. She won't be a problem, either, for long. We're finished whatever happens between you and me. If it really doesn't work, we'll both know. That we still feel emotion after thirty years means something. We shouldn't throw it away.'

He spoke slowly and quietly. Not a rehearsed speech, not a clever trap, just what he felt at that moment. And it touched Kate.

'Alright. But you need to sort out your relationship with Joanne first. It will be hard enough with the younger two without having her fighting me.'

When they parted an hour later, Kate kissed Jonathan softly on his lips and stroked his ear. She still felt unsettled but there was hope for the future.

**

She went straight to her Excel spreadsheet. She removed, "Jonathan would be a good father". After staring at the screen for several minutes, she highlighted the whole spreadsheet and pressed "delete". Decision made. She would phone a clinic she knew in London and make an appointment. It needed to be soon.

Chapter 23

Neil looked at the two suitcases in the hall. They were his suitcases. And they were full.

'What's this?'

'Just helping you out. I've packed some things for you. Not all your possessions. Didn't have the time or the patience to sort through your clutter.'

'Bloody cheek.'

'I told you to go. Becky will have you. You don't live here at the moment. And certainly not in my bedroom.'

'It's my house as much as yours. I'll go when I want to. If I want to.'

'You should have thought about that before you started a serious affair with my best friend.'

'Best friend? You don't have one. You are the only friend you have. You use Becky. She's a convenience to you.'

'She won't be much of a convenience to you now. She's pregnant.' Kate smirked, a look of triumph distorting her face.

'Don't look superior. I know. She told me. You could have some sympathy. Becky has gone through a torment of indecision trying to sort out her life. What a situation to have to deal with! A touch of friendship would go a long way, a kind word of support, even a shoulder to cry on.'

'I've heard her problems, I've talked to her, helped her even. That was before I discovered your nice little relationship. Now she's on her own as far as I'm concerned.'

Kate slid her hand across her own stomach. She could

have been smoothing her skirt, stretching her muscles, caressing her own baby – or cursing it. No words of comfort for me, she thought, no advice or help. I'm on my own. Becky can be, too. What would Neil say if I told him? Well, Neil, it's not just Becky who has a decision to make. You're my husband, not hers. If you want an infant in your life, there's a choice for you! What a lucky man! But she bit her lip and the words remained in her head, tormenting her, reminding her of the appointment she was about to make.

Kate picked up a knife from the stand in the kitchen and waved it slowly in front of him. 'Do we have to fight about this?'

'Put it down, Kate. Neither of us is a violent person.'

'You know something? I may be. Violent, that is. I cut Louise's arm. It gave me a weird sort of satisfaction.'

Neil looked at her with horror. 'You attacked Louise?'

'It was an accident. I was trying to stop her larking about here and a knife happened to be in my hand.'

Neil looked incredulous. Kate explained the sequence of events, Louise's apparent obsession with her, the continual visits and the knife incidents.

'She's a disturbed child. You could lead her to do stupid things. It's irresponsible. Not professional behaviour. I can't believe you enjoyed violence. What's the matter with you these days, Kate? You're not a person I recognise. You've changed so much of late. You shouldn't encourage Louise.'

'I don't. And what do you know? I don't need your advice.'

Neil walked away from her.

'Where are you going?'

'Upstairs. Like I said – it's my house as much as yours. I can go where I like.'

'Out, Neil, out! I don't want you here. I can't stand having you around me. You and your messy habits, your untidiness, your laziness, your... being in my space!' And to herself she screamed, your happiness, your success, the control you have of your life.

'Fuck off, Kate. I don't want you around me either.' The composure in Neil's voice was more irritating than if he yelled at her.

'It's not so appealing now, is it? Your lover carrying another man's child. Has she told you who the father is? I can tell you. Colin. The Chief Pharmacist. A fling at the reunion last September. Such a naughty girl!' Kate was desperate to get a reaction from Neil. 'I told you at the time, she relit an old flame. Well, the ashes remain!'

Neil said nothing; the silence from upstairs assaulted Kate's head. She shrieked obscenities at him, threw the knife into the sink, cutting her finger in the process, grabbed her handbag and slammed the door as hard as she could when she left the house. She was reversing the car out of the drive when Louise called to her.

'Stop, Kate, stop. I'm coming with!'

She rushed across the front gardens, treading on flowers and jumping a fence. Kate had to slow down to avoid hitting her as she ran behind the car. She pulled open the car door and was inside before Kate realised what was happening.

'Not now, Louise. Get out.'

Louise fastened her seat belt and stayed where she was. Kate was not in the mood for argument and needed to get away. She drove off with a sigh and a roar of the engine, ignoring her passenger.

'Wow! Love the noise! Where are we going? Always wanted a ride in your sports car. I don't mind where we go. A short ride, a long ride. To the shops, to the countryside. To a café, to a supermarket. Can I drive? I have a licence, you know. Took my test recently. Almost passed it. I'll be alright next time.'

There was a constant stream of comments and questions. Louise never waited for an answer. She could have been alone, a performance monologue.

'If I'd known we were going out, I'd have changed. These're old things. I put them on to colour my hair.' She looked at her baggy trousers, ragged at the edges, worn and stained on the knees. 'D'you like the new colour?' She pulled down the visor to look at her hair in the mirror. There was a pink streak down one side.

'Caused trouble at home. Mum came into the bathroom when I was doing it. Made an almighty fuss about the mess. Said I look like a tart. And she spotted the tattoo when I was bending over.' She fiddled with her hair, moving the pink stands around to get the best effect. 'She and Dad are having a "serious discussion" in the kitchen. That's why I ran out. I didn't want to hear the outcome. Bound to be bad.'

She wriggled around, getting comfortable.

'Have you had the car long? I'd love one. It would be red, like this. Makes a statement. Don't suppose I'll ever be able to afford one, though. How much did it cost? Maybe Dad would buy one for me. Huh! Don't suppose so. Perhaps I'll buy one later on, when I've earned loads of money.'

'Shut up, for God's sake.'

'Can we have the roof down? It's quite sunny. No, it's not really. I don't mind if it's a bit cold. It'll be getting dark soon so perhaps we'll leave it up. I know, we'll have the radio on.'

She found some music and turned the volume up. She sang loudly to something Kate did not recognise, constantly changing her position, adjusting the angle of the seat, moving it backwards and forwards. Then she opened her window so that the wind lifted her hair and chilled her face. She rubbed her cheeks and pulled up her collar. Spots of rain started to fall and she stuck her hand out to catch them. She pointed out someone she knew and tried to call to them but the moment passed. They went towards the school she used to attend and this set her off on bad memories and tirades against her teachers. It seemed life always conspired against her.

'Peppermints! Can I have one, Kate? She popped one into her mouth and leaned across to put one in Kate's. Kate pulled away from the sticky fingers and shook her head. The pale sun went behind a cloud and dusk came closer.

'Hey, Kate, there's something I wanted to ask you. You know you had a "secret ingredient" you put in the cocktails at your party. Tell me what it was. I won't tell anyone else. But I'd just love to know. It got everyone talking. Some thought it was dodgy doing that, making them drink unknown things. Have the police been round to talk about it yet?'

'I didn't make anyone drink anything. It was a free choice.'

'Yeah, but well…you know. People just joined in. It was fun. But lots of us were ill the next day. Was it kind of poisonous? Was it a drug? Did you get it from your pharmacy? '

Louise was talking faster and faster, the anticipation of learning a secret making her breathless and wide-eyed.

'Have you ever heard of Angostura bitters?'

'No. Is it what you used? They sound fantastic! Do they give you a high? Where can I get them?'

'Forget about it, Louise.'

'Why? I could make cocktails for my friends. Wow, I can't wait. What did you say these things were called?'

Kate did not reply but put her foot down and revved the car loudly; conversation was difficult. Louise carried on talking. Kate could see her mouth moving as she glanced sideways but could hear nothing.

She had no plans. She simply needed to get away, remove Neil from her existence and have time to herself. And now she had this irritating passenger, more parasite than companion. I'll frighten her, she needs a good fright, Kate thought to herself. I've had enough of her. Maybe she'll leave me alone then. She speeded up, taking bends faster than she should, rushing through amber traffic lights, ignoring speed limits. The rain splattered the windscreen and the wipers struggled to cope. This was her territory. She started to enjoy herself, counting how many times other drivers sounded their horns at her, how many fists and V-signs were waved.

197

Louise gripped the sides of her seat and squealed in delight like a small child. She stopped talking. Occasionally, she squeezed Kate's arm and gasped. As they left the street lights of the town behind, Kate roared down a long, straight strip of road, skidded on a patch of oil and span the car round one hundred and eighty degrees. Louise screamed as Kate tried to control the car. With some cursing she got them going in the right direction again. She felt a trickle of sweat run down her face and her blouse stuck to her armpits. Her mouth was dry and she licked her lips. In her head she was yelling, "Yes, yes!"

'Wow, that was scary! Do you always drive like that?'

Kate said nothing but went even faster. Relief that the road had been empty made her pant. But she wanted more. 'Adrenaline, adrenaline,' she whispered to herself and gripped the steering wheel until her joints ached and her nails made indentations in the palms of her hands. Her eyes were wide as she focussed intently. Comments and questions from her passenger were meaningless noise, unintelligible against the roar of the engine. Finally, Louise went quiet. They were on rough roads and the suspension rattled them around as they hit bumps and holes.

'Kate, I think I've had enough.' Louise tried to make herself heard. At the third attempt, Kate replied.

'I didn't invite you so you have no say in the matter. It's not up to you. Be quiet. Enjoy it.'

'But it's dark and raining. You can't see much on this road. I'm afraid.'

'Good.'

Louise started to whimper. She was a child again. 'I'm getting really scared!'

'Christ, Louise, act your age. You're the one who wants a life of her own! I'm an excellent driver. I know what I'm doing.'

There was a glow in the distance, the lights of a village. They were Kate's magnet and she put her foot hard on the accelerator. As they took a sharp bend, the headlights picked up the remains of an animal, perhaps a hare or a cat, on the road. It had been run over several times, its guts splattered randomly, a splash of red and gore on the wet road. Kate tried to avoid it but there was no place to go. They skidded yet again. The brakes locked on. Kate saw a tree advancing towards them, the bark silvery in the headlights. She pulled hard on the steering wheel and swore. Louise screamed. The tree would not get out of the way.

Chapter 24

Neil rushed out to the car and was half a mile down the road when he realised he should not be driving at all. He'd drunk several glasses of wine to calm himself down after Kate's hasty departure. He hadn't lost his temper, knowing that was exactly what Kate wanted. But he was boiling inside. As she marched away, he headed for the open bottle in the fridge. God, he needed a drink! He took it into the study, stopping dead when he discovered Kate's vandalism, the obliterated smile. The bottle did not last long.

Too late now. He had to get to the hospital. The policeman had told him little. He spoke in a voice used for bad news. Staccato sentences, bald statements, no emotion. Kate had been in a car accident. Neil should get there as soon as he could. He did not know if any other car was involved, if anyone else was hurt or how serious it might be. She was alive. That was all.

Would she survive? What consequences would she have to live with? He had visions of wheelchairs, of a disabled Kate who could no longer walk, of a Kate who had lost her mental capacity, a twisted mind and body. A Kate he did not know and could barely contemplate. A dependent, helpless Kate. What had she done? Maybe she was the innocent victim of a drunken driver. He shivered and slowed down, an eye on the speedometer. She was a skilled, experienced driver. She did not make silly mistakes.

He was bathed in guilt. She stormed out because of their argument. It was his fault. Could he have stopped her? Should he have tried to get her to reason with him? Maybe, but he was glad to see her go, to be alone. He wanted to anger her, to state his claims, to be dominant just because she hated that. To be a different Neil from the laid-back man she knew. While the thoughts formed a throbbing knot in his head, he tried not to drive too fast, to control his instincts. Be careful, don't attract undue attention. Whatever his blood alcohol, shock sobered him up. But a breathalyser would tell the truth.

He parked in a side street, guessing the hospital car park would be full. Half running, half walking, he got to A & E in five minutes, gasping. His sweaty hair stuck to his head and his throat was dry, a sour taste in his mouth. He stopped at the doorway to focus his mind and glanced down at his dishevelled clothing. Emergencies took people as they found them.

Kate was unconscious. One of the doctors described what he knew. There were no witnesses. A passing motorist found the car crashed against a tree with two passengers in it and called an ambulance. No other vehicle was involved. Kate had identification with her. As yet, the passenger was unknown.

'How bad is it?'

'I don't know yet but it could be serious. In addition to the blow to her head, there's a broken arm and lacerations. Possibly other injuries. But we are most concerned with potential brain damage. We're dealing with her breathing at the moment.'

Neil was shown into the resuscitation bay where Kate lay on a trolley. There were people around her – doctors and nurses, he assumed – a sense of calm urgency, machines, activity. Someone was coordinating what was happening, giving instructions. He wore a tabard with "Trauma Team Leader" on it. Neil was told to stand to one side. He was afraid to look, terrified of what he might see. All colour left his face. It was a relief to find she looked almost normal, a bloody cut on her forehead and wounds on her arms but otherwise asleep. Neil went back into the corridor, nausea overwhelming him.

They were about to move Kate. There was a discussion about a CT scan to find the extent of the damage, talk of the Intensive Care Unit. He took in fragments of conversation but most passed him by. He knew little about clinical terms; Kate had given up trying to explain anything medical to him long ago.

'Excuse me, sir? Could I have a word?' A policeman approached Neil. 'Do you know who was in the car with your wife?'

'I didn't know there was anyone with her.' Neil was in no mood to talk to the police.

'A young lady. She's also unconscious. If you could come with me as you might know her…? We need to contact her family.'

Neil followed the officer, not thinking of anyone but Kate, having no idea who she might have given a lift to. She didn't usually pick up hitch-hikers. It was a shock to see Louise. She looked more battered and bruised than Kate, a waif, a child. A crumpled, little body. He explained who she was and left the officer to contact her parents.

Neil felt light-headed. Kate had stormed out, an unexpected exit. How could Louise have anticipated that? Did Kate plan to take Louise for a ride? Their being together was a mystery. Had Kate been showing off in front of her gullible admirer? Normally, he would deny such a possibility. Kate was a responsible professional. She used to be a responsible professional, he reflected. But lately she was a different person. What had Annie warned him about? She had seen Kate taking tablets. She had access to so much. Was that the issue? His head was a maze of unanswerable questions. Kate taking illegal drugs? Kate taking legal drugs, but in excess? Every part of him thought it could not be true. Almost every part of him.

There was nothing he could do. The doctors needed to attend to Kate and they asked him to leave. He wandered around the corridors and ended in the café, alone among worried others, sharing the same fearful anticipation but isolated from any common consolation. The hospital-cream walls bore down on him, a solitary picture of a vase of flowers garish and overbearing. The chairs were grey plastic, no upholstery, functional and washable to fulfil hospital requirements. He perched on one. It was as uncomfortable as it looked. People were in constant movement, keeping themselves busy doing nothing. A faint smell of cleaning liquids was everywhere.

He looked at his mobile phone and realised he had told no-one what had happened. He should tell Annie. It was not a conversation he wanted to have. How could he break the news when he had no idea what the news was? But if the worst happened, she had the right to be there. It was late. She might have gone to bed.

'You never phone me, Neil. Is something wrong? It's Kate, isn't it? Is she ill?' Her voice turned into a high-pitched squeak.

He explained what had happened as slowly and unemotionally as he could. Annie panicked.

'I have to get there. Should I drive? I did it quite recently, but it was in daylight. I don't think I could do it in the dark. In fact, I'm not sure I should try in the state I'm in.' Her voice was breaking up, hiccups and gulps interspersing her words.

'It's much too late for you to come this evening. The best thing for you to do is to get the long-distance bus tomorrow morning like you did once before. Get a taxi to the bus station and another at this end to the hospital.' He spoke slowly, making sure of every word, like giving instructions to an inattentive child. 'Can you manage? I'll pay for the taxis so don't worry about the cost.'

'As if I would! What a thing to say, Neil!'

Neil ignored her outburst. 'I'll check the bus times and phone you back. Is that okay?'

'Yes, yes, thank you, Neil.' She hesitated. 'Sorry I was a bit rude. This is such a shock. I don't know what I'm saying.' Neil could hear sobs.

'The doctors are doing everything they can. She's in good hands.'

Why do we always produce such hackneyed platitudes when we're stressed? Neil could not help himself. Maybe platitudes were what Annie needed. She rang off, pleading with him to phone if there was any news.

The café closed so he moved to a waiting area by A & E. Time crept along like a prisoner dragging a ball and chain. Neil felt like that prisoner, trapped in a tiny world where his thoughts had a single focus. Would Kate survive? If she did, what sort of survival would it be? An elderly man walked by carrying a coffee in a plastic cup, a Kit Kat in his other hand, a bag of crisps sticking out of his jacket pocket. His face was weary and he dragged his scuffed shoes.

'There's a machine down the corridor, mate, if yer want one.' He raised the cup to Neil. 'Tastes rubbish but I s'pose it's better than nothin'. There's snacks as well. I spend so much time in this place, I know where every sodding machine is.' He laughed without humour and shuffled past.

Neil nodded. The thought of anything in his stomach made him heave. He hoped the passer-by was not hoping for a conversation; he would not get one. His mobile rang.

'I thought you said you'd pop round this evening. Help me throw out some of my stuff to make room for you. Have you changed your mind about moving in? Thought I'd call before I go to bed.' Becky's voice bounced out of his phone, a cheeky, intimate, inviting voice, the voice he loved.

'Oh, Becky, I'd totally forgotten. Really sorry. I'm at the General. Kate's had a car accident. She's unconscious.'

'Oh, God! How serious is it?'

'They don't know yet. It happened this evening. Not sure the exact time. My head's a mess. I can't think straight.'

'I'll come over.'

'You don't need…' Neil stopped when he realised he was talking to himself.

Becky arrived in half an hour. She had sandwiches and a flask of coffee, saying she knew what hospitals were like late at night. Impossible to get anything decent to eat or drink. Neil appreciated her thoughtfulness but declined her offerings. She held his hand, kissed his cheek and said the food would keep until later.

Later came. Neil had a cup of coffee, and another, realising how thirsty he was. Becky ate most of the sandwiches. He leapt to his feet when he saw a doctor approaching. But there was no news, nothing had changed. He was told to go home.

'Come back with me, Neil. I don't want you on your own.'

'I gave them our home phone number, not my mobile. Stupid of me. I'll have to go home. They'll ring if there's any news.' If she's worse, he thought.

'I'll come back with you.'

'No. Don't ask me why but it wouldn't feel right.'

He could see the expression on Becky's face, the look of rejection, and he hated himself for it. He wanted her, wanted the comfort she gave him but could not accept it. He could not let her sleep with him, could not let her lie in Kate's place while Kate lay unconscious in a hospital bed. Being alone was his choice; something told him he had to go through this, suffer this, on his own. At that moment, he had to think of Kate.

Chapter 25

Why is life so hard on me? Becky drove home in a shroud of foreboding, fear her passenger and companion. Recent events helter-skeltered through her mind. She knew Neil was pleased to have her there even though he hadn't asked her to join him. She felt it. The presence of a caring person was what mattered. They had not spoken much. Unsaid words and a squeeze of his hand were enough. But his rejection when they left the hospital was a surprise, a scare. She was the only person who could help him survive this, persuade him he wasn't at fault for Kate's accident, but he wouldn't let her. And worse, was this a temporary emotion or was the rebuff the start of something permanent?

Don't be stupid, she told herself. You're over-analysing the situation. Neil hasn't had time to think anything through. This is all gut reaction. Take it one day at a time, one hour at a time. But she could not shake off the veil of uncertainty that descended on her. If Kate needed a carer, would that person be Neil? Would he sacrifice his future because of guilt?

The happiness she felt when she planned their evening together – sorting out her possessions, deciding how the nursery would look, a light supper of risotto – seemed like the distant past. It was a worried Becky who tossed and turned for the remainder of the short night, waking with no answers to her questions. Again, she made sandwiches and a flask of coffee, found a chocolate bar and biscuits, and packed them into a canvas bag. There was a compulsion to take food, a physical act she could perform, whether or not it was needed. She called Neil before leaving. He answered immediately.

'I thought you might be the hospital.'

'I called your mobile so you'd know it couldn't be.'

'Of course. Didn't think. Not thinking at all. Just reacting.'

'Have you heard anything?'

'No.'

She was about to make an inane comment about no news being good news but thought better of it.

'I'll join you at the hospital'.

'I called her mother yesterday. She's arriving today. Not looking forward to it.'

'Have you let anyone else know?'

'No. Oh, God, what about the shops? I've no idea where she's supposed to be today. Could you possibly sort it out, Becky?'

'Leave it with me. Don't worry. I'll handle it.'

Not what she wanted to do. But she phoned the six premises, spoke to the managers, sorted out an emergency locum for one of them and ensured the others were functioning. She could rely on the staff. They were competent. As she flopped into a saggy armchair and gulped back a strong cup of tea, she realised there was one other person she should contact. Jonathan would want to know.

She was certain there was still something between the two of them. Strange he had been at the party – and with an elegant woman who drank too much. Was she his wife or the latest female in his life? She had not bothered to think about it. There was something in the way Jonathan looked at Kate, something in Kate's expression when he was near her that said theirs was not a passing flirtation. Whatever – she ought to let him know. She had his phone number. She made the call.

****

Becky was talking quietly to Neil, her hands holding one of his, when Jonathan arrived. The two men stared at each other. Neil frowned. Becky looked from one to another.

'I thought I should let Jonathan know.'

'Why? It's not something to broadcast.'

'He's a friend. I just felt I should tell him.'

Neil shrugged. It seemed the effort of working out what was happening was too much.

A stilted conversation interspersed with oppressive silences followed. Jonathan wandered off several times and returned, unable to stay in one place. He made phone calls on his mobile in a hushed voice. Annie was due at one o'clock. Neil went out to the main door of the hospital to wait for her.

She struggled out of the taxi, forgetting one of her bags and going back for it, fumbling with her purse for the fare and then remembering she had put it in a special envelope. She had to count it out, the taxi driver sighing and moving from foot to foot with his hand out.

'I can't stay 'ere long, lady. I'm in the way. D'ya want me to count it out?'

'No, thank you. I'm quite capable of doing it myself.'

When she saw Neil, she rushed up to him, abandoning the driver.

'How is she, Neil. Is there any change?'

'Annie, just sort out the fare and I'll tell you. The driver needs to go.'

She returned to the taxi, dropping some change on the ground. The driver made exasperated noises and picked it up. She looked suspicious and counted it carefully.

'Annie, please! Just let me pay.' Another taxi arrived and was queueing for the space.

'I'm not senile. If everyone stops fussing, I'll sort it out!'

She did, nodding haughtily at the driver. 'Now tell me what's happened, Neil.'

Becky and Jonathan were talking quietly, chairs pulled

together, when Neil and Annie arrived. They separated sharply as if caught out in a guilty secret. Neil introduced his mother-in-law.

'I know you, Jonathan,' she said in a flat voice, little expression on her face. 'And I think I remember you, too, Becky.' They both acknowledged her but then words died. There was nothing to talk about. No news, no point in going over old ground, no pleasantries.

Abruptly, Annie got to her feet and walked round the room, a random wandering with no purpose, a preoccupied look on her face. She clenched and unclenched her hands, rubbed them together, wrapped her arms around herself, wiped her eyes. There was constant movement, a hypnotic routine holding everyone's attention. Then she stopped and rocked backwards and forwards, heel to toe, heel to toe, before continuing her parade. At one point, she looked as if she was about to make an announcement or intone a mantra but nothing ensued. She continued on her pointless course. After several circuits, Neil stopped her.

'For God's sake, Annie, this isn't helping. Can't you sit down?'

'No, I can't. It's too distressing. I can't settle. I'm surprised you can.'

'If you're accusing me of not caring, you're out of order.'

'I didn't say that!'

'You implied it.'

'Just expressing my opinion.'

Neil stood up and glared. Becky interrupted what was turning into an unpleasant scene.

'Relax, both of you. We're all on edge. No point in saying things we'll regret later.' She placed herself between them and guided Annie away from her son-in-law, suggesting she went out for a breath of air or maybe a cup of tea.

Annie looked around wildly. Tears ran down her face. She dabbed at them with a ragged tissue. 'Air? Tea? How can I go out now? How can I drink tea? How can you possibly suggest a cup of tea? It would make me sick.'

She screamed at the shocked room, frantic with the pain of her own fears. She looked accusingly at the three faces in front of her. Words burst from her, words with a will of their own.

'What about the baby?' she cried. 'What about the baby?' With a gasp she turned and tottered as fast as she could on unsteady legs and sensible shoes towards the ladies' toilets, sobbing.

***

One of the medical team arrived. He called Neil to one side and told him there was good news. Kate was lucky. She had regained consciousness. They had done a scan and it appeared there was no serious injury although she felt dizzy and sick. And there was a degree of confusion. Possibly amnesia but it would improve. Her arm was now in plaster. There were no internal injuries although she was bruised badly down her left side. Yes, he could go and see her although she would probably be sleeping. Neil followed the doctor, glancing behind him at two people staring at each other in bewilderment.

***

'Becky, have you any idea what Annie's talking about?'

'No. None at all.'

'She doesn't call Kate "baby", does she? Very odd. Seemed like she was referring to an actual baby.'

'I can't imagine Kate putting up with a pet name like that.'

'Wasn't there someone else in the car with her – the neighbour's daughter, the strange girl? She was hardly someone you'd call a baby. But she could have been expecting one.'

'How would Annie know that? Silly idea. Oh, Jonathan – we've been neglectful. We should find out how Louise is. We've been so concerned about Kate, we forgot about her. Not very caring of us.'

Becky hesitated and then touched Jonathan's arm. 'I know you two have been seeing each other. Kate hasn't said much – we're not exactly on good terms at the moment – but I'm not stupid. She couldn't be pregnant, could she?'

'Kate? Pregnant? She can look after herself. And anyway, it seems Neil has a low sperm count. That's why they didn't have kids. One of the reasons. Probably shouldn't have mentioned it. But there you go. It's out now.'

'He wouldn't want it advertised but I was aware, anyway.' She didn't know how much Jonathan knew of their relationship. 'I wasn't thinking about Neil.'

'Does she make a habit of sleeping around?' There was an edge to Jonathan's question, a tinge of sarcasm. 'Are there a string of potential fathers?'

'She doesn't keep me informed. But I assume she slept with you.'

'My God, Becky! You're not suggesting I got her pregnant, are you?'

'Seems to me it's one explanation. If there is a baby.'

'But we haven't had sex. Okay, we've seen each other but we're still trying to sort out our relationship. She doesn't look pregnant.'

'She's fit, good muscle tone. It would be a first pregnancy. Probably wouldn't show until five or six months.'

'If it's the case, why hasn't she told me? Why would she keep it secret?' Jonathan had the look of someone who could not be fooled, someone with determined views that were not going to be changed. 'I'd know. I'm sure I'd know. I'd be able to tell.'

'You're saying it couldn't possibly be you?'

'We haven't had sex since the reunion when…Oh, Christ!' Jonathan sprang to his feet. The air vibrated with unspoken thoughts, impossible possibilities. He turned pale, bluster and confidence falling off him like a discarded fancy dress.

'Becky, you know more than you're saying. Come on. What's the real situation with Kate?'

211

'I'm just guessing. Honestly. I've told you all I know. When I told Kate I was pregnant…'

Jonathan opened his mouth to speak, a picture of incredulity.

'Yes, something else you don't know. Anyway, she was supportive. We were getting on well at that time. She had the perfect opportunity to confide in me. We had a long chat about the risks of pregnancy later in life, the choices and decisions to be made. But she said nothing.'

'So why do you now think she's pregnant?'

'God, Jonathan, we're going round in circles. It was Annie's comment that prompted all of this. I suspected nothing beforehand. Don't be naïve. It's a possibility.'

'Maybe Annie's confused. Worry has tipped her over the edge. She could be rambling. Early stages of dementia?'

'Believe what you like. She was certainly distressed. There's a simple way to find out. We can ask her.'

Annie stayed in the ladies' toilet. When Becky looked in and called her name, there was no answer. She left, having no wish to carry on a conversation through a locked toilet door.

Chapter 26

Louise was in Intensive Care. The news was not good. Gwen and Barry had seen her and were sitting in the café when Neil found them. They looked at him with vacant eyes as if their entire beings were with their daughter and only their shells were drinking coffee.

'She's still unconscious. She looks so damaged, so frail. She's on a ventilator. For her breathing. Our little girl.' Gwen had trouble saying anything, the effort of talking provoking more tears from her swollen eyes. Barry sat gaunt and grey, patting Gwen's hand and occasionally pulling her towards him. He spoke in a whisper.

'The police say the car skidded on a dead animal. A Detective Sergeant spoke to us. Called Mont…something… Montford…Montgomery. That's it – Montgomery. The road was wet. How can you protect yourself from something like that?'

'Do you know anything else about the accident? Was Kate speeding?'

'There were no witnesses as far as we know. The police are putting out an appeal. It'll be on the local news tonight. And maybe in the papers. You mustn't blame Kate. We're not blaming her. Like I said, there was this carcass spread over the road…' He swallowed, unable to finish his sentence, and shook his shoulders. 'Montgomery said they'll examine the site, do some measurements, skid marks and the like. Routine stuff, I suppose. I need to go and look. But not yet.'

'I'll come with you if it would help.'

Barry nodded. 'Louise was obsessed with Kate. Idolised her. Couldn't get my head around it but thought it harmless enough.'

'Do you know where they were going? Why they were together?'

The question caused Gwen to sob more loudly and Barry made soothing noises, telling her to calm herself.

'It's our fault, you see. There'd been this row. She's a rebel, our Lou. Just her age, a phase she's going through. She'd coloured her hair pink and made a mess. Gwen gave her a right telling off. Then she noticed Lou had a tattoo. A butterfly. On her bottom. She knows we both hate tattoos. It tipped Gwen over the edge and she yelled and yelled at Lou.'

Barry stopped to catch his breath. Emotion was not helping his laboured breathing. He held his sides as if his lungs might burst. 'I was in the kitchen and heard the rumpus upstairs in the bathroom. Louise charged out of the front door. She must have gone to your house. To see Kate. Why they were in the car, I don't know.'

He let his head drop on to his chest, the effort of explanation exhausting him. Neil said nothing. What was there to say that could possibly help? He sat for a few more minutes then left, giving them both a half-hug. Physical contact was easier than words.

Their guilt compounded his own. He felt sick with the burden of it. Two vulnerable people in a sports car. He had helped to put them there. His body weighed him down and it was an effort to put one foot in front of the other, to make any progress along the corridor ahead of him. He wondered how much he should tell Kate. Whether knowing about Louise would harm her recovery. But she would ask.

He went back to sit beside her. She stirred occasionally but her sleep was deep. After a long silence, he tried talking to her. Hesitantly, at first. Then the words flowed as he recounted his regrets. It was easier, knowing she would not respond. He told her

214

he was sorry if he had driven her to act foolishly. He was sorry if she was so preoccupied with their argument that her judgement was impaired. He was sorry if his indifference made her turn to a silly teenager for admiration. He paused and thought for a while before continuing.

He said he was saddened if his behaviour had driven her to deface his photographs. He felt wretched their marriage had ended like this. Because he knew, in spite of his guilt and distress at her condition, it was over. It worked for a long time. They had been good together. But love was finite and theirs had run out. He did not hold her hand.

He whispered mostly. Sometimes he was unsure whether he was thinking or saying the words. It cleared his head to put thoughts into proper sentences. It helped him make his mind up.

'I'll do all I can for you, Kate. I'll support you. I'll help to make you better. But not as your husband.' He spoke the words loudly, a surprised burst of sound ringing around the room. It made his decision real. He did not apologise for loving Becky; he was not ashamed of it. When he stood up he felt stronger. He carried himself with a determination he had not felt when he entered her room.

'I can see beyond today, Kate. I hope soon you'll be able to do the same.'

Becky was walking up and down outside the room. When he emerged, she looked at him with uncertainty in her eyes.

'It's alright, Becky. Don't look at me like that. It's alright.'

He put his arm around her and led her down the corridor, telling her of the conversation he had with the silent, unhearing Kate and holding her tightly against him.

Becky listened for a while but then interrupted him.

'Neil, I'm glad I've got you back. I feared you'd gone. I thought a misplaced sense of duty was anchoring you to Kate. But we still have a complicated situation. What "baby" was Annie talking about?'

'I don't know. It's been worrying me. We have to talk to her. Where is she, by the way?'

Becky explained what had happened. 'She might still be in the toilet.'

'She's not.'

They saw her sitting in a corner of the waiting area, twisting her scarf round and round her fingers, turning it into a screwed-up piece of rag. Her face was as wrung out and worn as her scarf.

'Come along, Annie. We're going home.'

***

Annie spoke when necessary. She listened to information about Kate, agreed to fish and chips for supper and said she would stay for a few days to look after her daughter when she came out of hospital. She took no part in the general conversation. She moved around in a daze, her body present but her mind elsewhere.

'We have to talk, Annie,' Neil said as gently as he could.

It was as if he had threatened her with violence. Silent tears flowed and she bit her knuckles. Her eyes widened and her shoulders trembled.

'I don't know what's bothering you. But there's something you need to explain. When you shouted out, "What about the baby?" what…' Neil stopped as Annie got up and made for the door. 'Annie, stay here. I have to know.'

'I shouldn't have said anything. It was a mistake. It slipped out because I was upset. I can't explain. It's something I can't talk about. It's confidential.'

'Then sit down again. I won't force you. But if it's to do with Kate, you need to consider if there's something you should tell the doctor.'

This seemed to frighten Annie further and she started walking around the room.

'Stop it. You don't need to pace backwards and forwards.'

216

Annie stared at him and sat down again, perching stiffly on the edge of an armchair.

'I don't want to talk to the doctor.' Annie pressed her lips together to signify the end of the discussion.

They were the quietest fish and chips Neil had ever eaten. Annie went to bed as soon as she could.

'I've been thinking,' Neil said when he and Becky sat together with their coffees. 'Kate isn't close to her mother. If she were pregnant, I can't believe she'd have told her. They don't share confidences. She'd have been more likely to tell you than her mother.'

'Well, she didn't.'

'I wonder if Kate mentioned your pregnancy and Annie got the wrong end of the stick? Thought she was referring to herself? She is woolly-headed at times.'

'That's pretty far-fetched. Inventing scenarios isn't going to help. I think you may have to accept your wife is pregnant by another man.'

Neil went quiet. 'She's just been examined by a doctor. He didn't say anything. Wouldn't he have spotted a pregnancy?'

Becky shrugged. 'They were more concerned with her head injury.'

'Surely I'd have realised if she was having an affair.'

Becky laughed. 'Oh, Neil! You don't notice anything when you're wound up in an exhibition. She could have brought a lover home and you probably wouldn't have seen him!'

Neil was not amused.

'Do you have any idea who the father might be?'

Becky hesitated. 'Actually, I do. The question is – do you want to know?'

Chapter 27

Kate felt empty, without sensation. And totally exhausted. She settled herself into the corner of the train seat and put her handbag and a newspaper beside her to ward off any potential company. She could not bear the thought of the physical presence of another body near her. Now, on her own, she could replay the events of the week – and that particular afternoon – in her head.

***

Annie put her coat on to walk to the shops. It was only bread and milk they needed, she could carry them. And a breath of fresh air would do her good. She explained this slowly and carefully, treating the recovering Kate like a five-year-old. Kate had mentioned the possibility of a walk several times, leading her mother to think it was her own idea. Five days of constant maternal attention were not helping her patience even if her physical well-being had improved. Annie had taken over the running of the house. Not in a major way – Annie was not a major person – but in a trivial, detailed manner. She was tidy but cluttered; Kate was tidy and minimalistic. The two clashed.

Annie would put her knitting carefully on the arm of the chair, the knitting pins pushed through the ball of wool to prevent the stitches from dropping off. She would take ages getting this right and the knitting would sit there, an offending ornament, until required. Kate's suggestion she put it in a cupboard or upstairs in her bedroom was met with an uncomprehending frown. Why would she do that when she would undoubtedly knit again later?

A similar conflict happened in the kitchen over her teacup. She liked a spotted cup she had once bought for Kate. Not Kate's taste but she kept it in case of a maternal inspection. Annie had dug it out making grumbling noises about wasting her money if her gifts were not used. She placed it prominently by the kettle where it remained in spite of Kate's attempts to put it away.

'Useful to keep it handy,' her mother said. 'I don't understand your obsession with clear surfaces.'

Another matter: there was the cleaning of the toilets. The house reeked of bleach and Annie walked around with a milder version of the perfume clinging to her clothes. Only a suicidal germ would dare to go near her. Kate complained the smell was making her feel ill. It was not untrue and succeeded in slowing down if not stopping Annie's sanitary fixation.

'We're both precise, clean and tidy people, Kate. You get all that from me. So I really don't know what you're complaining about.'

Trying not to snap made Kate morose and moody. She spoke little. When her mother encouraged her to chat, she left the room. She both recognised and scorned her mother's good intentions; they were intolerable but she had no choice. On one occasion, Annie embarked on a serious conversation. She put on her formal voice and sat close to Kate, coughing to clear her throat and wriggling around as she prepared herself for her performance. Kate feigned tiredness to avoid the topic she knew would emerge and said she was going to have a nap. Annie hovered nearby, her eyes fixed on Kate. Kate could feel them like the glare of a torch, could sense the words her mother was struggling with. She resolutely kept her eyes closed.

Privacy became like gold. She knew she had to get her mother out of the house.

Annie's fear for Kate's health was like a tether linking them together. It was as if a moment's absence would cause a relapse. To shake off her shadow, Kate forced herself into activity, did a few chores, made cups of coffee or tea; with effort, she spoke cheerfully and laughed at silly comments her mother made. It worked. Annie recognised Kate was getting better.

The prospect of getting Annie out of the house became real.

As soon as Annie had gone, Kate made a brief phone call and scribbled a few words on a slip of paper which she left in the kitchen by the teacup. Her broken arm was a nuisance. She draped a loose coat round it as best she could. The taxi she called took her to the railway station. There was a further taxi from Paddington station to the clinic. The compelling thought in her mind all week was the necessity to keep this appointment. And she had.

Neil had told her about Louise. Her memory of what happened was vague. Why was the girl in the car? She had no recollection of offering her a lift. She had little memory of the journey although when she thought back, feelings of anger and frustration were there. Yes, she remembered her annoyance at Neil. But she had been annoyed with him many times. That memory, that shadow over their relationship, could have resulted from a different occasion.

She was sad about Louise. Unhappy she was still unconscious. But it was like reading about an accident in the newspaper, a troubling event but not one that impinged on her life. It was similar to the illnesses and complaints she dealt with daily. She could not afford to get too involved. She told her staff they could not and should not weep with everyone. That was unprofessional. It was sympathy expressed but not suffered, an emotion separated by a curtain from her personal feelings.

Neil made comments about "a damaged life" and "an uncertain future" for Louise and she asked him if he was trying to make her feel guilty. Of course not, he replied. She was the one who had to decide on that. What a dreadful comment to make! Why did he provoke her? Did he consider she had done something wrong? It was a question that ran through her head as she fell asleep like the sub-text to a foreign film. Both she and Louise were victims of the accident. The squashed body of an animal on a wet road caused the loss of control, the police said. She felt sad about the animal, too. She felt distraught about her written-off car. These were simply events. They were all damaged. So why should she feel guilty? The thought would not, however, go away.

There was the usual questioning at the clinic. She sat in the patient's chair and faced the doctor. She knew she would have to go through it. It was standard practice before any termination. When she explained what her profession was, there was an understanding nod and the interrogation speeded up.

To her surprise, she found herself explaining about the accident. She had not intended to but a comment about the arm in plaster triggered it. She cursed silently when a further salvo of questions hit her. Was she in the right frame of mind to go through with this? After all she had suffered recently. She could have died; there was the question of her passenger. Was it affecting her judgement? Had she properly thought this through?

Silent panic hit Kate. If I don't do this now, I won't be able to go through with it. I've almost killed myself. I might have hurt Louise permanently. Should I end another life? She calmed herself by forcing away raw emotion and telling herself logic must prevail. She deliberately went through her list of pros and cons in her head. It was created for moments like this. She thought of sticky children, irritating teenagers and the prospect of being an aged parent at the school gate. She thought about Down's Syndrome.

'I have made up my mind. I am not changing it now. I made the choice before the accident. I will go through with this termination.' The words were out, the decision was stated. She felt relief.

A lady trundled a trolley with coffees, teas and snacks down the train, a bored expression on her face. Kate bought a coffee and, on impulse, a Snickers bar. Her head felt light. Maybe her blood sugar was low.

She could not believe what the doctor told her. But he was

a reputable, experienced obstetrician. He could not be wrong. Yes, she had been pregnant. But there was no foetus there now. No, she had not lost it during the accident; he would have been able to detect that. When she asked, 'Are you sure?' he had trouble disguising the look of disbelief that she questioned his expertise.

'Ms Shaw, no termination is necessary. You are not pregnant. Of that, I am certain.'

He asked about blood loss and Kate remembered there had been a little. But she had still felt pregnant after that, still had occasional nausea, her waistline had expanded and her breasts were sore. They were still sore. How could it be?

'Symptoms can persist for a while after a miscarriage. The pregnancy hormones are still circulating. But they disappear. As a pharmacist, you know these matters.'

He did not mention phantom pregnancies but Kate knew the unspoken words were hanging in the air. He would not insult her by making them into solid sentences. Nor could she bear to utter them. No intelligent woman could think herself pregnant when she was not. Could she? But she had been pregnant. She had been. The test was positive. The necessity of this being true was paramount. And he agreed there was evidence of a pregnancy. How could she still feel pregnant, how could she still be certain, if the baby had gone? Tomorrow, she would repeat the pregnancy test. She would buy one from Boots at the station on the way home. She knew what the result would be. But she had to prove it.

As she spoke to the receptionist on the way out about sending the invoice, she felt hollow. There was an understanding nod and a gentle voice. A practised conversation. Probably most people leaving here felt like she did, she thought. Because they are hollow, they have lost a part of themselves. That is not the case for me. There was nothing to lose. I should be pleased. I've got the outcome I wanted. This is why I came here. So why aren't I happy about it?

As she tucked herself further into the corner of her seat on the train and ate her chocolate bar, she felt an enormous, inexplicable loss.

***

Annie demanded an explanation. Kate refused to say where she had been. Annie was in turns furious and tearful, blaming herself for trusting Kate and Kate for being untrustworthy. She should not have gone shopping, should not have left the house!

'Whatever will Neil say?'

'He's not here so he doesn't need to know. You're a fool if you mention it at all.'

'Don't call me a fool. You were up to something. I was terrified you wouldn't come back.'

'I'm an adult, Mum. And I'm not an invalid. I've got over the accident well and I'm simply getting back to normal. I left you a note saying not to worry and I'd be home this evening. I've done exactly what I said. I don't need your permission to go anywhere.'

'You don't when you're properly well. If I'm here to look after you, it's what I'll do.'

An irritable silence clung to the room. Kate picked up a magazine and turned the pages without reading. Annie fussed around, plumping cushions that were already plumped and rearranging candlesticks she'd carefully placed in position just minutes before. A shaft of weak sunshine came through the window illuminating a few specks of dust on a side table. She rubbed them away with a tissue. She started to knit but after a few rows, put the knitting down on her lap.

'Kate, I have to ask you one question. Just one, then I'll shut up. I promise.' Annie took a deep breath but no voice emerged when she tried to speak. She went to the kitchen and returned with a glass of water. She sat down, put the knitting on the arm of the chair in its usual position and smoothed her flowery skirt over her knees.

'Did you go somewhere because of the baby?'

'What was that?' Kate frowned and carried on looking at the magazine. She sighed and turned over the page.

'The baby. Jonathan's baby. I don't know what you decided.'

'Whatever are you on about, Mum? What did I have to decide?'

'Whether or not to keep the baby.' Annie leaned over and pulled at Kate's sleeve with a shaking hand to get her attention.

'Kate, stop being silly. Just listen. You came to see me and we talked about it. Later on, I came to see you. I drove, don't you remember? Come on, Kate, stop this. You know what I'm talking about. It happened at the reunion.'

'I think you're confused, Mum. Maybe I wasn't clear. It's not me who's pregnant. It's Becky. But you're right about the reunion. She had a fling with an old flame. Not Jonathan. He was my boyfriend, not hers. Naughty girl! Did I confuse you? Sorry.'

'I'm not confused. I know what you told me. I'm not a senile, old woman so don't make me out to be one.'

'Then stop making ridiculous statements or folk will think you're losing your marbles.'

'But you came specifically to ask my advice. I couldn't give it. I told you that. But I also told you about the babies I lost. We talked in a way we'd never done before. It was hard. Probably the wrong conversation for both of us. Maybe it shouldn't have happened but it did. It did! You can't deny it.'

'You really are in a fantasy world, Mum! That conversation never happened.' She spoke each word distinctly. 'Come back to reality!'

'No, no, no! Don't say such things, Kate. Don't lie! I remember exactly what you said!'

Annie was crimson. She stood up and shouted at Kate in a way she had not done for many years, not since Kate's childhood. She waved her arms and pointed a shaking finger at her, called her a hypocrite and a cheat, an unloving, cruel daughter who had no idea what damage she was doing.

'Why would I invent such a story, Kate? I know what you told me! I know precisely what you told me! I've been worried for weeks about you. I haven't dreamt all this up.'

Kate did not answer. She got up nonchalantly, said she was going to check her emails and went into the study. Annie pressed her face into one of her over-plumped cushions and howled. When the tears subsided, she rummaged around in her cardigan sleeve to find her crumpled handkerchief and blew her nose.

What should she do? She thought of calling Neil but Kate would never forgive her. She could not talk to Jonathan. That left Becky. But what would she say to her? If Becky was also pregnant, she would have enough on her mind. Was she really pregnant or had Kate invented it? Round and round the room she circled, as if stopping her motion would prevent her from thinking. She rubbed her face with her hands and almost ran her fingers through her hair but would not let herself; even in her distress she could not spoil the shampoo and set.

Suddenly she sat down. She put a hand over her mouth as she gasped. Of course! Kate had a severe blow to her head. She was unconscious for hours. That's what caused this issue! Her memory is damaged. Oh, why didn't I realise? I shouldn't have shouted at her. She doesn't know what she's saying. She thinks she's speaking the truth. The doctor mentioned amnesia. She's simply forgotten the pregnancy. What an unkind mother I am! She seems much better but she isn't. Inside she's still wounded. My little girl, my little girl!

She felt burdened with guilt. She could have curled up and cried herself to sleep but she composed herself. 'Come on, Annie, this is no way to behave,' she muttered. 'You need to be strong for Kate. You need to help her.' She took a mirror from her handbag and looked at her face, wiped away traces of tears and put on a fresh smile of lipstick. If she looked better, she felt better.

But there was still a problem. Was Kate pregnant? And what should she do about it? Maybe Kate had already "dealt with it". The word "abortion" made her shudder. She shut her eyes and shook her head at the idea.

She jumped when she saw Neil standing in the doorway.

'Oh, Neil! You surprised me. Didn't hear you arrive.' She glanced around the room to make sure there was nothing out of place.

'Is Kate pregnant?' His words were harsh and clipped.

'What? I don't know. No, of course not. Please don't ask me!' Annie got up and started to parade around the room, her slippers making a scuffing sound on the wooden floor. Neil stood in front of her, blocking her way. He took her by the shoulders and sat her down on the sofa.

'Not again, Annie. This constant parading doesn't help. I know this is difficult but think of Kate and what is best for her.'

Annie closed her eyes. The decisions she made in life were simple ones. What to wear, what to eat, how to spend her day. The dichotomy of choosing between honesty and loyalty was outside her scope.

'I believe Kate is pregnant. Why else would this be such a difficult question for you? We need to think of the health of mother and baby.' He sat closer to Annie and turned her face towards him. 'Even if it means breaking a promise.'

Annie looked at the flowers on her skirt and pulled at a loose thread. She fidgeted around, coughed, extracted her handkerchief and patted her nose. Her breathing was laboured as if she had been running. Neil waited. Annie did not like silence. Normally she would fill any pauses in a conversation with random gossip, trivia and inane comments. This time, she filled it with truth.

'I think Kate has memory loss. She seems to be getting better on the outside but she's denying things she told me a few weeks ago.'

'What things?'

'She said she was pregnant. An accident. A bit of a fling. She came to me for advice but I let her down. We never talked about things like that. I was shocked. I found it too difficult. So we haven't said much about it. I did try to make amends. I drove here, you remember. To see her, to talk things over. But it didn't help. I don't know what she decided to do.'

Annie felt exhausted. Her struggle to force out the words was visible on her face, a pallid mask with a red, clown's mouth. She made a final effort.

'I've just asked her about the baby. She says she doesn't know what I'm talking about. She's ill, Neil. The accident had a bigger impact than we realised.'

Annie got up; she had finished and would say no more. She gave Neil a shake of her head and made for the stairs. She felt old and worn out.

Kate passed her in the doorway. Annie averted her eyes, said she needed a rest and would be down later.

Neil watched Kate as she came into the room. 'How are you feeling?'

'Not bad. A bit tired. I think I should be back at work soon'.

'Don't rush. Make sure you are really well.'

'Ever the concerned husband! I can look after myself, Neil. What are you doing here, anyway?'

'I came to see how you are.'

'Well, you've seen. Not sure if I'm happy with you wandering in unannounced. Maybe you could hand back the key.'

'It's our house. I own half of it. It's a discussion for another day.' He stayed where he was as Kate pointed to the door.

'I'll go when I've asked you one question. Are you pregnant, Kate?'

Kate forced out a harsh, unamused groan. 'You've been talking to my mother. I don't know what's wrong with her. She's confused. Got some odd idea I told her I was pregnant. I probably mentioned Becky and she muddled everything up in her head. I worry about her.'

'She's not senile. A bit forgetful, a bit random and often

an annoying nuisance. But she wouldn't get something major wrong, something like her daughter expecting a baby. Have the decency to be honest, Kate.'

'I am not pregnant. It is the absolute truth.' Kate faced up to Neil, the force of her gaze crushing him into silence. He turned and left.

***

Word spread. The phone rang and concerned voices asked how she was. An array of "Get Well" cards stood on the sideboard. The neighbours called round. Kate hated it. Illness was something that happened to her customers. She was not ill. She was simply getting over an accident. She said, 'I'm fine now, thank you.' She repeated, 'All is going well. Thanks for your concern.' She got rid of everyone as rapidly as she could with barely hidden impatience.

'You could be a bit more appreciative, Kate. Don't sound so ungrateful. These folk are being kind.' Annie was putting yet more flowers into a vase and finding space for another card.

'I don't need concern and compassion. Or cards and flowers. I'm well. I'll be back at work soon. The doctor will tell me that when I go for my check-up next week.'

However, when Colin arrived on the doorstep with a bunch of grapes, she invited him in. Annie looked puzzled and disappeared into the kitchen.

'I'm not a cause for anxiety, Colin. Look at me. Do I look ill?' She placed herself in front of him. He tipped his head to one side and examined her, smiling.

'See, I don't look ill at all. Maybe we'll talk about a different topic: Becky.'

'You're aware of her pregnancy?' He was serious now.

'Of course. As, it seems, are you.'

'She came to see me. I realised as she left there was an ulterior motive. As you probably know, we had sex at the reunion.

228

I think she believed I was the father.'

'Seems like a valid assumption. Unless she has a stream of lovers. Which I doubt is the case.'

'Valid, yes. But possible, no. I had a vasectomy years ago. It worked. I'm not aware of any other offspring and I've not been exactly celibate!'

'Oh, God!' Kate looked at him with wide eyes. 'Did you tell her about the vasectomy?'

'It came up in the conversation – she asked me. I thought it odd. It was only after she left I realised the significance of the question.'

'I assume you have no urge to be a father?'

'Too right! Becky has to look elsewhere. Must have had a good time with someone else. Not unlikely. She's an attractive woman. There's a surprise for him.'

'So a cosy little relationship between you and her is no longer on the cards. Never really saw it happening. Although I did put in a word for you. Your wandering eye will have to look elsewhere.'

Colin raised his eyebrows.

'I didn't mean me.'

In the kitchen, Annie was tidying up the non-existent mess, being busy, keeping out of the way. But nosiness got the better of her and she decided the cupboard next to the door needed attention.

At the mention of Becky, she stopped what she was doing. Moving china around made too much noise. She remained fixed like an impromptu scarecrow, a cup in each hand, arms wide to keep her balance as she bent forward to catch the words. It was true. Becky was pregnant. Could she have got confused? No, of course not. Kate said she'd ended up in bed with Jonathan. She remembered the words distinctly. She remembered her own reaction, her shock, her disgust, her feeling of helplessness. But two of them being pregnant at their age? It seemed impossible.

And it seemed she was the only one who knew about

Kate's pregnancy. Neil did not know. Surely Kate confided in someone other than her? The more she thought about it, the more she doubted her own memory. Who was the one who was ill? Herself or Kate? I need to go home. Being here is not helping. Kate did not appreciate her efforts, anyway.

She left the following day.

Chapter 28

Barry told his wife he'd not be long and walked the short distance to Kate's house. He was shaking. There was stubble on his chin and his wear-weary clothes were creased. One of the buttons on his shirt was undone. The dapper man had departed and left a poor quality, second-hand replacement. He stood on the doorstep in the gloom of early evening. Kate waited for him to speak. He said nothing.

'You'd better come in, Barry. You've not got a sweater on and it's chilly. We can't stand here.'

She did not want him, did not want any more enquiries about her health. But he had the look of a messenger and she felt there was a reason for this visit. Barry shuffled across the hall into the sitting room, the energy to lift his feet being more than he could summon. He crossed his arms and rubbed his bare elbows, gnarled rings of skin that looked like knots in the bark of a tree. He folded into himself as he sat on the sofa. He looked ancient.

Without asking, Kate went into the kitchen and made him a mug of tea. He put his hands around it, still saying nothing.

'Why have you come?'

His pale face seemed to go paler, greyer.

'Is it about Louise?'

He nodded and tears spilled from his watery eyes and ran down his face.

'Is she worse?'

Kate had been so preoccupied with herself Louise had faded into the background. A flutter of guilt passed through her.

'You'll have to explain, Barry. I know she's still unconscious and in hospital but no-one has given me any more information.'

He found his voice. Like a radio springing to life, he cried out, 'She's gone, Kate. We've lost our little girl. She's gone. She's gone.' The shout died and he whispered, 'We lost her last night. She didn't recover consciousness. They tried. They said the pressure in her head was raised and they put something called an intra-cranial bolt through her skull to measure it. It sounded horrible. They talked to us about it. I hated the idea. A dreadful thing to do to our precious daughter.'

Once he started to talk the words flooded out like a torrent. 'I don't know what use it was. In the end it didn't help. They were about to move her to another hospital, a bigger one with more neurosurgical facilities. But it was too late. She died.'

He blew his nose on an overused handkerchief. 'They asked us about organ donation. I'm in favour of that. I carry a card I signed. They can have my body. But I couldn't bear the thought of them cutting Louise up. Nor could Gwen. Do you think we were selfish?'

Kate shook her head. It wasn't the moment for such a discussion. She had dealt with bereavement before. It was part of her job. She produced all the right phrases of comfort, patted Barry's hand and soothed him. But it felt uncomfortable and she stepped away. This loss was different. She knew Barry as a friend; she knew Louise. She shared in the grief.

Fragments of memory returned. She remembered driving fast. She heard Louise's constant chatter and felt the irritation of the unwanted passenger. Again, a frisson of guilt. But only a frisson.

'I'm sorry, Barry. I truly am. Although I don't think it was my fault, she was with me and I feel partly responsible.' It was a hard sentiment to produce. Perhaps she should feel worse than she did; she could not feel as devastated as Barry.

'I've not come here to blame you, Kate. I thought you'd

232

want to know. Louise loved you. You meant a lot to her. Of course, we don't blame you.' He looked at Kate with sorrowful, imploring eyes. 'You are our last link with Lou. You are important to us.'

He rose slowly to his feet and walked towards Kate with his hands outstretched. She wanted to back away but was unable to move; there was nowhere to go. He rested his head on her shoulder and wrapped his bony arms around her. His hair was greasy with flecks of dandruff and his rough face caught on her cashmere sweater. There was an artificial pine smell about him, the aroma of hospital. She patted his back rhythmically as if he were a child seeking comfort and then held him at arm's length.

'Go back to Gwen. She needs you.'

'Yes. You're right. She does. I'll see you again soon, Kate. Very soon.'

Kate poured herself a large brandy as soon as Barry had gone. She did not want to see Barry very soon. She did not want to see him at all if she could avoid it. She hated sharing his sadness, the fate of a parent who loses a child. She hated the very thought of being a parent, of putting herself in such a vulnerable position. Her handbag was lying on the armchair and she took out an envelope from the zipped pocket. It was a note Louise sent her several days before the accident.

Hiya Kate

I dont write letters so this is funny – somethings making me tell you how special you are

I want to be like you. Dont think I could do pharmacy or what ever but I want to talk like you and be brave and confidant and not be afraid of anything

Please let me be with you please help me to be like you

Love

Louise xx

She'd brought it on herself.

Chapter 29

It was a dismal affair. Kate knew she could not avoid going. There was an obligation. Neil collected her. He offered and she agreed. They sat in silence in the car. She refused to wait with him at the crematorium, telling him to go ahead and join the others. She needed a breath of air. There were flowers everywhere, neatly placed in sections with the deceased's name on a small card beside them. Yesterday's already looked like yesterday's, rose heads hanging at their loss. She cringed at the elaborate floral versions of 'DAD' and 'GRANDMA', fervently hoping nobody ever commemorated her passing with such ostentation.

An elderly couple walked by and she heard them saying what a lovely service it was, what a glorious celebration of Doris's life. They seemed in high spirits and she could hear the strains of Vera Lynn's 'We'll meet again' creeping out of the exit door, trying to persuade listeners that life went on. The mourners, if they could be called that, seemed comforted such a meeting might not be far away. She followed them along the pathway looking at Doris's flowers, reading the cards. Doris had reached ninety-nine.

Kate sighed. Louise would make a different farewell to the world. The hearse drove slowly up to the door where a group of people gathered. She could see Neil talking to Becky. Jonathan was there, with Colin. She scowled. Most of the neighbours huddled together, talking in whispers, faces moulded into funereal expressions. Several younger people stood uncomfortably to one side, fidgeting in ill-assorted clothing, an attempt to dress in what they thought a funeral demanded. One stood out in a scarlet coat and glamorous high heels. Barry and Gwen got out of the over-large black saloon that followed the hearse, both drowned in black. Gwen was wearing a hat that shaded her face and a scarf high up round her neck. It was as if she had sent her clothes to the service instead of going herself. She held on to Barry with gloved hands as they led the group of people into the crematorium behind the coffin.

Kate decided to sit at the back. She wanted to be on her own, with her own thoughts. Her non-participation would be less visible to the congregation. But she was guided by Neil towards the front where he and Becky planned to sit. She did not have the energy to resist and, anyway, it was not crowded so maybe she was less conspicuous among the others.

One of Louise's friends read a poem. Barry stood up and stumbled through something he had written on a piece of paper. Kate could hardly hear him; he spoke quietly and her head was resounding with "I don't want to be here, I don't want to be here". The noise blocked out the words, the music and the hymns. Fragments of the service floated past like motes of dust. She heard the words "sure and certain hope" and thought what a ridiculous expression it was. Hope was hope and by its nature uncertain. The service was over in the time it takes for a service in a crematorium but Kate did not measure the time. Perhaps it was quick; perhaps it dragged on forever. She did not know. She remembered Tina Turner singing "Simply the Best" as they emerged into the dull afternoon.

They filed out, passing by the coffin, some people touching it and muttering a few words of farewell while dabbing their eyes. They nodded at the vicar. Was he a vicar? Kate had no idea what a man who commits the dead to everlasting life in a crematorium was called. Some people shook his hand and murmured their thanks. What for? It was his job. Barry and Gwen stood together at the door, saying how kind everyone was, speaking in little voices. Barry invited everyone to join them at the Horse and Hounds.

Kate asked Neil to take her home.

'You can't go home, Kate. They expect you to be with them. It's just too rude.'

'I don't feel like going to the pub.'

'If you'd still been unwell, I'd understand. But you keep insisting you'll be back at work soon. There's no excuse. You were with Louise in the car, the last person ever to talk to her. You must come. It's your duty. I'm going to join them. If you want a lift home with me, you need to stay.'

'I can take a taxi.'

Neil was trying to control his voice, not to make a show of their disagreement, when Barry put his hand on Kate's shoulder.

'You're coming along, Kate, aren't you? Louise needs you. Gwen and I need you. But you know that. You'll come. I don't need to ask.'

Kate had no choice. She would rather have been at the wake of ninety-nine-year-old Doris whose life was a celebration.

But at least there was alcohol. Barry was generous; everyone drank. Toasting Louise behind a blurred veneer of fellowship was easier than discussing the facts of her death. They ate sandwiches, neither bad nor good ones. Just funeral sandwiches with ordinary fillings, fit for ordinary funerals. Kate ate a small one but did not taste it. Barry said he would call round the following day. He might bring Gwen. Kate nodded in a daze.

He had called round daily since Louise's death, a faithful dog, a dependent follower. He talked only about Louise. Of course, he talked about Louise. As the days moved on, he forgot her more irritating qualities, the tattoos and the piercings, and she became the daughter he wanted her to be: "Simply the Best". The song was a favourite of Gwen's. The reason they chose it. He had no idea if Louise liked it or not. He seemed surprised Kate asked.

Kate had to remind him to go home, to spend time with his grieving wife. He obeyed with a sigh, looking forlornly behind him as he walked down the path and along the road to his house, leaving his spirit behind. It lurked in the house, haunting Kate, a constant reminder of the change in his life which was impinging on hers. Things will be better after the funeral, she told herself. It will bring a closure of sorts and we will all move on.

It seemed they had not moved far.

Alone in her house, she made a large gin and tonic, and took a couple of tablets. It was not a problem; she knew all about benzodiazepines. She could control her usage. She had barely taken off her shoes when the doorbell rang. It was tempting to ignore it but she could see Becky's car outside. Becky knew she was home.

'Well?'

'Can I come in?'

'I don't think we have anything to say. But okay, you can.'

The two women sat down in silence.

'I'd offer you a G and T but you'd refuse and, anyway, I'm not expecting this to be a long, cosy chat.'

'I know whatever friendship we had has disappeared but I do need to talk to you. Why didn't you tell me you were pregnant?'

'Why would I invent something like that?'

'Come on, Kate. You were pregnant. I realise it now. The way you talked about the issues of pregnancy at our age, the way you advised me. You'd been thinking about it. It was personal. And when I look back, there was a different air about you.'

'I didn't stop drinking. I didn't stop eating all the "forbidden" foods as you did. My shape didn't change. This is pure imagination. You're jumping to the wrong conclusions. And it's none of your business, anyway.'

'I know, I know. But you've either had a termination or your fit body is producing a good disguise.'

Kate groaned, a forced, ugly denial.

'If you are expecting, you need to talk about it. Please talk to me. I've come on my own. It would be in total confidence.'

'If I were pregnant, you'd be the last person I'd turn to.'

'I'm at high risk of Down's Syndrome. The doctor told me. You could be, too. You need to think about it.'

Kate opened the sitting room door. 'I said it wouldn't be a long chat. I think we're finished.' She finished her drink in a gulp.

'Even if you've had a termination, you should confide in someone.'

There was no reply.

Becky gave Kate a long, searching look and left. She saw Colin arrive as she drove away.

'Colin, what are you doing here?' Kate's greeting was terse.

'That's a friendly welcome! I can't say I was just passing but I'd had enough of the wake and knew there'd be a drink here.'

She provided the alcohol. Colin chatted about nothing much to Kate's intense irritation. She wanted to be alone, to get rid of him. Colin put his head to one side, as he did in his more pensive moods, and looked intently at Kate.

'What do you remember about the accident?'

'Not a lot. I recall leaving the house in a fury at Neil and simply needing to drive away. I expect you know we're separating.'

'How did Louise end up in the car?'

'I think she ran across from her parents' house as I was leaving. But it's hazy and it might not be a true memory.'

'What happened next?'

'I don't know. Why are you quizzing me?'

'I'm nosy, you know me.' He hesitated. 'And, to be honest, I thought talking it through might be therapeutic for you. You didn't seem yourself at the cremation or the pub.'

'Nobody was normal. It wasn't a normal situation. I don't need therapy.'

'Everyone needs a helping hand at times. It's no weakness to admit it.'

'I'm fine. I'm in control of my life. I'll be back at work next week.'

'It was a serious accident. You can't shrug off something like that. I want to help.'

'There is no shrugging. I'm simply better.'

She turned away in case Colin's perceptive eye detected the lie. She could now remember most of what happened in the car. And it haunted her, plagued her sleep in the early hours, a half-nightmare, a blurred reality.

'But Louise died.'

'If you're trying to help me, introducing guilt isn't the way to do it.'

'Why do you deliberately misconstrue everything?'

'If you go on about her death, what is it but a way of blaming me? You've finished the wine, Colin. Go.'

'Barry mentioned a witness has just come forward. Someone parked in a lane nearby. Didn't want to get involved but saw the death announcement in the paper and felt obliged to say he'd seen the accident.'

'So? What difference does that make?'

'I don't know, Kate. I really don't know. Just thought you should be aware.'

'I can't stand this, Colin. Go! I don't need your information, your fussing, your criticism masquerading as help. Just leave me alone.'

'If you change your mind and want to talk…'

'I won't.'

***

Kate went upstairs to change. She felt clammy, coated in the concerns of others. Standing in the shower, her face turned into its power, she relaxed. She knew there were plans to be made. So many changes in her life but there would be more. She needed to put the accident, the funeral, the whole bloody business behind her. Her head was swimming with ideas and alcohol and she tripped as she stepped out of the shower. God, I must have had a few, she thought, nursing a sore elbow.

As she emerged into the bedroom, a towel partly wrapped around her, she heard footsteps on the stairs. The door opened and Neil entered.

'Christ, Neil! I need to have your key back. You can't just walk in. This isn't your home.'

'We've already had that discussion. I didn't expect to find you undressed. As it happens, I've come to collect the rest of my clothes.'

'You could have got them when you dropped me off.'

'I didn't think.'

She was standing in front of the wardrobe and did not move when he went to open it.

'Kate, just let me get on with it.'

She blocked his way and moved towards him, dropping the towel, putting her arms around his neck and pressing her breasts against his shirt. He pushed her to one side.

'It's ages since we had sex.'

'Stop it, Kate. Those days have gone. Don't you remember you threw me out? Put some clothes on. Act decently.'

'For old time's sake? You smell delicious. Aren't I still attractive to you? I bet I am. We were good in bed.' She stroked his face and moved her hand down his body. He sprang away.

'What is this? A means of getting revenge on Becky? Or are you simply drunk?'

Kate laughed, a silly, unaccustomed giggle. 'Probably a bit of both! Definitely a bit of both! You'll regret it, you sad man. Just pregnant Becky and the potential for a damaged child. Another man's child.'

Kate picked up the towel and went back into the bathroom. 'I bet you'll wish you'd taken me up on the offer when you think about it. Your loss!'

But it was her loss, too. She needed to be held, to be caressed; she needed the physical closeness of a man.

'I simply don't understand you, Kate. The day of Louise's

funeral and you behave like this.'

'Life has to go on, Neil.' Kate was determined to cram so much into hers that she didn't have time to think. On her way downstairs, still pulling her sweater on, she called back.

'Oh, by the way, Colin isn't the father. Has Becky mentioned it? He had a vasectomy years ago. Your lovely lady has been generous with her favours.'

Chapter 30

Joanne had gone. When Jonathan returned home, there was a note on the kitchen table.

Dear Jonathan

I'm leaving. It's inevitable. I don't want to be thrown out so I'm going of my own accord. We had good times. Without your girls, there'd still be good times for us. But I can't handle the bad atmosphere and antagonism – from them and from you. I think we've run our course. I'll remember you fondly for the love you once gave me. Try to do the same for me.

Move on, Jonathan. I shall. I suspect you have my successor lined up. I saw how you and Kate looked at each other. There's unfinished business there. But she's not the mothering type, so beware! There'll be problems with the girls. You're not a man who can exist without a woman so I don't expect you to heed my words.

Yours with memories

Joanne

Beside the note were her house keys.

Jonathan walked round the house to see what traces of her were left. He could not find a single personal item. Her clothes were gone, drawers and wardrobes like empty shells. A faint perfume of her presence remained in the bedroom but it would be gone if he opened the window. The dressing table bore no lotions or cosmetics, a bare, challenging space glaring at him. There was little enough of her personality downstairs. She had chosen the grey silk cushions for the lounge and had left them behind. They belonged to the house and Jonathan had paid for them. A tiny reminder she had shared his life. The kitchen was as it always was, functional and tidy. He wondered if she had thought to take her gardening gloves. He could not be bothered to check but expected they would be gone from the shed.

She had been thorough. That was her way. His life with Joanne was over. All that remained was a conflict of feelings. It was too easy. He needed the anger of disagreement and the frustration of incompatibility to give him closure. Joanne denied him that. She knew she had; she had chosen to go. Her own, small, final triumph.

He was staring at the emptiness that had been her presence when Lara rushed in. She was singing to herself, a good mood around her like a puff of steam.

'Hey, Dad, just been listening to K T Tunstal. Love her music. D'you like it? You do know who I'm talking about, don't you?'

She stopped when she saw her father's blank face. 'You okay?'

'Yeah. I think so. Yes. Just getting used to the circumstances. Do you notice anything different here?'

Lara looked him up and down.

'You've had your hair cut. Big deal.'

'I have, but I meant something more significant.'

Lara walked round the room as if they were playing a silly, child's game. 'You've moved the cushions – is that it? No, there's a new plant on the windowsill. Or maybe I just didn't notice it before.' She stopped by the bookcase. 'Something's missing from here. What is it?' She thought for some seconds. 'It's Joanne's silver candlestick.'

She rotated to face her father. 'That's it, isn't it? She's gone! I knew there was a reason for my good mood. Thought it was the music – wrong! The air feels lighter without Joanne here!'

She grabbed Jonathan's hands and twirled him round, whooping with delight. He laughed; it broke his introspection. He enjoyed dancing with his daughter, even if it was a clumsy gallop with little style and poor rhythm. The weight of Joanne's disapproval had fallen heavily on them all.

'Well, we can now start on the next phase of our lives, you, me and Sheena. We've been on our own before and we can do it again.'

'I like it when there's just the three of us. Sheena does too.' She gave her father a hug. 'Not sure you do, though.'

Lara turned off her merriment and looked seriously at Jonathan. 'I'm old enough to understand now, you know. Relationships and the like. I know you prefer to have a woman in your life. Other than your daughters, that is! Don't look so uncomfortable. I'm not a little girl anymore. I realise being just us won't last.'

Jonathan hesitated and nodded. 'I do like to have a woman around. It gives a balance to life. If your mother had lived, things would have been different.' They both took a deep breath. 'Hard for me to talk to you about women.'

'And odd for me to say this. Daughters don't usually give advice to their dads. Choose a bit more carefully than last time. Don't rush. Let's enjoy being the three of us. Just for a bit.'

'Okay, I'm listening. I'll try to do the best for all of us.'

The burden of handling teenage daughters hung about him like a yoke. Jonathan thought about Kate. Lara liked her. Would she still like her if she moved in?

Timing, timing.

Chapter 31

'Keep forgetting to ask you – what's the due date? Must be sometime in June.'

Becky ignored the question and continued painting the wall. Neil was on the floor, varnishing a skirting board.

'Bugger, I've just dripped paint down my trousers. Can you pass me some kitchen roll?'

'You do have a date, don't you? You said you were having a scan.'

'Just pass me some paper, will you?'

There was a pause.

'Becky, why won't you answer my question?'

'It's towards the end of July. Twenty-third, actually.'

Neil sat back on his heels. Becky could see him calculating.

'But the reunion was at the end of September. The baby should be due in June. Did you tell the doctor that?'

'Yes. The scan is the most accurate means of confirming dates.'

'Bloody hell, Becky! I thought we were being open and honest with each other. It wasn't a one-off! You carried on seeing Colin after the reunion. How long did it go on for? Is it still going on? You must think I'm a real fool.' He threw his brush across the floor. 'You said there was no relationship there. Or did he get cold feet and run when he discovered about the pregnancy?' He walked out of the room and out of the house.

Becky tried to stop herself from shaking. She put the lid

on her paint tin, wiped the brush and put it into a polythene bag, carefully sealing it with a rubber band. She moved methodically and slowly, the only way she knew to contain the feelings within her. A quick action and emotion might rush out like water from a burst pipe. This was the inevitable conversation she had been avoiding. Neil would return. He had left his car keys, his phone, his coat. It took him an hour. He returned cold and pale.

'You're being unfair, Becky. I'm trying my hardest to do the right thing by you, struggling with emotion and practicality. And you persistently lie.'

'I haven't lied, Neil. I haven't lied at any point. But I am guilty of not telling you the whole story.'

'Comes to the same thing. Splitting hairs.'

'I've kept things from you because I'm scared. I don't know how to make you believe me.'

'I don't see your problem. I've trusted you up to now. My mistake, it seems.'

'We can't talk like this, standing on the doorstep.' She led Neil into the kitchen and they sat at the table, in their usual chairs, as if everything was normal and they were having a cup of tea, a break from decorating the nursery. But the atmosphere was not normal.

'Listen to me, Neil. Don't speak.' Becky waited until she judged Neil was listening. 'Everything I told you is true. I did have a one-night stand with Colin at the reunion. It was once. Just once.'

She saw Neil stiffen at her words.

'I believed he made me pregnant. It's what I told you. However, I don't now think he's the father. In fact, I know he isn't. He had a vasectomy years ago.'

'Okay. I was wrong. I'll accept that. Seems Kate was right. She told me about Colin's vasectomy. I thought she was winding me up. Just making life difficult. Turns out she was telling the truth. Nice to know she does sometimes. So someone else is the father. Is that supposed to make me feel better?'

Becky scowled. Why were Neil and Kate discussing her? When did it happen? She would ask later on; there were more important matters to deal with now.

'As I said, I didn't sleep with Colin again, but nor did I have any other random partners.' Neil looked as if words were about to burst out of him. 'And don't start making comments about angelic visitations. I don't need any wisecracks.'

Becky reached across to take Neil's hand. She could feel the tension in his arm, his unwillingness to touch. 'The only person I've slept with since Colin is you.'

After a long pause, Neil said, 'How can I believe you?'

'Because it's true. Perhaps now you'll understand why I've been avoiding this conversation. I knew you wouldn't believe me. I knew you'd think it impossible you could be a father. I knew you'd accuse me of sleeping around. And I was frightened. Frightened of losing you.'

Neil walked around the kitchen. 'I need to get this straight. Colin had a vasectomy. I assume vasectomies don't fail?'

'They can but not after so long.'

'And your dates are wrong for the reunion, anyway?'

'As you've just pointed out.'

'So Colin can't be the father.'

'I've just explained that.' Becky recognised Neil's need to go through everything he had just heard, like the revision of a difficult maths exercise.

'You conceived towards the end of October?'

'Yes. We had a weekend away in the Cotswolds if you remember.'

'But I have a low sperm count.'

'I know. But there are sperm there. The count isn't zero.'

'Why haven't you got pregnant before?'

'I don't know. I discussed it with my doctor. She couldn't explain. Just said men with low sperm counts have fathered children before.'

'Kate and I tried and gave up.'

'As I said, I can't explain.'

Neil wiped a hand across his eyes. 'This takes a lot of absorbing. Most men prepare themselves for fatherhood. It's usually a process with planning and discussion.'

'We've got time, Neil. July is a long way off.'

'I want to trust you. But there is still the uncomfortable shiver of doubt I feel when I think about the situation.'

'We could prove it by DNA testing. Would that convince you?'

'Of course, it would convince me.'

'So we don't need to do it. The fact I would do it just to satisfy you is enough. I want you to believe me unconditionally, without a test. I want trust to be fundamental.'

'I'll try. I need some time. This is a huge shock.'

Neil walked out into the garden and Becky watched him pacing around, sometimes rubbing his hands against the chill, turning up his coat collar, sometimes stopping and staring into space. He picked up a twig and broke it into tiny pieces. He sat on a bench for some time, immobile.

'Come back in, Neil. You'll freeze out there.'

He returned to find Becky opening a bottle of wine.

'I think we should celebrate. I'll even have a small glass, my first since I discovered I was pregnant. A little one won't hurt. This warrants me breaking my rule.'

Neil put his arms around her and soaked up her warmth. He slid his hand across her abdomen.

'Just think. You might have had a termination. If you'd done that, and then discovered the truth of the situation, I'd have been heartbroken. We'd have lost our baby.'

'Does it mean you're glad the baby's yours?'

A slow smile crept across Neil's face, spreading out without his help. 'I suppose it does. There was a time I wanted to be a father. Expected I would be. Discovering the low sperm count was dreadful, hard to get my head around. A real shock. I felt less of a man.'

'I remember you telling me that soon after we started seeing each other, when we used to meet for coffee in town, before we started a proper relationship. And I remember saying you seemed a pretty good man to me.'

They both relaxed into the memory.

'But if I'd had an abortion, you'd never have known about it, Neil. I wouldn't have told you. I may not have known the truth about the father myself. I might not have discovered about Colin's vasectomy and dates would have been irrelevant. I'd probably not have told Kate about us either – that happened because she caught me at a vulnerable time. So we'd have been exactly as we were. Apart from a secret held by me.'

They raised their glasses to each other. Neil sighed.

'What's the problem now?'

'You do realise all this personal upheaval is creating problems in my work life. I'm losing motivation, doubting the value of my project. Is it beneficial to these kids and their parents to single them out? The exhibition is approaching fast and I'm not ready.'

'You must get on with it. It will help significantly in removing some of the awful ideas about Down's. Honestly, Neil, it's worthwhile.'

'I've lost focus.'

'Only temporarily. You and Kate have parted. We've had our most serious discussion ever. And the outcome is good. What's stopping you getting back to work with your usual vigour?'

Becky was on a high, relief and happiness fuelling a burst of enthusiasm for Neil's work, life, pregnancy, everything. She rushed round the kitchen, put some nuts in a dish, ate a few, opened and closed a couple of cupboards and became busy doing nothing in particular.

'Come here and let me say something.'

Becky wrapped her arms around Neil and kissed his neck.

'I love the bouncy you but I have to be serious for a bit.

It's about the exhibition. I need to ensure I have balance. Above all else, it must ring true. I have an excellent selection of photos of young kids with Down's who are coping and of their capable parents. I have a good series with Daisy-Lee to represent an adult who's managing brilliantly. But not everyone does well and I must show the other side, too. Otherwise it's a skewed picture.'

'I know. We talked about it ages ago.'

'I wish I'd already done those interviews. They're the hardest. I need to see parents who are having a bad time, to appreciate how difficult it can be with a child with multiple problems. And take the photographs.'

'It's because of me, isn't it?'

Neil nodded. 'You're high risk. Worst case scenario is that the baby will have Down's Syndrome and various associated, serious problems. It's personal. I could be independent before. Sympathetic and understanding, yes. But I was an observer. That's what a photographer is. There's a blur now. I'll have a word with Karen to see if she can put me in touch with someone.'

'You have to do it, Neil. Now it's more important than ever. Your story – our story – can be bound up in the exhibition. It makes it more poignant than before.'

Neil stood up, gasped and rushed out to his car. He returned with a camera.

'A few trial photos, Becky. I can do them again if necessary, probably when the pregnancy is more apparent. You can write the text. I want to show your bump but not your face. You'll represent the nervous anticipation of a high risk mother as well as being yourself.'

He was already in his professional world, positioning Becky, muttering to himself, moving clutter out of the picture, planning, biting his lip.

'That transformation didn't take long!'

'You triggered it, Becky!'

They talked about the best angle for the photo and the probable lighting although Becky was the passenger not the driver for decision-making.

'You'll get it right. Just as you did for the "Love Bite" photograph.' She paused and faced Neil. 'The one of Jonathan.'

Neil turned to Becky in amazement. 'Why do you say it's Jonathan?'

'I know it is.'

'But how?'

'My secret, Neil. Always important to keep your partner guessing. To be able to spring a surprise. A touch of unpredictability. Keeps the relationship alive.' Lively Becky was back.

The expression on Neil's face showed more apprehension than belief in surprises.

***

'I've spoken to a few mums but I don't think I can help you, Neil.' Karen, the diligent go-between, had done her best to find a family where Down's Syndrome was not something they coped with, a family willing to talk to Neil.

'Are you saying all families with DS kids are happy and successful?'

'No, absolutely not. I'm saying no-one wants to talk to you about their problems. No-one with multiple, complex problems.'

'Understandable. Can you tell me anything about them?'

Karen told him about two situations. In one family, they were trying so hard not to be different from any other parents, they refused to be associated with any groups, meetings or activities to do with Down's Syndrome. Said it did not help, just made them all the more obvious.

'I hope you said I was trying to represent the Syndrome fairly and sympathetically?'

Karen gave him a "Why are you asking such a stupid question?" look.

'So do you think this family is coping?'

'No. They are making life harder for themselves than it need be. But it's their choice.'

'And the other family?'

'She has two children, both with Down's. Both have what is called low functionality. Neither can talk, at ten and seven years. They are still in nappies. She sees absolutely no point in parading her children as objects to be looked at and pitied. She loves them too much. Mixing with Down's kids who are doing well just emphasises her problems. And the pride of the parents who say it's rewarding to bring up a DS child rankles when she looks at her own life – their lives. They have a bad time.'

Neil took a deep breath. 'I shouldn't ever have asked.' He felt guilty, as guilty as if he was the cause of this parent's problem. 'God, I've got a lot to learn.'

'You're okay, Neil. Don't beat yourself up. But I don't think I can help any more. I'll come along to the exhibition, though. Most of the mums from our group will, too.'

Neil nodded, distracted. His fervour abated. The exhibition felt secondary to his life, a poor pastime, a trivial distraction. He phoned Becky.

'I don't think I can go ahead with the exhibition.'

'We went through that, Neil. Don't be silly.'

'I spoke to Karen.'

'Did she give you any more contacts?'

Neil went through what Karen had said.

'I'm worried, Becky. If we had a child with severe disabilities, how would we manage? We know nothing about being parents, let alone knowing what to do in the circumstances some of these parents face.'

'I thought you said you'd support me? I thought you'd want to support me more knowing the baby is yours.'

'Of course, I'll support you. But I want to do what is best for us and the baby. I'm struggling to decide what that is. You know, we'll be among the ten-percenters. Termination rate is around ninety percent among those who know the foetus has Down's.'

'How do you know?'

'Part of the research I've done. It's just more personal now. I think I've been blinded by only talking to parents who cope, those with high-functioning kids. The worst case scenario is bad, really bad.'

'You're not telling me anything new. We don't actually know the baby will have Down's.'

Neil forced himself to continue. 'People always think about the baby, the child. How it will cope, what the problems will be. I've looked more closely into the adult situation. An adult unable to speak, not able to live independently, low mental age, possibly autism. What happens when the parents are no longer there? Alzheimer's disease is more likely in people with Down's and at an earlier age. Something to do with chromosome twenty-one. I've got info about…'

Becky jumped in. 'Stop it, Neil. Stop it! Are you trying to scare me? I know all this! I've done the research as well. Don't make life harder than it is.'

Neil wished this conversation had not started. It needed face-to-face contact, the closeness of an arm's reach away. He spoke more sharply than he intended. 'Christ, Becky! We're over fifty; I'm nearly fifty-two. Are you sure you want to go through with this pregnancy?' Tears blurred his vision.

'And possibly abort a healthy baby?' Becky burst into tears and cut the line. Neil was not the only one overwhelmed with emotion.

When he called in at the supermarket on the way home – Becky's was "home" now – he was not expecting to bump into Kate. She was wearing a navy suit he had not seen before with an emerald green scarf and matching shoes. Her hair was sleek, tucked back behind one ear to reveal crystal earrings, and her make-up perfect. She looked Neil up and down. He was aware of the age of his jacket, his scuffed shoes and his day-old beard.

'Life with Becky seems to be taking its toll.'

'You seem somewhat overdressed for buying groceries, even if they are top of the range.' He glanced at the expensive olives and the smoked salmon.

.   'I've just had a couple of business meetings. With my lawyer and accountant. I'm in the process of buying another pharmacy. Doing what I'm good at.'

'Congratulations.'

'How's Becky?'

'She's well.'

'And you? Looking after a child with Down's Syndrome won't be easy. Especially someone else's child.'

Neil did not reply.

'Oh, of course, you know all about Down's. You've done the research, spoken to the mums. Everyone copes these days. No stigma at all. Your exhibition will make all that clear. It's a walk in the park.' She laughed artificially. 'Sorry, that's an exaggeration. Looking after any baby is a huge undertaking. Are you reading all the parenting books, Neil? Spoiled for choice – there are shelves of them. You can probably get one here.'

'Stop it, Kate.'

'Just showing interest and concern.'

'I wasn't going to tell you this, Kate. I decided it would be kinder to say nothing. But seeing as kindness is not a sentiment you're familiar with, I've changed my mind.'

Kate looked at her watch. 'Make it snappy, I need to get a move on.' Kate dressed her face with boredom and pulled a neat shopping list out of her handbag.

Neil moved nearer to Kate in an attempt to speak privately. 'I'm worried about Becky. I'm worried how we'll manage. I'm unsure if she's made the right decision, especially with the high risk. We need to discuss it further. But I'll support Becky all the way. And the reason is this. Becky is carrying my baby.'

It took Kate a few seconds to register what Neil said. She

took a step away from him and tossed her head backwards.

'Huh!'

'Is that all you can say?'

'You don't expect me to believe you, do you? And if you believe her, you're a fool. How long did we try for? How many times in our lives together did we have sex?' Two passing shoppers looked at her in amazement. They continued to stare and muttered to each other.

'She knows the baby isn't Colin's. Maybe she thought you'd overlook a fling at the reunion, forgive her for that. But sex with someone else points to another life, to secrets and liaisons beyond your knowledge. And she wants it to stay that way. Of course she doesn't want to lose you. She needs all the support she can get. It's a lovely story, Neil. But calculated. I'm surprised you were taken in.'

Kate consulted her shopping list, put a jar of asparagus tips in her basket and walked away.

Neil reflected on Becky's words about trust. Then about springing surprises and wondered again what she meant. Was she just being the teasing, unpredictable Becky he loved or should he be worried? He wanted to believe her; he thought he could. But Kate's reasoning was sound. He had to admit that, too.

***

Neil went straight to Becky's, hating the conversation they had on the phone.

'I'm putting a hold on the exhibition.'

'What do you mean?'

'Delaying it. It will cause some problems and probably cost me financially but I simply can't go ahead just now.'

'But you're not cancelling it?'

'No. Gut reaction was to run away but I thought about the people who shared their stories with me and I felt it was unfair on them. They need me to represent them. They need me to present their case in the only way I can. I've made a commitment.'

'I'm glad. It's the right thing to do.'

'But I'm aware I'll only be giving part of the story and it bothers me.'

'Perhaps it's the part that has to be told.'

Neil sighed and took Becky's hand. 'Making a decision on the exhibition is one thing; deciding what we should do is another.'

'The decision's been made.' Becky took an envelope from her handbag and removed a photograph. It was her twenty-week scan. The foetus was grainy but its details were there – a small, curled-up baby with fingers and toes.

'How can I get rid of this living creature? And anyway, I'm getting close to twenty-four weeks. It's legally almost too late. For me, it is too late.'

Neil thought about Tina's story and pulled Becky close to him.

'It's alright, Neil. Really. Truly.'

Chapter 32

It was out of character. Annie knew that. But she had no choice. She was not going to live the rest of her life with everyone thinking she was mad. She had to brace herself and be brave. She listed down all the actions she needed to take. Seeing them on paper made it seem more real.

1. Book train (return)
2. Book taxi to station (and return)
3. Book Bed and Breakfast (one or two nights?)
4. Contact Becky and arrange to see her
5. Contact Neil and arrange to see him
6. Decide if she needed to talk to anyone else

She looked at the list. Fear showed in the wobble in her handwriting. And everything was in the wrong order. She was not thinking straight. But it would do. She phoned Neil's mobile number.

She had her script ready. She did not want to get flustered and she knew the effect phone conversations had on her. So she had made some notes. Long notes. Sentences, really. She could read them and not get lost or be persuaded from her plan. She did a few breathing exercises she learned at a yoga class long ago.

When Neil answered she tried to speak slowly and casually but her voice cracked. She told him she was coming to see him the following Tuesday.

'It's important, Neil. We have to talk privately.'

'I've got meetings Tuesday. I'm not here.'

It had not occurred to Annie Neil might be busy. There was no note to cover this. Panic prickled her stomach.

'But I could see you on Wednesday if you really think it's essential.'

She agreed. 'I need to talk to Becky as well. Could you give me her phone number?'

'Becky? Well, I could. But there's something I need to tell you as it seems Kate hasn't. I am now living with Becky. You can see her here, at her house. Kate and I aren't together any longer.'

After a silence, Annie asked him to repeat what he had just said.

'I don't know what to say, Neil. I really don't. The world has turned upside down. Why didn't Kate tell me?'

'I assumed she had. Kate isn't herself at the moment. A lot on her mind. The funeral and everything. I expect she hasn't got round to it.'

Why was he making excuses for Kate? Inconsiderate bitch. He was not defending her; he was softening the blow for Annie.

Annie refused to give Neil any more information in spite of his prodding and would not let him help with her travel.

'I'm competent, Neil. Just give me Becky's address. I can sort myself out.'

She did. It was as precise as a military campaign, from rising at five o'clock to arriving in a taxi at Becky's house several hours later. She clutched her folder with its plans and notes for the whole journey like a child with a comfort blanket.

Becky had a light lunch ready and they sat around the kitchen table waiting for Annie to explain.

'Becky, you're a pharmacist. You must know about senility – they call it dementia now, don't they? Or is it Alzheimer's? What are the symptoms?'

'Why ever are you asking?'

'Just tell me the symptoms.'

'Well, there are many. It can start with memory loss,

258

difficulty in performing familiar tasks, losing things, problems with time and place…do I have to go on?'

'That's enough. Would someone with dementia be able to organise a journey for themselves, including booking train tickets, organising taxis, linking the various parts of the journey together and travelling on their own?'

Neil and Becky looked at each other.

'Annie, you don't have dementia so don't worry.' Neil placed his hand on Annie's arm as he spoke.

'I *am* worried. Either I have severe memory loss and confusion or Kate is suffering from the effects of the accident and has wiped out all knowledge of her own pregnancy. I needed to test myself, to see what I could do. So I came here.'

She sat with her mouth slightly open, ready to consume comforting words from her audience.

'None of us knows the truth of the matter.' Neil shook his head.

'It seems extraordinary to me anyone could forget they'd been pregnant.'

'Kate vehemently denies a pregnancy. It seems you, Annie, are the only person she told.'

'So you don't believe my story?'

'I didn't say that. Why did she decide to tell you?'

'She asked for advice. I thought it strange. We've never been close. And I let her down. I found the subject too difficult.'

'Kate is behaving oddly. I think we have to put it down to the accident. But there's nothing wrong with your brain, Annie.'

Neil stood up to signify the topic was finished. 'When are you going home?'

'I have a local B & B booked for tonight. The train is in the morning.'

'Why don't you stay here?'

'Thank you but no. It's all part of the test I set myself.' She did not add she was struggling to cope with the signs of affection between Neil and Becky. She kept looking at Becky's

259

rounded stomach. Seeing the two of them go upstairs to bed together would be too difficult.

Chapter 33

Barry was there again. He had made one of the kitchen chairs his own. Said he preferred to be in the kitchen so Kate could get on with whatever she was doing. He felt less like a visitor than in the sitting room. He brought offerings: a packet of chocolate biscuits or crisps, sometimes a plant, popping them in the trolley along with his regular shopping. Said he felt he should contribute as he visited so often. He devoured the biscuits and crisps himself, brushing the crumbs off his sweater on to the floor. Kate rarely ate any.

He did all the shopping now. Gwen could not face the looks people gave her and stayed at home. She came once to see Kate, sitting stiffly beside her husband. Her wide, surprised eyes were now heavily guarded slits. She had lost weight. A faded dress hung in folds around her and her hair was reverting to grey. Colour, like the spirit of her daughter, was disappearing from her life. Kate could feel the arrows of antagonism behind the bland and infrequent words. At one point, she let out a wail, a tearless screech that bounced off the walls and killed the conversation. Then she sat in silence, in her own world. As they were leaving, she turned abruptly to face Kate.

'The police will be round. Be sure of that. They'll come eventually. My brother's in the force and knows about the poisoning. He's a sergeant. They'll listen to him. Those cocktails that tasted funny. He said there wasn't enough evidence for a case. But he knows the sort of person you are. And now there's the witness. The man parked in the lane. Doesn't want his name made public 'cos he was up to no good with some woman.' She stopped and took a deep breath. 'He said you were driving too fast. That means you killed Louise.'

Barry tried to move his wife along, told her to shut up and stop exaggerating, that Kate was their friend.

'So sorry, Kate. She's upset. Doesn't mean it. Take no notice.'

Barry hurried his wife out of the door. Kate heard her mumbling something about 'an evil woman' and 'a wicked influence'.

She never visited Kate again; Barry had no wish to take her, nor Kate to see her.

***

'I'll be back at work on Monday, Barry. We won't have much time to chat.'

'Well, I knew it would happen. I'm glad you're better. I can come in the evening. We only sit and watch telly at home. Gwen usually falls asleep. Then complains she can't sleep at night. She won't miss me.'

'I expect I'll be tired.'

'Well, I won't stay long. To start with, anyway.'

'I have meetings in the evenings sometimes, accounts to do.'

'I can fit around those, I'm sure. We'll manage something.' He patted her arm as she walked past.

There was no getting rid of him.

***

Gwen was right. Two days later a police car pulled up outside Kate's house. Detective Sergeant George Montgomery showed his identification and asked if he could have a chat. Kate wanted to close the door in his face, to shut out this cheerless

262

inquisitor, this invader in her life. She led him into the sitting room, a trail of stale tobacco smoke and fried food following him. She took a step back as he spoke to avoid the blast of his lunch.

It wasn't a chat; it was a grilling. He made notes of every word Kate said. What could she remember? How fast was she driving? Had she been drinking? Had she taken any drugs? How was she feeling? The questions were endless.

'I went for a drive because my husband and I had just argued and I needed to get away from him.'

'So you was angry, preoccupied?'

'Angry, yes. Preoccupied, no. I concentrate when I'm driving.' She resisted the temptation to correct his English.

'What was the argument about?'

'Is that relevant?'

'It could be. Please answer the question.'

'We have marital problems. I don't remember what that particular argument was about.'

'Do you think your emotional state might have affected how you drove?'

'I told you. I'm a good driver however I feel.'

'Why was Louise with you?'

'I didn't invite her. The memory is vague but I think she must have seen me leaving and got in the car.'

'Did you often take her out?'

'No. Never before.'

'Where was you going?'

'It was just a drive around local roads. A chance to get out of the house.'

'How much do you remember about the drive?'

'Little. It's hazy. You must know I had a head injury.'

'Was your speed appropriate for the wet conditions?'

'It was. I'm a pharmacist, a responsible person. I drive sensibly.'

'If your memory is hazy, how can you be sure?'

'I know how I drive, how I always drive. My memory

may be hazy on some points but I'm well on the way to recovery. You can rely on what I say.'

'I expect you know we have a witness who claims you was driving too fast.'

'I've heard. I also heard this individual was parked in a lane nearby with a woman. I hardly think he would have been concentrating on the speed of a passing car. Otherwise occupied. An unreliable witness. Hardly a witness at all.'

'We've measured the skid marks. There was rubber from your tyres on the road.'

'The road was wet and an animal was splattered all over it. Of course, I skidded.'

'The extent of the damage on the car helps us estimate the speed of impact.'

'I hit a tree. There is no give in a tree. Unsurprisingly, there was extensive damage.'

The officer continued to scribble, splaying his ungainly legs wide and leaning on one of his thighs.

'Why ask me about this now? If you have a case against me, why haven't you already arrested me? If there is evidence I was speeding – and I'm certain I wasn't – you don't need this new witness.'

'Thank you for your co-operation. We may have to bring you in for further questioning. Maybe you'll remember more in a few days' time.' Innocent until proven guilty did not seem to be DS Montgomery's philosophy.

Kate let him out and poured herself a large brandy. She flopped on to the armchair, weak but triumphant. I feel detached from the whole event, she thought, justified in all I said. The nagging feelings of guilt were disappearing. Is this how madmen vindicate their actions? She enjoyed the thought of a deranged Kate, mentally unstable, a case for treatment. She laughed out loud. I told him nothing, she thought. Stupid, ill-spoken, malodorous man. I should have been a lawyer.

On his second evening visit, Barry asked where Neil was.

'Such a busy man. I expect it's that exhibition coming up. Wonderful talent. Heard him interviewed on the radio a while ago. Making a name for himself. Haven't seen him for ages. Thought he might be here tonight.'

'Neil and I have split up.'

'No! It can't be possible! You always seemed such a happy, well-suited couple.'

'We didn't advertise our problems.'

'Not very nice of him, after all you've gone through, to leave you on your own. I always thought what a genuine fellow he was.'

Kate prevented herself from making the comparison with Barry's treatment of his wife.

'It was a mutual agreement. He didn't leave me, we left each other.' I won't tell you I threw him out. Nor that he might come running back!

'So where is he?'

'He has another partner.'

A volley of tutting followed this discovery. Then a stream of exclamations, mostly to himself. Kate made no comment. Barry started to ask questions, nosiness making its way through indignation. Who was this new lady? Did Kate know her? How did they meet? Where did the pair of them live? It was something to tell Gwen, possibly even the neighbours. Something to say in a world that had lost its words.

'It's my friend, my ex-friend, Becky.'

Kate was able to leave Barry alone for a full five minutes while he expressed his opinion. She could hear him putting forth his views on current morals, the state of the nation, the respectability of professional people and the value placed on marriage. He was so preoccupied, she was able to push him out of the door somewhat sooner than usual.

She was expecting Jonathan in an hour. Since the funeral, when she had barely spoken to him, he had kept away. No phone call. No email. She remembered their last proper conversation, when he talked about leaving Joanne and wondered how matters had progressed. He was never far from her thoughts and a future that included him was becoming more positive. That morning he'd sent a message asking if he could call round.

He arrived with a bottle of Rioja. 'It feels like a red evening.'

He told Kate Joanne had gone and she looked expectantly at him. Was this an invitation?

'The girls are pleased, as I expected. They're looking forward to the three of us being together.'

'The three of you?'

'Yes. Lara and I had a serious talk. Almost like adults. Felt odd. Can't think of her as grown-up with real opinions. But I'll have to. She's changing.' Neil paused. 'She's worried. Worried about another woman in the house. Worried I'll move on too soon. A repeat of the Joanne experience.'

'What do you think?'

'I think I have to consider what I do, and how quickly I do it. Timing's important. Don't want to hurt the girls.'

Kate got up and walked to the window, playing with her glass.

'This is a different tune, Jonathan. What happened to the persuasive man who told me Lara thought I was "cool"? The weekend we were going to have together to test things out?'

'We'll do that. I'm sure Lara likes you. You are not Joanne. It'll all work out. It'll just take longer than I expected.'

'I recall in the brief conversation I had with Lara that she was pretty laid-back about your women. Said something about it not being her business.'

'I wasn't aware you discussed my "women". Lara is fourteen. She has the emotions of a teenager. Don't be taken in by her attitude.'

'Thought you just said how grown-up she is. Have you talked about me since Joanne left?'

'To Lara? No. It wasn't appropriate.'

'Oh, I'm sorry I'm no longer appropriate. Perhaps you'll kindly inform me when my appropriateness will start? Then I can work on pleasing your difficult daughters. Decide on what would suit them regarding my behaviour, my relationship to them. Perhaps even my relationship to you.'

'Stop it, Kate. Sarcasm doesn't suit you. I truly believe we have a future together. That the four of us have a future. I want to give it the best chance.'

'How very selfish of you.'

'You're calling me selfish? You're probably the most selfish person I know.'

He marched over to Kate, removed the glass from her hand and kissed her. She was expecting a barrage of words, an outpouring of fury but his passion took a different form. And she gave in. She enjoyed Jonathan as much as she had over thirty years ago.

They were on the second bottle of Rioja – Jonathan had back-up in the car in case of necessity – when Kate saw Neil's car pull onto the drive. He had refused to hand over the key but she was not about to let him walk in. And Jonathan's car was obvious. She went to open the door.

'Someone here?'

He had come for his CDs, he said, walking roughly past her into the living room. The two men stared at each other. Neil took in Jonathan's dishevelled look, his partly open shirt and the absence of shoes and socks. He had no need to ask what he was doing there.

'Right. This explains a lot.' He stood facing Jonathan, his feet apart, braced for action. 'I was confused when you arrived at the drinks party we had. Didn't know why Kate invited you. But you brought your wife, woman, whoever she was, so I wasn't suspicious. I'd not really understood why you came to the hospital after the accident. Becky said something about you being a caring person. But – stupid, innocent me – I couldn't put two and two together. How long has this been going on?'

'Does it matter? It's no different from you and Becky.' Kate spat out the words, jumping in before Jonathan could say anything.

'You could've been honest. It would've made life easier all round.'

'I play by my own rules, Neil. You know that.'

Jonathan watched in silence. But when Neil walked up to him, he put up his hand.

'Hang on there. Think what you like, but there hasn't been an ongoing relationship. Not at all like you and Becky from what I hear.'

'Okay. You just came round for a fuck.'

'An oversimplification. But we had a good one.'

'Take her. I don't need her any longer. I think our separation is now permanent. She's not part of my life.'

'I will. Kate and I are similar people. We both look after ourselves. We will have a future.' He watched Kate as he spoke. 'And, in fact, we do have a past. A distant one with recent repercussions.'

'You're talking in riddles. I really don't care.'

'You should, Neil, you should. You don't know to what extent your fame is due to us.'

Jonathan turned his back on the conversation. Neil left with an armful of CDs and a frown on his face, unable to work out what Jonathan meant.

'Jonathan, you shouldn't have said that.'

'What does it matter? It did once, perhaps, but not now. And it wouldn't be difficult for him to guess.'

'Do you know what? Neil says he's the father of Becky's baby. It's what he told me, anyway. Not sure if he believes it.'

'Could it be possible?'

'I don't think so. Anyway, I'd prefer to talk about us than

about them.'

'Can you be patient, Kate?'

'No. It's not one of my skills.'

***

Patience was definitely not one of her skills. She wanted Jonathan now. She had enjoyed his chasing, whatever impression she tried to give him. It made her smile when she thought of Verona. She laughed at the memory of their garage encounter at the drinks party. They were meant to get back together. For Christ's sake, she had carried two of his babies! She did not believe in fate unless it suited her and it suited her now. But his coolness was uncharacteristic, not part of the man she recognised.

She picked up her phone and found Lara's number. The way to Jonathan had to be via his girls. What should she say? This was a new challenge. What would appeal to a teenager? She did not know any. Then she thought of Louise. She knew the message to send.

Hi Lara. I expect you remember me, remember our chat at your house. Picking up my new sports car next week. I've chosen British Racing Green this time. Just wondered if you'd like a ride in it? We can go out whenever. Let me know. Kate.

Another potential follower.

Chapter 34

Someone had spoken to the South Midlands Echo. An article on the front page speculated about a potential manslaughter charge. It was flimsy; few facts, little evidence, nothing new. About the standard usually achieved by this low-budget, scandal-searching paper. But it worked; it got folks talking. "Local pharmacist involved with death of neighbour's eighteen-year-old daughter".

Jonathan phoned Kate to ask about it. She was furious.

'Christ, Jonathan, how do I know where it came from? Could be that cow, Gwen. Louise's mother. She's hated me since the accident. Hated the fact Louise got on better with me than with her. Always blamed me. I wouldn't put it past her to talk to the press. Anything for revenge, whatever the truth is. No-one seems to realise I could have died, too. I was unconscious, for God's sake! Anyway, how do you know what's in our local rag?'

'Becky told me.'

The news spread. Kate went round to the corner shop for some milk and felt the eyes of the shop-keeper drilling into her. She heard whispering, someone mentioned her name. She left quickly.

Later that day, Colin called. 'I know you said you didn't need help but maybe you do now.'

'I'm fine. Just angry such rubbish is circulating.'

'Have the police spoken to you?'

'Yes. An officer came to see me a week ago. Detective Sergeant fucking Montgomery. A horrible, biased, smelly man who assumed I was guilty before I uttered a word. He said I may have to answer further questions. But there's been nothing since. They have no case against me, insufficient evidence to take me to court. It was an accident, an accident!'

'Let me come round over the weekend. Now if you like. I'm really concerned.'

'I don't need you. I don't need anyone to visit me.' She started to shout. 'You know something? I'm sick of this. I don't care any longer about Louise. I don't want to show continual sympathy to her father. I wish her mother would take an overdose. I wish my own mother would stop treating me like a sick child. I wish everyone would forget about it and let me get on with my life. I don't want to talk about it any more. I've had enough!'

'Kate, Kate – I think you've just very clearly made the point that you do need to talk to someone. If not to me, then to a doctor. I think you need emotional help. Mental support.'

'I said I've had enough, Colin.' Kate cut him off and threw the phone on to a chair.

'Enough, enough, enough,' she screamed to the unlistening house. 'I want my world to start again. I want to forget about stupid Louise. I want Neil and Becky to get out of my life. I want their relationship to fall apart. I hope she loses her baby. I want Jonathan's girls to keep away. I want some happiness for myself.' She stopped shouting and burst into tears. 'I want Jonathan.'

***

Neil was watching Becky. He smiled at her rounded shape, at the way she rested her hand on her small bump. They were discussing the article in the newspaper when her phone rang.

'Why call *me*, Colin? Kate's hardly my favourite person and she's refused to discuss anything. I did try. You stand more chance of getting through to her than I do.' She put the phone down and sighed. 'I can't get rid of her, Neil.'

'What's she done now?'

'Colin's spoken to her and he's worried. Said she sounds unhinged, in a bad way. Wouldn't let him visit her. Why he's telling me, I don't know. Maybe I should call Jonathan.'

'He doesn't need to be involved.'

'He's already involved, Neil. We can't change that. And it might help us both if he takes over. We have enough to think about without Kate's troubles. I'll phone him.'

She called his number.

'Hi Jonathan, it's Becky. Just a quick call. Not sure if you've contacted Kate lately but I think you should be aware of the state she's in.' She described the situation as briefly as she could.

'Okay, but shouldn't we do something now?' A few minutes later she returned to Neil, shaking her head.

'Jonathan says it's probably just "difficult" Kate being "extremely difficult" Kate, making sure she's heard, going over the top. It's what she does. He says watch and wait.'

Neil pulled a face, disappointed at Jonathan's attitude and afraid of Becky's involvement. 'I'm not a watcher and waiter, Becky. I need to call round. I feel a sense of responsibility. If she's in a bad way, I need to know. I'm still her husband, estranged, unwanted and despised but her husband, all the same. Maybe I can help. I'll go now.'

***

To avoid another dispute, Neil rang the doorbell rather than using his key. Kate appeared brandishing the broken neck of a decanter.

'Neil – what a timely visit! I didn't know hatred could act as a magnet. I was just revelling in how much I loathe you.' She picked up a full glass of brandy with her free hand.

As she wobbled on her high heels, Neil put out a hand to steady her.

'Don't touch me!'

272

'Kate, maybe we should sit down.'

'Why would I want to sit down with you? No. No. I'm just doing something important. Wiping the last traces of you from my life.'

She waved the jagged edge of the broken decanter nearer his face.

'Be careful, Kate. That's dangerous.'

'I know it is. I could spoil your handsome face forever with it.'

'Give it to me, Kate. If you've broken something, we can clear it up.'

'Oh, yes, I've broken something. It wasn't an accident, either. You thought you'd removed all your belongings from here. Empty wardrobe, empty drawers, nothing left in the bathroom, photographs gone. Even taken your toolbox!'

Kate screeched; a weird cry, too loud, artificial.

'But you forgot the most valuable thing you possess. Your precious family heirlooms – the antique decanter and glasses. Well, you can have them. They're all here. You'll need a lot of glue to put them back together again.'

Kate paraded out onto the patio and pointed to the glinting glass scattered everywhere.

'I broke each item individually so I would get maximum pleasure. I threw each piece as hard as I could and cheered each time. I finished with the best.' She waved her weapon in the air. 'The beautiful decanter.'

'Kate, what a despicable thing to do! I'd forgotten about the glassware. You know how much I treasured it. It's been in our family for generations. You know that!'

'It wasn't important enough for you to take. So I decided to dispose of it.'

She came closer, waving her glass weapon and drinking her brandy.

'If I tried to cut your face, Neil, would you be able to stop me?'

Neil backed away, his heart thudding in his chest. 'Put it down, Kate. This is ridiculous, stupid behaviour. Not like you at all. You'll regret it.'

'I never regret anything I do.'

As Kate followed him across the patio, a movement by the house caught his eye. He pointed over her shoulder and, to distract her, shouted, 'Look!' A large man had just marched through the side gate.

'What are *you* doing here, Detective Sergeant Montgomery?' Kate screamed out his name, a bold, capital-lettered shout, his title an insult. 'How did you get in? You're an intruder. This is trespass. I shall report you.'

'Put that broken glass down.'

'Out of my garden! Go! I didn't let you in and I don't want you here. This is private property and a private matter.'

'An attack with a broken bottle is a police matter. Put it down.'

With Kate focussed on the policeman, Neil grabbed the hand holding the decanter and tried to wrench the jagged glass from her. There was a struggle and a scratch of blood appeared on Kate's arm. She shouted and released her hold. Neil threw the weapon into a bush. They both looked at the blood not knowing whose it was. Kate was suddenly still.

DS Montgomery put his hand on Kate's shoulder. She jerked away as if scalded.

'We received a phone call from a neighbour of yours. She saw you smashing glass and heard you shouting. Having read the local paper, she was worried about you. Justifiably, it seems. That's why I'm here.'

'I'm fine. No problems. You can go. And you can tell that nosy busybody to keep out of my affairs.'

'I find you threatening this gentleman with a weapon. A broken bottle or something similar. That's a criminal offence. You'll have to come to the station with me.'

Kate backed away, her eyes flashing from one man to the

other. 'You can't do that, Montgomery! I'm a pharmacist. A responsible member of society. If I choose to lose my temper in my own garden, that's my affair.'

Montgomery took a step towards her.

'Neil, Neil!' She yelled. 'Get rid of this man for me! I'm not going anywhere in a police car!' Her usual demeanour shattered like the decanter and she flung her words around like shards of glass.

'Ms Shaw, this is not normal behaviour. Even in your own garden. We need to question you further. About the car crash. Like I said before. We'll go to the station.' He spoke in a strained, agitated voice, a cop from a second-rate film.

'Neil, tell this guy I wasn't serious. I wasn't going to hurt you. It was just a way of making a point. I've never been violent. You know me. I'm your wife.'

Neil shook his head. 'You're not safe, Kate. You need help. Go inside while I talk to the officer.'

'No! I'm not having you talking behind my back. I'll sit here.' She perched on a garden chair, looking wildly around for her lost glass of brandy.

'Officer, you're aware of what Kate's been through.' Neil chose his words carefully. 'She's unstable, not herself yet. It's a doctor she needs, not a police charge.'

'She told me she was recovering well.'

'Possibly. It doesn't mean it's true.'

'I am well, Neil, I am well!'

'Kate, be quiet. This isn't helping.'

She got up and went into the house, indignation a hot cloud around her.

'We can call the police doctor on duty.'

'Fine. But I shall call her GP, too.'

'Nevertheless, we're going to the station. You can follow. I shall caution Ms Shaw.'

The two men went into the house where Kate had curled up on the sofa. She heard words familiar from TV dramas, about not saying anything, about harming her defence if she relied on something later in court that she'd not previously mentioned. She heard them, but they were about someone else. Not her. There would be no case against her.

She dragged herself up from her nest of cushions. Her anger had disappeared but there was terror in her eyes. She walked alongside Montgomery, glancing anxiously back at Neil. He trembled as he watched this person he thought he knew, this intelligent, capable person he once loved, once understood and admired, being led out to the waiting car.

As they drove away, Gwen appeared outside her front door, arms folded across her chest, a look of triumphant bitterness on her face.

***

The prospect of a night in the cells. Not something Kate thought she'd ever experience. The police doctor talked about bringing a psychiatrist in to see her. They talked about charging her. Possession of a dangerous weapon, dangerous driving, possible manslaughter. They talked. They talked. It was like white noise; she couldn't take it in. She wasn't guilty of anything – there was no case against her. They would quickly realise that. And, without a charge, they had to let her go. In the morning, she'd walk away, go home. It would be the end of the whole ludicrous business.

Then Neil arrived with Neelam Patel, her GP. More talking, talking, talking. She didn't want to go to hospital. It wasn't necessary. She told them again and again. But the choice was clear. A private ward was preferable to a police cell.

She slept badly and woke with a start in the early hours. A firework had gone off in her head. She was instantly alert, her heart thumping, but the room was silent. She dreamt she was expecting Neil's baby. She put her hands across her flat abdomen, knowing there was no baby there.

She had been so dismissive of Neil's claims of fatherhood; sure Becky was leading him on, telling him what he wanted to hear, disguising her infidelities. It all made sense. But perhaps she'd been wrong. There was a slim possibility it might be the truth. Men with low sperm counts do have children; it wasn't unknown. He might be the father of Becky's child.

She felt hot, delirious almost, sweat soaking her hair and nightshirt. Her head thumped from the many brandies of the day before. Acid rose up her throat from her stomach and she put her hand over her mouth to prevent herself from vomiting as she realised the implications. She got up and walked around the confined space, gulping in the dry, stale air.

If Neil had made Becky pregnant, he could also have fathered her child at around the same time. She bit her lip and dragged her nails through her hair. How different life might have been if she'd even considered that! Maybe she wouldn't have lost the baby. She had been pregnant, she had. The obstetrician confirmed it. Would that have altered her marriage? Would Neil have stayed? Was that what she wanted? He would have had a choice between two pregnant women. Her head swam with the complexity of what might have been.

Now she didn't want Neil near her; she wanted Jonathan. She was certain of that. But it may not have been Jonathan's baby after all. It may not have been his baby…it may not have been his baby…it may not have been Jonathan's baby…

That was definitely something to think about.

Post-Script 2010

She sat in the Piazza Bra, a glass in her hand, watching the locals go by. A few nodded at her, the eccentric, possibly mad Englishwoman with her halting Italian and expensive tastes. Verona was the perfect place to be and she was starting to fit in. She liked the climate, the food, the wine, the clothes. She liked the men. After selling the house and the pharmacies, she had more than enough money for an enjoyable, enviable life.

Neil visited once; they had financial matters to discuss. It was relaxed and amicable. They got on well. He took her out to dinner, showed her a photo of his daughter, a beautiful, happy child. It reminded her of earlier photos she'd seen for the 'Ups and Downs' exhibition he'd done so well.

She thought of him mostly with affection. Although there were times when she remembered his bad habits and how his untidiness irritated her and that made her angry. Last time it happened, she threw a vase of flowers on the floor. It was a mess to clear up. But her temper made her do it.

Generally, though, she was grateful to Neil. He'd helped when the objectionable policeman barged in. Detective Sergeant Montgomery, it was. Montgomery the Miserable. He'd carted her off to the police station, horrible, incompetent man. As if it had been necessary! Neil knew she wasn't dangerous and hadn't pressed charges. Of course, she wasn't dangerous. They kept her in hospital all the same. For far too long. Recovery time, they said.

She thought of the broken, jagged neck of the decanter. She could remember wanting to disfigure Neil, to make sure he would never be attractive to a woman again. It was a powerful memory, a disturbing, recurrent memory. Perhaps she *had* been dangerous. It made her uncomfortable, agitated, so she forced herself to think of something else. The glass of brandy helped.

Her neighbour, a gentle lady called Sofia, walked by and Kate called to her. She was helping Kate with her Italian and they enjoyed being together, speaking a strange mixture of the two languages.

'A drink, Sofia?'

'Not now, Kate. I'm off to visit my daughter. But soon. Ciao!'

On one occasion, Kate told her about the car accident and that she'd almost been charged with manslaughter. She relished the telling, liked a touch of notoriety. Sofia looked horrified then chuckled in her fat, wobbly, Italian way and said it was all too much imagination. But a good story! She'd tell her friends; a bit of fresh gossip to pass on. Kate said no more.

There had been insufficient evidence for a case against her.

She contacted Jonathan frequently. He was always on her mind. Their relationship fell apart after she'd been fined for speeding with Lara in the car. He decided they were better apart. She asked him to visit her in Verona. He would come. She was certain of that. She thought of him particularly when she visited the statue of Juliet or the Castelvecchio. A link that was hard to break, an ache she could not shift. He would definitely come. It was their city.

Once she bumped into Maurizio in the restaurant where they first met. He greeted her with delight, but she had no interest in him. He was simply a fragment of her past.

That's what they all were. Fragments of her past. To be forgotten most of the time. Except for Jonathan, of course.

This book is a sequel to

A Taste of His Own

Medicine

If you haven't read it, there is a taster here…

She didn't think about him anymore. She hadn't thought about him for three decades. In truth, she believed she'd exhausted her thoughts where he was concerned; she protected herself from him.

There was a time when it was different. A time when she enjoyed mundane tasks because completing them got her minutes closer to their next meeting. A time when she would find herself skipping like an excited child as she walked along the street, smiling at strangers because she was inwardly smiling at him. A time when all her thoughts contained him.

It was years since she woke in the night imagining she felt the touch of his fingers brushing her spine. She stopped reacting with a start if a man wearing his fragrance happened to come near. And the phone could ring without causing a jolt to her stomach.

But joy turned to bitterness and vengeance. Desire for him became the desire to hurt him; to scar him as much as she could.

Then nothing.

He was in a locked compartment in her mind. He was her past; he was no longer her everyday.

Chapter 1

'I thought you would come.'

'Confident in your power, I see.'

'That's not what I meant. Something is sweeping us along this evening. This is a special encounter, a one-off. We're unable to stop it.'

He pulled her towards him as she expected and placed his lips softly on hers. He kissed her twice and then ran his tongue slowly over her lips. 'You used to like that.'

'I still do. But I have to say something before we go further.'

She walked across the room and stood with her hands resting on the back of a chair, feeling his eyes on her, his scrutiny. 'You need to know how much you hurt me.'

'Kate, enough. I wasn't expecting you to come to my room to lecture me.'

'It's not a lecture. But you need to understand what you did. You intended to finish our relationship but gave me no clue it was about to happen. When I needed you most, you gave me no support, no sympathy. Awful as that was, the events afterwards compounded the hurt.'

'What events?'

'Don't be naïve, Jonathan. The succession of women you paraded before me. Everywhere I went you were there with a female, usually a different one from the previous time. The wound went deeper with each encounter. I hated you for that.'

'It wasn't deliberate. We were students on campus, bound to see each other. I was lost, Kate, and confused. Don't you know that? I was being honest when I told you I loved you. But then it got too much for me. I had no idea what I wanted from life. So I sought simple pleasures.'

'Sex, you mean.'

'Well, yes, I suppose so. And company. Certainly no commitment, nothing serious. Situations where I could live for the moment and start again tomorrow. I was suffering, too, I felt insecure and afraid.'

'It didn't appear that way. I hope you're not expecting sympathy! You were usually laughing, drinking and in control of life. While I had so much to cope with.'

'I don't display everything I feel. I didn't leave you for anyone else. I had no other lover, not even the glimmer of a relationship, when we split. Surely it would have been worse if I'd fallen in love with someone else?'

Kate paused and said, 'I suppose so but at the time I don't think you could have hurt me more than you did.'

Jonathan searched for words as he looked at Kate, a question on his lips he couldn't ask.

'There is no discussion, Jonathan.'

'I did try to talk to you but you ignored me. I tried to congratulate you when the results came out.'

Kate knew it was true. She remembered looking away when he came near. She hadn't trusted herself to speak. Now she turned from Jonathan, wondering if she was saying too much. The atmosphere in the room changed, as if a cloud was hiding the sun. She put her head in her hands.

Jonathan went over to the table in the corner. The silence throbbed around them like a headache.

'I ordered more drinks before you arrived. Do you want one?'

Kate took it from his hand and sipped it. He took a large gulp from his and then sat playing with the glass. Gradually they both relaxed and looked at each other, neither daring to break the gaze.

3

'Have you had your say?'

'Yes. No more.'

'Are you staying?'

'Do you want me to?'

'Yes.'

'Then I will.'

He moved slowly across the gap between them, the physical and the emotional gap.

'Perhaps we need to go back to where we were,' he said, putting his glass down and removing hers.

She reached out for Jonathan's hand and put it against her cheek. He drew her towards him.

'You'll taste of brandy. Luckily I like Rémy Martin.'

He kissed her again, licked her lips again, held her face in his hands, then buried his own face in her neck and breathed deeply.

'You smell the same. Do you still use the same perfume?'

'I can't remember what I used then. A cheap scent, I expect.'

'Then it's pure Kate I'm inhaling.'

She licked his neck, tracing circles with her tongue and nibbled his earlobe.

'That used to drive me wild.'

'And what does it do now?'

'It drives me wild.' He pulled her tightly against him and she could feel the warmth of his body.

'Slowly, Jonathan. You were always a teasing lover, you never rushed things. I want it to be exactly like the last time.'

'Can you remember the last time?'

'Of course I can. Making love to a person you adore – and I did adore you – isn't easily forgotten.'

Jonathan slid his hands under the straps of her dress and over her shoulders. 'Just as smooth as I remember. You always had peachy skin.'

'So you remember, too.'

4

'Kate, you were important to me once. I wasn't playing with you.'

Kate undid the buttons on Jonathan's shirt. She took her time over each one and carefully eased the shirt open. After each button, she kissed his chest. Then she ran her fingers through the light covering of hair, trailing her long nails so he could feel the pressure. She slid her arms round him and ran her fingers up his spine. He closed his eyes and moaned softly. It was working; her scheme was working.

'Kate, I don't think it can be like last time. Thirty years more of experience has to make it better. You are doing wonderful things to me.'

Kate had now removed Jonathan's shirt and started to remove her dress.

'Let me.'

'Soon. First, I want you to watch.' Slowly, she stepped out of her dress and he smiled at her still seductive shape.

'Stand there for a moment. I need to relish the temptation.'

Kate did as he asked, then walked towards him. She held him against her, enjoying the way they fitted together and then undid his belt, unzipped his trousers and slipped her hand inside. I'm having the required effect, she thought. No doubt of that.

'I think it's time we removed a few more clothes,' Jonathan said, stripping down to his underwear. Still the male model physique, she noted.

'Did you ever model underwear?'

'No. The guys who did that got into other things. Made plenty of money, but porn wasn't my scene.'

'You still look amazing. Sales would have rocketed if you appeared in a magazine like that.'

'You're talking too much. There are better activities for your mouth. Come here.'

He kissed her properly and Kate struggled to keep control of her emotions. I mustn't get too involved, I mustn't lose focus on the job to be done. She stepped back from him and told him to remove her bra. He undid the hook and she let it drop to the floor.

Slowly she turned to him and he held her breasts gently in his hands, then pressed his face against them. He rolled one nipple between his forefinger and thumb, feeling its erection. I should not enjoy this, Kate thought. But it's hard to avoid the pleasure. Keep control, keep control.

It was her mantra.

Jonathan slid his hands down her hips hooking his thumbs inside her knickers and rolling them down so that she was naked. He picked her up.

'This is what I always did.'

You usually said you loved me as you did it, thought Kate, and winced at the memory.

Laying her down gently, he knelt beside her, now naked himself, and started to stroke. Kate closed her eyes and let his hands wander at will. He knew where to touch and how to use his fingers. He remembered what she liked best. This could have been my life, Kate thought, and the pain of it made her bite her lip and gasp.

She started to caress Jonathan. At first, like feathery wisps of air, then with forceful bursts of wild passion. Or so it seemed. She went through the repertoire of what excited him; if it worked all those years ago, it would surely work now. Such a danger of getting carried away. This could be the most wonderful sex in years; I must control my passion, she told herself. I must follow my plan. There is a task to be completed. Jonathan was breathing heavily and whispering her name when she suddenly pushed him away.

'I can't do this, Jonathan. I thought I could but I can't.' She threw her legs off the bed and stood up, wrapping her arms around her body.

'Kate, come back. Don't be ridiculous. You were enjoying it.'

'I can't, I can't!' She grabbed her clothes, struggled into her dress and rushed towards the door, avoiding Jonathan's eyes.

That was the problem; she was enjoying it too much.